D1084836

DOPE THIEF

DOPE THIEF

Dennis Tafoya

MINOTAUR BOOKS

NEW YORK

This is a work of fiction. All of the characters, organizations, and events portrayed in this novel are either products of the author's imagination or are used fictitiously.

DOPE THIEF. Copyright © 2009 by Dennis Tafoya. All rights reserved. Printed in the United States of America. For information, address St. Martin's Press, 175 Fifth Avenue, New York, N.Y. 10010.

www.minotaurbooks.com

Book design by Jonathan Bennett

Library of Congress Cataloging-in-Publication Data

Tafoya, Dennis.
    Dope thief / Dennis Tafoya.—1st ed.
      p. cm.
    ISBN-13: 978-0-312-53115-7
    ISBN-10: 0-312-53115-X
    1. Crime—Fiction.   I. Title.
    PS3620.A33D67 2009
    813'.6—dc22

                          2008045665

First Edition: May 2009

10 9 8 7 6 5 4 3 2 1

For Cori

ACKNOWLEDGMENTS

THIS BOOK OWES its existence to a chain of remarkable and generous people: Cori Stern, who found me wandering and set me on the right road; the invaluable Laurie Webb, whose insight made the work better and stronger; my manager, the wise and endlessly patient Brooke Ehrlich; and Alex Glass, my literary agent and brilliant advocate, who not only found my work a home, but made crucial suggestions about the shape of the book. My editor, Kelley Ragland, and her assistant Matt Martz were incredibly kind and patient with a neophyte during the process. My family, Jill, Elena, David, and Rachel Tafoya provided love, support, and infinite tolerance. I also have to thank Dick, Karen, Caroline, Lucy, Olivia, August, the Rebel Writers workshop, Jonathan Maberry and the Liars Club, and all the other friends, teachers, and writers who helped me learn and kept me going.

DOPE THIEF

CHAPTER ONE

August

RAY SAT IN a van on Jefferson Avenue in Bristol in the rain, watching people come and go from the white corner house with blue shutters and a cast-iron bird feeder in the yard. A kid in his late teens sat on the stoop eating candy from a bag and talking to the people moving in and out. Sometimes they handed the kid something; sometimes he just waved them up the steps to the door. Nobody stayed more than a few minutes. Ray's partner, Manny, climbed from the passenger seat into the back and pulled binoculars out of a gym bag. He sat on the rear seat away from view and watched the kid and the front door, then moved the glasses along the street. Looking for open windows, young lookout kids watching the traffic, anyone that might signal the long-limbed teenaged boy on the stoop that there was trouble coming.

Ray took the glasses back for one last look. The people coming up the steps were black and white and brown, young and old. The only thing they had in common was that nearly all of them looked like shit. Hair uncombed. Lined faces the color of ashes. It reminded him of that movie where the dead are walking, coming to beat their way into this little farmhouse in the country. Only instead of breaking down the doors, the zombies stood quiet on the porch until there was an exchange through the door, and then the zombies went away.

Ray combed his mustache with his fingers and shrugged. "What do you think?"

He handed the glasses back to Manny, who stashed them under the seat and brought out a blue windbreaker with DEA spelled out on the back in bright yellow letters. He pulled it on while Ray slid over to the passenger seat and opened the glove compartment, taking out a black semiautomatic pistol, a big, ugly Glock with an extra-capacity magazine. Manny heaved himself into the driver's seat and Ray climbed around him and put his own windbreaker on, crouching in the cramped space by the side door of the van.

"Wait for a break in the traffic." They watched two young girls on the stoop, one of them doing that little nervous dance of waiting for dope, like bees Ray had seen in a documentary, vibrating with some kind of insect ecstasy of anticipation. When they were away down the street, Ray touched Manny's arm.

Manny put the van into gear and drove down the block, stopping at the corner and making a right onto the side street next to the house with the blue shutters. Manny reached into an oversized gym bag and handed Ray a pair of fifteen-inch bolt cutters and then took out a short-barreled Remington shotgun. He pulled his badge out of his clothes and let it dangle at the end of a chain over his shirt.

It was August, and it had rained every day for a week. Ray thought the bad weather was making everyone edgy, tense. Stuck indoors when they wanted to be out. Maybe it was just him. He looked up and down the side street from the side window, fingering the badge on his chest, then jumped out and ducked behind the house and pressed himself against the wall next to the basement door. He put the bolt cutters on the chain holding the padlock on the door and looked at his watch and counted in his head.

Manny ran up the street to the front of the house and swung over the fence without a sound. He put his shotgun against the side of Candy Kid's face and spoke quietly. "What's your name?"

The kid stopped eating and clamped his mouth shut. "Jerome."

"What you eating, Jerome?"

"Jolly Ranchers." The bag began to shake slightly in the kid's hands.

Manny looked at his watch without taking his hands off the gun. "Is there enough for everyone?" Jerome swallowed and tried to see the barrel of the gun out of the corner of his eye. "Let's go inside and share our Jolly Ranchers, okay?" Jerome stood up and turned awkwardly around, the gun glued to the side of his face. He was tall standing up, taller than Manny, who was more than six feet, and he bent slightly at the waist. They walked slowly to the front door; Manny stayed off to the left and moved the gun down to Jerome's side, keeping out of view of the peephole cut in the door. He looked at his watch and whispered to Jerome. "Okay, let's not make any mistakes. Knock twice and wait. Tell them you gotta use the can."

Jerome lifted his arm and banged the door twice.

AT THE BACK door Ray lowered his watch and cut the chain. He hit the door hard with his body and it gave slightly, so he backed off and put his shoulder into it and the door popped open, banging against the wall. He was in a basement, the only light coming down the stairs from the first floor, where Manny was inside now doing his thing, yelling, "Down, down, down, federal agents!"

Ray hit the stairs in time for a teenaged girl with her shirt tied at her waist to appear at the top step, moving fast. Ray lifted the big, squared-off Glock with both hands and pointed it at her head. "Federal agents! Back up the stairs, now! Hands on your head!"

She shrieked and fell back into the kitchen, knocking over a bulked-up kid with a diamond earring who was right behind her with his arms full of small plastic bags. The kid was wearing an oversized black Sixers jersey with IVERSON on the back. Ray reached down with one hand and pulled them apart and pushed them out of the kitchen toward the front of the house. He heard Manny telling someone named Jerome to lie flat. They came out to the living room, where Manny had two tall kids stretched out on the floor, the sprawl of their long legs eating up all the space.

Ray pointed down. There was a small metal box on the floor near the front door next to an ancient double-barreled shotgun with the stock cut down. "You two, on the floor right now."

The boy and girl lay flat, between a bright green couch and a glass-topped coffee table supported on the backs of metallic gold elephants. The living room was neat, with photos of a smiling kid in a cap and gown from Ray guessed thirty years ago on the wall near the stairs. There were doilies under the knickknacks on the end tables.

Manny pointed to one of the kids near the front door. The kid was impossibly long stretched out on the floor, wearing faded jeans and a hoodie with a stenciled picture of a fist clutching a pistol. "This is Jerome."

Ray stood over him. "Jerome, who else is in the house?"

"No one."

"Don't lie to me, Jerome."

"I ain't lying."

" 'Cause if I go looking and I find someone upstairs I'm going to be pissed off, you understand me?" Ray opened his jacket and pulled a half-dozen sets of plastic flex cuffs out and began restraining the kids on the floor.

Manny moved the pump gun in a slow arc, covering each one in turn. "I'm gonna go look now, okay? What am I gonna find?"

The girl murmured something under her breath.

"What was that? What did she say?"

"She said maybe Ronald upstairs."

"Ronald, now? How come she's helping the police and you're not helping the police, Jerome? I'm about done with you, son. Who else is in this house?"

"Maybe Ronald."

"Maybe Ronald." Ray sighed theatrically. "Jerome, when you are standing tall before the judge I am going to be your only friend, do you understand that? What am I going to tell the judge,

Jerome? That you lied to the police and made them go looking for Maybe Ronald, or that you helped resolve this situation?"

"I don't know." The kid's voice was muffled by the carpet.

"What?"

"I don't know."

"You can be a hero, Jerome. You can be the one makes sure no one gets hurt, that the police get the money and the drugs off the street. Believe me, Jerome, you want me to tell the judge you were a hero and not an uncooperative dirtbag. You know the difference?"

There was a long silence.

"I don't know."

The kid with the Iverson shirt said, "Heroes get a beatdown."

Ray looked at him. "Shut up. Heroes get to finish high school, and dirtbags go to jail." He finished cuffing the kids on the floor and straightened up.

Manny took a hand off the gun and yanked Jerome awkwardly to his feet. "Talk to Ronald, tell him to come down here with nothing in his hands." He walked Jerome to the foot of the stairs.

Jerome leaned against the wall, unbalanced with his hands cuffed behind him. He called up the stairs. "Ronald!"

Ray waggled his eyebrows at Manny, who put a cupped hand to the side of his mouth.

"Ronald! Come on down here with your hands up." Manny kept Jerome between himself and the stairs, lowering his body to use the tall kid as a shield. "Ronald!"

"What?" The voice was high-pitched, quavering.

Manny slapped the wall. "Don't 'what' me, you pain in the ass. You get down here on the ground right now. You want to get shot?"

"No, I don't."

"Then come on down." There was another silence. Ray trained his pistol on the stairs and waited.

"How I know you won't shoot me?"

Manny said, "We're the police, Ronald. The police don't just shoot people."

The kid with the Iverson shirt said, "Bullshit, they don't."

After a long minute, brilliant white Jordans appeared at the top of the stairs; then Ronald slowly walked down, looking all of about twelve in an oversized red jeans jacket and gold chains. When he reached the bottom step, Manny stepped from behind Jerome and laid Ronald down next to his friends, and Ray took another pair of flex cuffs out of his jacket.

Iverson said, "Punk," under his breath.

Ray flicked the back of his head with the plastic cuffs. "Shut your mouth." He ratcheted the cuffs around the smaller kid's skinny arms. "Maybe Ronald is my hero."

Manny stayed in the living room, his long, thin frame bent over the shotgun like a pool hall sharper draped over a cue. Ray went back into the kitchen. He opened a few cabinets until he found a roll of big plastic trash bags, jammed his pistol into his belt, and pulled a bag off the end of the roll. He dropped to his knees and began scooping the dropped Baggies off the floor into the green trash bag. He held up one and inspected it—tiny vials, each one with a few rocks of blue-white crystal—and then shoved it into the trash bag. He opened the freezer, the oven, the dishwasher. In a drawer near the back door he found a pistol, an Italian .32 with rust on the handle, and he pocketed it and went out to the front room.

Manny was going through their pockets, turning out rolls of bills and tossing them over by the stairs. Ray grabbed them up and shoved them in the bag. He went to the front door and retrieved the metal cash box, open and showing stacks of fives and tens. Ray upended it, spilling the money in with the vials. He picked up the old shotgun and broke it open, throwing the shells into a corner, and tucking the gun awkwardly under one arm.

His eyes kept going to the picture on the wall. A light-skinned black woman in a yellow cap and gown, cheeks wide with her smile. Even white teeth and almond-shaped eyes with a kind of fierce intelligence that made Ray feel uneasy. Guilty. For standing in her house, maybe, for waving a gun. Probably at one of her children or grandchildren.

Ray leaned over the kids. "Jerome, where's the rest of the money and the stash?" The big kid was silent. The kid with the Iverson jersey shifted, glaring at Jerome. Ray snapped his fingers. "Don't look at Iverson, look at me. Where's the rest?"

"I don't know."

"You do know. Don't look at him. Is he going to do your time? Is he going to take care of your mom while you do ten years upstate? Is he going to talk to the judge for you and get you home tonight in time to watch *The Gilmore Girls*?"

"No."

"No is right." Manny pulled Jerome to his feet by his cuffed hands and propelled him into the kitchen. Ray followed, keeping the pistol where the others could see it. Ray stood in the doorway and saw Manny put his head close to Jerome's and whisper. Jerome looked over his shoulder toward the room where his friends were laid out, then whispered something back. Manny grinned, then stood back and banged his hand on the kitchen table hard. "Goddammit, tell me something." He smiled wider and Jerome shyly smiled back at Manny's game.

Manny ducked into a bathroom off the kitchen while Ray made a show of marching Jerome over to his friends and laying him down on the floor. "Looks like Jerome don't want to help the police. I guess he's going away upstate for a while. See his uncles out at Camp Hill." Ray picked up the trash bag from the floor and threw it over his shoulder like a pistol-toting Santa. "Nobody move, now."

He backed into the kitchen. Manny was holding up two wet plastic bags, one filled with vials, the other with cash. Ray pulled the bag from his shoulder and handed it to Manny, who moved silently down the stairs. Ray stuck his head into the doorway to the front room and looked over the prone bodies. He heard the girl ask Jerome how Ray knew his uncle was at Camp Hill and Jerome telling her to please shut the fuck up.

"Keep your heads down and be still. Since Jerome isn't telling us what we need to know, we're searching the rest of the house. I'm leaving Maybe Ronald in charge." He ducked back into the kitchen and followed Manny down the stairs, through the basement and out to the street. Manny was starting the engine on the van, the side door open. Ray threw the double-barreled gun under the seat, jumped in, and slammed the door.

They drove in silence for a minute, Manny keeping it at the speed limit and making quick turns, Ray spinning in his seat to look behind them. After a couple of blocks, Ray opened a gym bag and dropped the pistol in; he reached over and took the badge from around Manny's neck. He leaned forward awkwardly in the seat and took off his windbreaker and stuffed it into the bag with the guns and badges and a couple of leftover pairs of flex cuffs. They turned out onto Route 13, and he reached over and grabbed the wheel and held it straight while Manny took off his jacket.

Ray thought about the kids lying in the front room, whispering to each other. He wondered how long it would take them to begin to move around, get up, tiptoe into the kitchen, their heads cocked for the slightest sound. He imagined Jerome peering down the cellar steps, his hands still cuffed, and realizing they weren't coming back. He rifled in the green trash bag for a minute, then held his hand out to Manny.

"Jolly Rancher?"

RAY WATCHED THE cars around them as they drove west on the Pennsylvania Turnpike. "That was a nice house. Whose house do you think that was?"

"Someone's grandma, I'd bet." Manny clicked the radio on, low. "Maybe Ronald's."

"Didn't stink, it was all kept up. It was like Crack House Lite." Ray picked up the trash bag and set it on his lap, running his fin-

Dennis Tafoya

gers through the loose cash and vials. He stuck a finger through the plastic bag of cash from the toilet tank and made a hole, thumbing the bills, looking at denominations.

Manny looked over. "How did we do?"

"We? Who did all the work?"

"Get the fuck out of here. Who got Jerome to spill?"

Ray waved his hand. "Oh, like I wouldn't have lifted the lid on the toilet. Doper kids like that only know two places to hide shit, and I already looked in the fridge."

"I have to admit I got a kick out of that 'help the police' stuff. How many times the cops tried to play me and my friends like that."

Ray shrugged. "They call it the command voice. It's a gift some people have. Your problem is you don't watch enough TV. One or two episodes of *Cops*'ll tell you anything you want to know about managing the criminal element."

"Please, the criminal element. They were all like fifteen. An episode of *Sesame Street* could have told you anything you needed to know about managing that bunch." Manny rummaged in his pockets and brought out a cigarette. He pointed with his chin. "Seriously, what did we get?"

Ray didn't answer. He kept thinking about the house, and the picture of the girl in the cap and gown. Someone's mother, or grandmother. One of the doper kids her son or grandson. The kids now stumbling around the house, their wrists still cinched by the flex cuffs. It made him unaccountably tense, wondering how they'd get out. They had cell phones, he knew; he had seen them when Manny turned out their pockets. Ray thought about whoever was supplying them. Conjured a hulking gangbanger with big shoulders from the joint, a shaved head. Would there be trouble when they came up short? He saw a big man stalking around the house with a baseball bat, Jerome and Maybe Ronald talking fast, trying to make him see how they got took by two guys said they were cops. Had guns and badges, looked like cops, sounded like cops.

Ray noticed one of those little roadside shrines that families build where someone has been killed in a wreck. Saw the shattered plastic flowers and rotted wooden cross, a tiny, faded photograph flashing by too fast to register. He began to feel a tightness in his chest, a hitch in his breath that felt like panic.

The girl in the picture reminded him of someone. The girl in the cap and gown. The name came back to him, and the accident, and a terrible pulse in his head that made him sick. Marletta. A girl he'd loved, who'd loved him. The brilliant girl with the open smile.

He got her back for an instant sitting in the front seat of a car on the day she graduated high school. The day he would have graduated but for Juvie and the time lost. Marletta sitting beside him in her cap and gown, looking like the girl in the picture in the house on Jefferson Avenue.

He stretched, turned on the radio. KYW came on, the announcer talking about Allen Iverson and his bad attitude. Ray snapped off the radio, opened the window, let the rain spatter his eyes, his cheeks, his open mouth. Manny watched the road, the traffic, occasionally looked his way. When they reached the exit,

Ray cranked the window back up and ran his hands over his face. He caught sight of himself in the mirror on the visor, and it looked like he'd been crying.

"Ray, man?"

But Ray was staring, now. His hands empty in his lap, his brain twisting in his head. "All good things," he said.

CHAPTER TWO

THE NEXT DAY, the morning of his thirtieth birthday, Ray pulled his Camaro up outside his father's house in Hatboro, hunched his shoulders against the rain, and ran to the open garage. He stood and watched the sky for a minute, the clouds low and dark as smoke. There was a faint sound of thunder, like cloth being torn, and a weak green light in the clouds. He could smell the wet asphalt and the cut grass caked on the old mower in the corner, the dust and oil and gas. The houses were shaded by leaning maples and oaks that muted the constant low roar from the turnpike but that darkened the streets and yards so that even outside Ray felt like he was behind walls. He walked through and opened the door to the house.

Theresa, who had raised him after his mother left and stayed with him when his father went upstate, was sitting at the kitchen table smoking a cigarette and watching the small TV he had gotten her for Christmas, squinting through a thin trail of blue smoke. In front of her were a cup of coffee and a game of solitaire. She waved her small yellow hand at him, leaving a smoke circle in the air.

"The prodigal." At her feet a white dog watched him, moving only his eyes as Ray moved into the kitchen.

"Hey, Ma. How's the reception?"

She shrugged. "Good enough."

He looked in her refrigerator and walked into the living room. "You fixed for everything? Eating right?"

"I got no appetite."

"Yeah? What's the doctor say?"

"He says I'm an old bag and I'm gonna die soon." She moved cards on the table.

Ray patted her on the head. "That sounds about right."

"Fuck you, too, chum."

He held up his hands as if to spar, and she flicked ashes at him, smiling a yellow nicotine smile. "You and what army, boyo?"

"My ma, toughest kid on the block." He walked through the narrow, paneled rooms into his childhood bedroom. He shook his head at the trophies topped with small gold batters with unreadable expressions that somehow frightened him when he was a kid and woke with night terrors. He got down on his hands and knees and pulled an olive drab duffel from underneath his bed.

Theresa called from the kitchen. "Raymond, you want coffee?"

He unzipped the bag and opened it, showing stacks of bills, some with the bank bands on and some ringed by grimy rubber bands. He took rubber-banded rolls of tens and twenties out of his jacket, his shirt, his pants and dropped them in the bag, then rummaged around under the cash.

"Nah, Ma, thanks. You stay put." He pulled out a Colt .45, a scuffed 1911A1 he had bought at a gun show in North Carolina, and laid it on the rug. He fished around in the bag and came out with two empty clips and laid them next to the Colt. He sat and did math for a minute, figuring the rent, the money he owed, food, gas, the money he'd have to front Manny until the next thing happened. He grabbed a stack of twenties, snapped off the rubber band and counted bills from one hand to the other, then zipped the bag and pushed it back under the bed, leaving a track in the dust.

"You working today, Raymond?"

He picked up the pistol and quietly worked the slide, then stuck it inside his jacket and pocketed the clips. "Yeah, Manny and this guy Rick Staley are picking me up."

"The degenerate Manny I know. Who's the other degenerate?"

He walked back out and laid money on the table, then went to the sink and washed his hands. The glasses in the cabinets rattled, and Ray ducked his head to see a pair of A-10s coasting into the naval airbase up the road above Maple Avenue. He had grown up to that sound, lain awake nights listening to the jets come and go and found it comforting.

"You don't need anything? Coffee, milk?"

She shook her head. "Walk Shermie for me." He watched her for a minute as if trying to fix her in his mind. "Shush, it's my numbers." She grabbed a pencil and two lottery tickets from the table.

"What you got, Ma, the Powerball?"

She screwed up her face in concentration. "Will you shut it?"

He pulled the leash from a peg on the wall near the door and grabbed a plastic bag from a coffee can. The dog sighed like an old man and rose stiffly, stopping to scratch himself. Ray watched Theresa leaning toward the TV, her eyes flicking back and forth from the screen to the tickets, the lenses in her glasses blue with the reflection. For a minute she seemed otherworldly, alien. Her tongue curled around her upper lip, flicking. Finally she threw down the pencil. "Not one goddamned number."

"Anytime today, Sherm. This fucking dog. You should put it to sleep."

"Who's going to keep me company, you?" He zipped up his jacket and led the dog outside. He heard her through the door. "Don't forget to pick up the shit! I'll put *you* to sleep."

He stood in the rain with an unlit cigarette while the dog sat in the shelter of a scrawny dogwood in the backyard. In the corner was a half-built brick barbecue; really just a hole in the ground covered with a piece of rotting plywood and a pile of bricks, a few stuck together with cement.

He remembered his father standing in the yard, a cigarette working in the corner of his face, a beer bottle in his fist. Picking up a brick and fingering it, putting it back in the pile. The next day he went off to court to answer a robbery beef and never came back. Ray was eleven, already unmoored from childhood by the disappearance of his mother the year before. That night, when he woke up (a nightmare about a dog coming for him), Theresa was sitting in the dark, smoking a cigarette. She sat on the edge of the bed, her breath sweet with his father's whiskey. She kissed him on the forehead and sat silently with him until he fell asleep.

Now the dog looked at him, and Ray said, "What?" and led him out to the front yard through a teetering gate. The place was falling down, and Ray felt guilty again about the long list of things Theresa needed done. Shit that Ray promised he'd do but never got around to. He had lived in the house for a while after getting out of prison for his first fall as an adult. Driving a stolen car and getting into an accident.

Manny rolled up the street in his vintage Mustang, the old 390 making a drumming sound he could feel in his chest. Ray hooked the leash onto a low branch of an apple tree that overlooked a statue of the Virgin Mary and walked over to lean into the car, smelling Armor All and cigarettes. He shook Rick's hand and waved at Manny, who pointed at Rick, a muscular guy with long hair and a tattoo of a clock on his bicep.

"This is Rick Staley. He did a bit with Harlan Maximuck at Graterford." Rick was built up in his arms and shoulders the way some guys get inside. He had lank brown hair and licked his lips nervously. Manny was lean, tall, and stoop-shouldered, even behind the wheel of a car. His mouth was framed by a black goatee, and he wore sunglasses with blue lenses despite the sunless day.

Ray leaned in the window. "Harlan the Hillbilly. I haven't thought about him in, Christ." He felt a pang, thinking of big Harlan keeping him pure inside. Keeping the skells away from Ray, when he was in for the first time and just a kid. And Ray getting out and away and never looking back. He could have done something, looked in on Harlan's family, sent him some money.

"What's up with Harlan? Is he out?"

Manny frowned, shook his head. "He tried to burn some guy in segregation."

"Jesus."

Rick Staley's voice was low, and he looked up and down the street while he talked. "Yeah, he got shorted on some kind of deal, Christ only knows what. He got some cellie to smuggle gas in from where they keep it locked up for the lawn mower. Gets into Segregation, where they're keeping the guy, sprays gas through the bean chute, and was trying to light him up when the CO came up. So Harlan, being Harlan, tries to light up the CO, too. He got Buck Rogers time for that shit."

Rick laughed. "I told him, bro, you got to look on the bright side. By the time you get out there'll be flying cars and robot whores and shit." Rick scratched a dope bruise on the inside of his elbow.

Manny caught Ray's eyes and shrugged. "Fucking Harlan."

Ray had known some guys inside who had been killed or maimed that way. The bean chute was what the cellies called the slot in the door where the dinner trays were slipped through in places like Segregation, where the guys were in protection or were too crazy to be let out to eat with everyone else. The corrections officers, the COs, were a mixed bunch. Some were okay; some were humps who never missed a chance to smack you down. There were all kinds, holy rollers, drunks. He remembered one time when he was inside at Bucks County, awaiting trial on a car theft (dismissed). A skinny crackhead ran away from a work assignment and climbed up into the rafters of the warehouse and dangled his legs over into space, threatening to jump if he didn't get a helicopter. The CO that time, a morose diabetic named Happ, stood there for a minute banging his clipboard against his leg, looked up at the kid, and said, "Jump, pussy. I got problems of my own." Then he sent everyone back to work, and eventually the kid climbed down and they sent him to Segregation for a while.

Manny pointed to the door, where Ray's mother was standing at the door with a scowl on her face, lifted his hand, and smiled.

"How you doing, Mrs. D?"

"Just peachy, shitbird." She pointed with her cigarette. "Bring Shermie in before he gets away."

"Okay, Ma."

"Did you pick up the shit, Raymond?" She walked away from the door.

Ray shook his head. Manny laughed until he started coughing. "Yeah, Raymond, did you pick up the shit?"

He took the dog back in and took one last look around. Theresa opened her purse, releasing a smell of cheap perfume and tobacco that took Ray back to summers waiting for her to pick through her change for quarters for him to take out to the ice cream man while he hopped from foot to foot, whining for her to hurry up and come across.

She came out with an envelope and handed it to him. "Did you think I forgot?"

He smiled and took it, shaking his head. "You didn't have to do that, Ma."

"Who's going to do it if I don't?"

It was a good question. "Well, thanks."

"You seeing anyone?"

He shrugged. "Not really." Not unless you counted the girls at the Osaka Spa, a Korean massage parlor behind a pool hall off

Old Easton Road. The woman in the picture jumped into his head again, and he almost said something, made up a story about a woman with a hopeful smile and fierce brown eyes. Something dropped in his stomach, a lead ball moving down through him and pulling everything with it. He felt every minute of the life that had gone by. He felt like he could begin crying, and that if he did start he wouldn't be able to stop. The old house creaked like a ship going down.

Theresa tapped her cheek and he kissed her.

"Happy birthday, Raymond."

He nodded, couldn't get anything out. He could smell her, stale Arpège and Marlboros; and the house, something fried from last night, wet dog and dust and Lysol. The smell of home. He thought about staying there, sitting with Theresa while she watched her stories, playing poker for the pennies she kept in a glass piggy bank on the counter. Drinking the peppermint schnapps she liked, a beer from the fridge.

He wanted to ask, did she remember Marletta? Ray had brought her to the house, but maybe only when Theresa was gone, so they could be alone. If he brought it up, he knew, it would be a bad memory for Theresa, bound up with him going to jail and all these lost years since. He felt something slipping away, couldn't give it a name. He turned away, waved from the door, and was gone.

THEY DROVE OVER to Horsham and dropped Rick off at his car at the Best Buy in Willow Grove. Rick, it turned out, had done

Dennis Tafoya

some dealing, some B and E, passed some checks. He'd never done strong-arm but was willing to learn and didn't come across as an asshole with something to prove. On the way over they talked about people they knew in common, some locked up, some dead, some still hanging around getting high, and some just gone. More signs for Ray that he was getting older and had nothing to show for it.

Ray got lost in his head the way he did sometimes, thinking about prison and Harlan and feeling guilty he'd never visited him or really done anything for him since he'd been out and wondering what Harlan would think about that. Especially as Ray got older and knew better what it meant for a young kid to be inside with no one to look out for him the way Harlan had stepped up for him. Staring down the old lags who came for him, and half the time Ray too young and dumb to know what was going on until it was over.

Later Manny and Ray sat at a booth at a diner in Willow Grove across from the air base. A-10s dropped out of the sky, touched the runway, and took off again, the roar making things clatter slightly on the table. Out at the curb Ray watched two kids walking up 611 with their thumbs out. One kid was short and one tall and black-haired, and Ray smiled, seeing him and Manny. The short kid wore a surplus army jacket, and the tall, skinny kid had a black leather jacket with duct tape over one elbow. A car went by at speed, and the big kid flipped it off, screaming something Ray couldn't hear.

Manny covered his mouth with his hand and leaned toward

Ray. "What do you think?" He put sugar in his coffee and stirred.

Ray kept his head down, talked to the table in a low voice. "About Rick? I think I don't know anything about him except he's got a jones."

Manny said, "Or a bruise on his arm, supposed to make us think he's a hype. I could try to see Harlan, see what he says."

"Yeah, maybe, but if Harlan is jammed up he'll just lie. What does he have to lose?" The waitress came over and poured more coffee. They watched her go. Ray shrugged. "We need the third guy on this one. The thing is I'd rather have a junkie than a cowboy, if that's my only choice."

Manny nodded. "Some idiot who's shooting just to hear the gun. Scaring the shit out of the citizens."

"For a junkie it's a straight line. Money—" Ray drew a line in the air with his forefinger. "—Dope. The cops come, he runs away. What do you want, some guy's going to make a stand, shoot it out with the bulls? Get his name in the paper?"

"Fuck that."

"Yeah . . ." Ray said, but thinking: What am I, then? Not a junkie, not quite, or not yet. Not a cowboy. He used the gun, but didn't love it. He thought of himself sometimes as a professional. Or as acting like a professional, if there was a difference.

He and Manny had been robbing dealers for about a year. Had been in the life for a long time before that, of course. Stole cars, broke into houses. They had met in Juvie, a place called Lima, out in Delaware County. Taking off dealers wasn't something you could do if you didn't know who was who, what to look for. You had to score dope to know dope dealers, or know people who did. Where to go, what to watch for. Manny had been in rehab and knew people who were out copping every day.

They were careful, in their way. They would watch the houses they picked out for a few days or, if they were really hungry, a few hours. Watch the traffic, get a feel for how many people were in the place, who might be carrying. The trick was to go in strong but not crazy. Take control of the situation. Ray had found them the windbreakers with DEA in yellow letters on the back at a flea market in Jersey. They bought badges at an army surplus store in Connecticut and hung them on chains around their necks. It calmed the dealers down. No one wanted to get tagged, but only a stone retard was going to throw down on a Fed. Only when they were down on the floor, their wrists bound with plastic wire wraps, would they begin to get it. Who they really were, Manny and Ray. Why they were there.

At least the older or more experienced ones would get it. Then they would curse, spit, roll around, put on a little theater for their girlfriends, but it was over already by then. Manny would have the pump gun pointed at their heads, and Ray would be looking under the toilet lids and in the freezer.

The dealers made Ray feel like he had his life together. Dealers had their wives and mothers and girlfriends and kids in the houses with them holding dope and cash. He would tell them they were lucky he wasn't some crazy Dominican there to cut throats. They'd be cooking meth and poisoning their own fucking brats in the next room, the air full of charcoal smoke and acetone mist. Speed cookers, small-time Mexican coke dealers with *Scarface* posters on the wall. Hillbilly tweakers with wide eyes and bad teeth, what they called now meth mouth. Big crosses around their necks, smoking dope to calm their racing hearts. When they were in the cuffs, they'd sing hymns and cry and call down Jesus Fire. It made Ray want to laugh—conjuring up a Tweaker Jesus in his head, a Jesus with gray teeth and unwashed hair, tattoos reading BORN TO LOSE and BORN TO DIE.

MANNY WALKED RAY to his car, looking at the dark sky. "More rain?"

Ray went into the glove compartment and pulled out a short stack of twenties and put it in an envelope. He made a show of licking the gum and sealing it. Manny laughed and shook his head, let his long frame settle against Ray's car, leather jacket flapping open. With his arms folded he looked even more like some great bird poised to erupt into the sky in a blast of lost feathers and rushing sound.

"Fuck you." Manny put the money in his jacket. "Ever since you gave up smoking you fucking delight in being a hump. Anyway, I wanted to talk to you about holding the money."

Ray held up his hands. "Hey, anytime you want it . . ."

Manny looked at his hands. "The thing is, I asked Sherry to move in."

"No shit. Huh." Ray raised his eyebrows.

Manny stuck his hands in his pockets, awkward. "You think I'm making a mistake."

"No. No I don't. I like Sherry, she's a good kid."

26

"But?"

"Just, does she know, you know. Where the money's coming from."

Manny smiled. "She knows I ain't a housepainter." A dig at Ray, who in a moment of panic once told this dumb-ass lie to Theresa, who then spent hours on the phone digging up painting jobs around the neighborhood. "She knows I got money and don't work. She's been around the block. Shit, we met in rehab. Anyway, she knows not to ask too many questions."

"Great, then. She can dole out the money, get the rent paid and keep you from getting your legs broken by Dickie Lagrossa when the Sixers tank. What you owe him now, about twenty grand?"

"Oh, stop. It's a couple thousand. Anyway, I got a system."

"Yeah, how's that working?"

Manny pulled a medal from inside his shirt and kissed it. "And I got Saint Bernadine on my side."

Ray said, "You and Arnold Rothstein." He squinted through the smoke from Manny's cigarette. "You're the one asked me to dole out the money. Hey, though, you got to love that there's a patron saint for gambling degenerates."

Manny waved his arm expansively. "There's a saint for every fucking thing. My ex-wife's cousin, Deborah?"

"The good-looking one."

"She says there's a patron saint for meth cookers."

Ray held a palm up as if to stop the flow of bullshit. "Get the fuck out."

Manny held his hand across his chest, cigarette out. "I swear to Christ. Saint Cosmas, she says. He's like the patron saint of people who work with chemicals. She was dating that guy, you know the one. Jacques or Jocko or some shit."

"I remember. He's in Graterford now, right?"

"When she moves in and finds out he's dealing, she goes to the priest and asks what does she do. You can imagine that conversation."

Ray smiled. "He's cooking in the house, the kid's there . . ."

"But deep down he's a good guy."

"A sweet girl, not a smart one."

"No. But the priest comes up with Saint Cosmas. And of course that she should dime Jocko."

"Which she does."

Manny gave a half-shrug. "Of course, the asshole is also beating her and her kid, so . . ."

"Well, wherever he is, I'm sure Saint Cosmas is looking after him."

They stood in the lot for a minute. Ray watched tiny waves cross a coffee-colored puddle. "So . . . the Rick question."

"You really think the cops would get onto us and try to put a guy inside?"

"Don't seem likely, huh?"

"What are we, the Dillinger gang? I think we run into trouble, it ain't going to be that kind. I don't see nobody calling the cops."

They both thought about that. You could only do this shit so long. Someone was going to recognize them, or follow them, or just do something brainless when they came in the door. They wore the cop jackets and badges and they moved with purpose and told themselves they were smart, but there was only so much luck and then it was gone. At the end of the day they were as doomed as the goofy bastards they were ripping off. Manny and Ray would do lines in the truck before they went in, getting their edges sharp, making their minds fast. It couldn't go on forever. Everyone was high. Everyone was stupid. Everyone had guns.

CHAPTER
THREE

AT TWO O'CLOCK in the morning Ray sat upright in bed, his heart racing. He wiped at his eyes and found them wet. He put a palm on his chest, tried by force of will to slow his breathing, fumbled for the TV remote. He clicked through the channels, found an old movie about a man and a woman, carnival sharpshooters who end up robbing banks in cowboy outfits. He didn't recognize anyone in it, but it was good enough to keep him occupied. He liked how they were with each other, high in love the way you could sometime be, but he didn't get the cowboy outfits. Of course they were doomed, that was the movies, but he couldn't think of a lot of bank robber stories that ended up with they live happily ever after. Not a lot of any kind of stories. He wanted a drink but couldn't see getting up to get it, and he knew it wouldn't help him sleep or stop the nightmares. He wanted a cigarette, too, and thought how it was great you could tell yourself you were becoming a better person by staying in bed and doing nothing.

He tried to remember the dream that woke him up. There was something about a house floating on a lake and somehow the house turned upside down. Someone he loved was in the house and he was screaming, or trying to scream. The place was familiar, like some place he knew or had seen, but not the same. That's how it was in his dreams. The places were put together from bits and pieces of real life but reassembled in a crazy way that made him uneasy.

He couldn't think who would have been in the house. All he could bring back from the dream was that feeling of being helpless and desperate, but there was no one he'd feel that way about in his waking life. It made him jealous of his dream self, this other him with this other, richer life of strong connection and the kind of love that made you frantic.

After the movie ended (they killed each other, but it was the only way out), another movie came on, something with Danny Kaye. He muted the sound and drifted off.

He was standing up on the bleachers, after gym and Mr. Hughes blowing that fucking whistle to make them all deaf. Him and Pete Quirk and Pete's little brother Davey, who everyone said was retarded, but not to his face because he went six-two in ninth grade. They were high, drinking Mr. Pibb, which sucked but was the soda they had at the Indian's store, the only place they could get to and then back before fourth period, and now they were standing up on the bleachers and watching the girls come out of the locker room in their black and white leotards. Pete said, what the fuck lame school has black and white colors, and Davey snorted his Mr. Pibb out of his nose, and they all laughed even more at that. Davey and Pete jumped off the bleachers and walked out, enjoying the loud, echoing bang of their feet hitting the boards and the girls all watching them go, but

Ray slouched back on the bleachers and watched one of the girls pull herself up onto the balance beam into a handstand. She was small, dark, her eyes clear and focused, and she held herself straight, her back like the blade of a knife under the green lights of the gym. Ray moved down crablike over the bleachers until he was just a few feet away from the beam as the girl rolled over to stand upright, the muscles in her legs standing out, taut as wires, her hands frosted with chalk. Her body turned in flat circles, described fluent arcs that in Ray's eyes, half-closed by dope, seemed smeared against the bright blue of the mats.

She launched herself off the beam, and he held his breath when she came down, pulled into himself in a sympathetic motion when her feet hit the mat. She held her hands up over her head then but looked down at her own feet while her friends clapped and one of them, the tall red-haired girl he knew was Claudia, whistled and smiled and called out to her. Go, Marletta. Ray smiled, full of expansive good humor fueled by Pete Quirk's hash, and he wished she'd look up and see him so he could say it, too. Go, Marletta. But when she did look up, finally, her smile wide and her feline eyes flicking over his and then away, he couldn't get anything out. His dry lips worked, clicking, but she was gone that fast, head down, dark hair hiding her profile, and he sat a long time and looked at the small white handprints she'd left on the beam, and he repeated her name to himself, the way her friend had said it. Marletta.

The next day Ray drove up 611, through Doylestown and up into the country, following a map Manny had drawn on the back of an unpaid electric bill. The rain had slowed. He passed an ice cream stand with a woman smoking a cigarette under the shelter of the awning, talking animatedly into a cell phone, and it made him unaccountably lonely. He glanced at his own cell phone as if he expected it to ring. Someone calling just to say hello. It brought back that feeling he had had in Theresa's kitchen, that weight in his stomach, emptiness and a feeling of tears forming just behind his eyes. He put on the radio and found the college station from Princeton, drifting in and out with the effort of carrying all the way from Jersey. It was something he had never heard; a guitar drifting and echoing in a way that made him think of someone alone in an immense and empty space in the middle of the night.

Above Ottsville he followed a forking exit onto smaller roads lined with farms being cut up into developments. Patches of trees, their branches moving in the rain. He slowed, found a rusted mailbox and a gravel drive leading off over a low hill, and kept moving around a slow curve. There was a turnoff into the field, and he pulled off and stopped.

He grabbed his bag and got out, stretching as if he had come a long way, though he had only been in the car about forty-five minutes. The quiet, the unfamiliar greenness of things, made him feel he had made a long trip to a strange place. In the distance there were long fence lines and horse barns. A country of people whose lives he couldn't imagine. Getting up early, to do what? Feed the fucking horses. Tinker with farm equipment, maybe. The engine ticked, and water dripped from the trees. He looked up and down the empty road and then walked off into the field, up the hill along a line of trees.

He kept to the left of a screen of maples, moving quietly and staying aware of his position, ears straining. He began to sweat immediately, his legs getting wet from the high grass. There was nothing to see except the trees and the fields on either side of him. He looked at his watch and back down the way he had come to where his car was just barely visible now and began to hear a dog bark somewhere.

Near the crest of the hill he stopped and swung the knapsack off his back and kneeled down to rummage in it. He lifted the pistol out and quietly racked the slide, putting a round in the chamber and then putting it back in the bag. He took out a pair of binoculars and picked up the bag, moving slowly up the hill. Finally on his right a farmhouse came into view, partially obscured by pines. A dog was tied up outside to a stake in the ground, barking itself hoarse at nothing. There was a Ford pickup collapsing in on itself by the side of the drive and a kids' swing set with just the chains hanging, the swings long gone, the chains pinging off the rusted poles. There was a black barn with the doors rotting in.

Ray squatted by a tree and put the glasses to his eyes. The lenses fogged up, and he wiped them with the tail of his T-shirt. The wind picked up, and rainwater ran out of the leaves over his head, soaking his back. A man with a black T-shirt, a leather vest, and a ponytail came out of the house with a beer can in his hand. He threw the can at the dog and lit a cigarette. The dog sat and watched the man expectantly, his ears back. There was a blue van in the driveway and a motorcycle next to the rotting porch. One of the windows upstairs was broken, and a curtain hung through where the glass was gone. After a minute a woman with wild hair and thick hips came out wearing a green T-shirt and shorts and carrying two bottles of water. The guy with the ponytail took one and dumped it over his head and into his eyes, and the woman smoothed back his hair with her hands.

Ray ran the glasses over the house, the van, the yard. He could hear thunder far away, and the rain began to pick up again. He went into his bag and came out with a thin plastic parka and put it on and then settled onto a tree stump and picked up the glasses again. He smelled the faint, acrid odor of charcoal burning. The rain on the parka made popping noises close to his ears. He let his mind drift, thinking about decades ago when the house was new and someone brought a young girl here to show her where she was going to live. Someone thinking this was the place they would get old and die and maybe being okay with that. Christ, but he was getting strange in his old age.

After a while he walked back down the hill and along the road, back past the driveway and along a fence that bordered the other edge of the property. The ground was more exposed, open to view from the neighbors, and he walked just to the crest of the hill. He sat down in the wet grass and made sketches of the layout: the house, the barn, the dog, the tree line. This side of the hill had a view of a valley dotted with houses, stands of trees. Six or seven cows stood together on a hillside a hundred yards away. Horseflies found him and began to bite him through his jeans. He retreated down the hill, swatting at his legs.

LATER, RAY DROVE back down through the hills into Doylestown and parked on a side street. It was a Sunday afternoon, the day quiet and the air thick with humidity. He put a baseball cap over his wet hair and walked the main drag, stopping at a bookstore to get a paper. He stood near the door, feeling his wet clothes cool and holding his paper. There was a circular rack with ten-dollar DVDs near the register, and he stood and pushed it around. One of the faces looked familiar, and he picked up the case, finding it to be the movie he'd watched the night before. *Gun Crazy*.

A woman stood at the register holding her glasses up to the light, and then she breathed on them and wiped them with the tail of her shirt. She put them on and took them off again while Ray watched her. She swore under her breath, then noticed him standing there.

"Sorry about that." Her smile was crooked, and she looked down. "We're not supposed to, you know, swear in front of the customers." He smiled back and shrugged to show he didn't mind.

She pointed at his hand. "Ring that up?" she said, and he handed her the box, his mind blank. He felt his face coloring.

"This is a good one."

"I watched it last night. On TV. You know, not the DVD. Or why would I be getting it now?" Jesus Christ. "I never saw them before, the couple in it, but I liked it."

"John Dall, he never really did anything else that was, you know, famous. The girl, Peggy Cummins, she was in *Night of the Demon*."

"A horror thing?" He was conscious of the way he talked, the words forming in his mouth. Of not cursing, trying to seem okay.

She had a small mole near her mouth, and her smell was sweet and faint, like an apple smelled when you held it to your face.

"Oh, yeah, a great one, with Dana Andrews. Directed by Tourneur. Great stuff, very . . ." She waggled her fingers and widened her eyes in mock terror. "You don't get nightmares, do you?"

Ray thought she must be in her midtwenties, maybe thirty? Younger than him, he thought, but he was no good at ages. She came around from behind the register and went to another display and flipped through some more cases. She bit her lip and pulled her glasses off her face to use like a magnifying glass. Her hair was dark, and she wore it in a braid, something that always caught his eye. He thought of her in a room somewhere braiding her hair in front of a mirror. Putting on makeup, those little pencils and liners a whole branch of knowledge he knew nothing about. Not that she wore much makeup.

"Shit. Sorry. These things aren't worth a goddamn. Sorry. Doesn't look like we have it." She was tall, maybe taller than him, with a slim build under loose clothes. A gauzy skirt, one of those sweaters that looks like it has thread pulls all over it. Dark colors, like he wore. Browns and blacks and dark blues. Did that mean something?

He wanted to keep talking, had nothing to say. He nodded.

"Thanks for looking. I'll keep an eye out." He spent a long time looking through his pockets for the right change. *"Night of the Demons."*

"Demon, right." She smiled at him. There were lines by her eyes that made her seem like someone who would be nice to people. Ray looked down. He held up his bag, smiled, and waved on his way to the door, and she watched him go.

He sat in the car a while. The sun wanted to come out, he thought, but then fat drops started hitting the windshield and the roof, loud as pistol shots. It began to hail. Chunks of ice pounded the car, making a muffled roar that was somehow pleasant. He liked being inside and watching it come down. People ran by: two young girls, holding hands; a fat man with a bent umbrella. He opened his paper, closed it again. He was drawn to those women who wore long clothes and dark colors. He thought it meant something, dressing like that. It seemed to him they were protecting themselves against some possible danger, and he thought it wise to be onto the world, to know things could go wrong.

He wondered if he asked her out, how long it would take for her to get on his nerves, or how long until she got bored with him. Isn't that what happened? She seemed a lot smarter than he was. There were people he met who seemed to have a whole language he didn't know. He wasn't stupid, but what he knew was what he had taught himself. He haunted the bookswaps, buying paper bags full of Louis L'Amour and Zane Grey. Books about World War II, black holes. He had opened a book of short stories by a woman named Amy Hempel and couldn't stop reading it. Bought it for ninety cents and went to the library in Warrington to get more. Something in it made him wish he'd finished school, could somehow get to know smart women who knew there was a terrible joke inside of everything that happened to you.

He could only see clearly the end of the arc of wanting someone. He could feel gears turning inside him when he saw certain women, fell in love two or three times a week with women in shops or at bars or just stopped alongside him at intersections, but it was like he skipped too much in his head and got caught up in how the end played out. The screaming and cocked fists and broken glass. He had a vision of his mother carrying him into the bathroom and locking the door, holding him in the bathtub while his father screamed like a gutshot animal and smashed things in the kitchen.

THAT NIGHT HE lifted the lid on the toilet tank and pulled out a plastic ziplock bag with a foil package in it. He went into the kitchen and made a pipe out of a straw and aluminum foil and dumped a tiny hit of brownish, clotted heroin into the bowl. He sat on his old couch and fired it up and waited. His apartment was tiny, white walls and three rooms over a garage owned by an ancient Ukrainian widow who only left her house for funerals and bingo.

He had put on an album he liked, the sound track to the Bruce Willis movie where he finds out he's a superhero. The music was quiet but built to a point. Ray liked to think it suggested powerful things happening that were invisible to the eye. He put the pipe down and poured himself a Jameson. He became aware of a pounding in his blood, a repeating signal that spread warmth and light through his head and down along his arms. He lay back on the couch and let his eyes almost close, so the lamplight filtered orange through his lashes. Currents moved in his blood, and he thought of chemicals being conveyed through his system to his brain, like people in another time passing buckets full of water hand to hand to throw into a house on fire. He sipped at the shot, and the burning in his throat was like something being cleaned out of him. The woman from the store came into his head wearing blue and black, and he closed his eyes, trying to conjure the sensation of her fingers touching his forehead. Light, in the way some women's hands were light on your skin. He touched his own dry lips and felt his heart beating in the pulses in his fingers. His head moved with the low drumming of his heart, small lateral movements as if there were water under him. He drifted, drifted, waiting for the fire to go out.

"Hey, counter lady."

"Hey, you."

"How much is this hat?"

"You want that hat?"

"I don't know. Yeah."

"That is a ridiculous hat."

"It's cool."

"Take that off, it's making me laugh."

"I make you laugh?"

"Yes, you're laughable."

"Well, I like to make you laugh."

"I know you."

"Yeah. I know you, too."

"You're in Mrs. Haddad's fourth period English."

"I was. Fatass Haddad."

"You used to make us all laugh in there."

"Not Fatass."

"No. You're Ray."

"Yeah."

"You know my name?"

"Yeah, I know your name."

"You're a liar. You don't remember me."

"I remember you. You're Carole Quirk's friend."

"But you don't know my name."

"Carole's friend."

"I knew it. You don't know. Hey, what happened to you?"

"Ah, nothing. I got kicked out."

"I know that, everyone knows that. What for?"

"Ah, I boosted some stuff."

"Yeah?"

"Yeah, it was stupid. I don't know."

"Claudia Shaeffer said your dad . . ."

"Yeah."

"Is that true? Is he in jail?"

"Yeah, he's an asshole."

"Why is he in jail?"

"For being an asshole."

"They don't put you in jail for that. Half the world would be in jail if they did that."

"You don't say that."

"What?"

"Asshole."

"So?"

"I don't know. I just knew that about you. You don't say . . ."

"Swears."

"No."

"Well, it doesn't make me a bad person."

"No."

"I wasn't raised like that."

"You're from, like, the South, right?"

"Kentucky."

"Yeah. Isn't your dad like a cop or something?"

"A state trooper."

"Oh, man."

"You don't like policemen."

"No, I don't know. My old man sure hates them. One thing."

"I guess he would.'

"One thing, they always call you by your whole name. Raymond."

"Yeah, that's my dad."

"Raymond, is this any way to get ahead in life? And shit like that."

"Well, it's not."

"But you're laughing."

"I can't help it, you make me laugh."

"Good, I like to make you laugh."

"You going to pay for that candy bar?"

"No, I'm going to put it back."

"You already ate like half of it."

"Well, then it should be half price."

"Oh, you think you're super bad, huh?"

"I would be if I had this hat."

"You'd be super retarded. Anyway, Mr. Rufe just put in a camera over in the corner, so he can see when you juveniles steal from him."

"You think I care?"

"You should. He'll call my dad and my dad'll put you in jail."

"Like I'm scared."

"You should be."

"Maybe you should be scared of me."

"Why?"

"I was in jail."

"Yeah, but I'm not scared."

"Not even when I'm close up like this? In the middle of the night and you're all alone at the counter?"

"Not even then. Anyway it's like seven thirty at night. It's not even dark."

"What about now?"

"No."

"I think you should come for a ride with me."

"My shift is almost over."

"That's good, then come for a ride."

"I have to go home."

"Just for one ride?"

"You don't even know my name."

"I know it."

"You don't. Say it."

"Marletta."

"Say it again."

"Marletta."

"So you know my name."

"I know about you."

"What do you know?"

"I know you do gymnastics. I know you're smart. I know you like Carole Quirk but not her other friend, Amy."

"Everyone knows that."

"No, I know. I see you. I know your mom is black and your dad is white and that's why you moved up here."

"Who told you that? You think that's funny?"

"No."

"You better watch what you say."

"No, I know that's why you're so good-looking."

"I'm not."

"No, you are. I thought so the first time I ever saw you."

"No. No one says that"

"They're all dipshits."

"You think I am? Good-looking?"

"You are."

"Why did you do that?"

"Kiss you? I wanted to."

"You shouldn't."

"I can't help it. I'm a juvenile."

"You'll help it when my dad sees you."

"He protects you, huh?"

"Something like that. He gets pissed. And then he calls me by my whole name."

"What does he call you when he's not pissed?"

"You'll laugh."

"I won't. I swear."

"Like the swear of a juvenile is worth anything."

"What does he call you?"

"Mars."

'Uh-huh."

"You said you wouldn't laugh."

"I'm not."

"Yeah, you kind of are."

"You're laughing, too. Look at my arm and your arm."

"You're so pale."

"And you're like, I don't know. Honey or something."

"Watch the hands, mister."

"Your skin is soft, that's all."

"You shouldn't be back here. Mr. Rufe would be super pissed."

"I'm just keeping you company."

"Are you coming to junior prom?"

"No, probably not. When are you done?"

"Soon. I have to go home."

"Nah, you don't."

"You shouldn't do that."

"Kiss you?"

"No, you shouldn't."

"I can't help it."

"No?"

"No. I have to."

"You have to?"

"I see you and I just . . . have to."

"Well, if you have to."

"I do. Do you like it?"

"Yes. Say my name."

Dennis Tafoya

"*Marletta.*"

"*You like me?*"

"*I like you.*"

"*I like you, too. Ray.*"

On Tuesday he drove south through Philly, down 95 past the airport and the Burn Center. At Providence Avenue he got off and made his way to SCI Chester, the front looking like a factory or a school or something, if you didn't notice the coils of razor wire.

He filled out the forms using his own name, figuring if they didn't want him there they could kick him out. He wasn't sure he wanted to be there either, but the big bull with the gray flattop behind the Plexiglas just took his name and buzzed him through. He emptied his pockets and stood for a wand, and in about fifteen minutes he was sitting in the visiting room that stank of disinfectant and cigarettes, watching men in yellow jumpsuits trying to act casual with their wives and kids. He sat and watched the kids get tokens out of the change machines for sodas and candy, the same thing he had done the one time he had visited his father upstate all those years before.

He thought about riding the chain the first time, the way he did every time he saw coils of wire. When they sent him out to Camp Hill, his arms were busted, and he sat stiffly in the bus with his arms in the rigid casts while a guy with a lazy eye looked his way and moved his tongue over his lips in a pantomime of hunger.

He could remember little bits of the trial, but it was like he'd seen it on TV. The prosecutor looking pissed all the time and telling the judge how he had stolen a car from his drug buddy

Perry March and racked it up with Marletta next to him, but the trial went by in a rush, like ten minutes of bullshit before they locked him up. None of what the guy said was right, but Marletta was dead and he didn't care what came next.

It was like his life had run backward, the parts before Marletta died real and true and clear, and everything after just a long twilight, a half-life where none of his vague wishes or worst fears materialized and it was hard to come fully awake, to open his eyes and see things as they were. Harder still to sleep, with no one he trusted there to stand watch.

HE PICKED THROUGH different pictures in his head. His father, short but wide through the shoulders; jet black hair in short spikes, holding a can of beer at a ball game. His mother sitting at the kitchen table, her cigarette in the ashtray stained with her lipstick, looking as if it had been dipped in blood. Her blank, defeated look, her eyes fixed somewhere else. His father in handcuffs in the kitchen in the middle of the night, the cops looking embarrassed on his mother's behalf, their eyes down.

Now his father shuffled into the visiting room in a bathrobe, and Ray wasn't ready for the sight of him. His hair was sparse, gray and patchy, and his lips were sucked into his mouth like he was tasting something bitter. He leaned heavily on the long table as he sat, and Ray saw his hands shaking. His father smelled like cigarettes and sour sweat, the wave of it taking Ray back to his own time upstate.

"So," said his father, in a petulant rasp Ray wouldn't have recognized. "I thought you was dead."

Ray opened a pack of cigarettes and shook one out, and his father picked it up with fingers gone orange at the tips.

"Gimme some credit, Bart. I'm violating my parole to be here." He bared his teeth in a mirthless smile and lit his cigarette. He couldn't look directly at his father's face, like it was a too-bright light. "I'm not supposed to associate with criminals. Not even the ones that raised me."

The old man nodded as if Ray had made a valid point. "Ever hear from your mother?"

"I thought I saw her once at the Pathmark in Warminster. Just wishful thinking. What's with the robe, old man? Playing sick?"

Bart shrugged, looked him up and down, everywhere but in the eye. "Cancer. In the stomach. Drinking that shit they make in here, the raisin jack."

Ray looked away, not ready for any of this, and his father looked down, talked to the tabletop.

"The guys put all kinds of shit in it, trying to make it taste like something."

"Shit, Bart. What do they say?"

The old man shrugged. "Six months, a year. Over and out."

"Did you talk to your lawyer? Maybe you can, you know . . ."

His father snorted, made a motion like throwing something over his shoulder. "Can what? Go where? It might as well be here as anywhere. Like you give a shit."

Ray let that hang. He stubbed out his cigarette, lit another. His father grabbed the pack and tried to pinch one between his shaking fingers. Ray watched him for a minute, then took the pack and shook one out. Across the room, a man reached over to tousle the hair of a little girl, who slid away down the bench.

"What about Theresa? Does she know?"

Bart shrugged. "What do you think? She better off with me there, or here?"

Ray shook his head, things moving in this unaccountable direction. Why had he come? What did he need from the old man now?

"I keep remembering this thing," he finally said. The old man looked at Ray, and he pulled his lighter out and fired up his cigarette for his father. "We're in the old house on County Line, remember?"

His father nodded, looked at the tip of his cigarette.

"Anyway, I'm like seven or eight, I don't know. It's the middle of the night and I'm half asleep, but you got me down the kitchen in my pajamas. You been beating the old lady, showing her the errors of her ways. She's crying, but what the hell. I don't remember her doing nothing else. I'm out of it, and slow on the uptake anyway, like you used to point out. But after a while I get that I'm supposed to take a swing at her. You know, get in the habit. Learn how it's done. Take a lesson."

"Yeah, it was all me. I was the one ruined your life."

"Did that happen, really? Like I remember it? Would you even admit it now, you old fuck?"

The old man's breathing was shallow, his face red, the busted veins standing out on his cheeks. "She'd have ruined you."

"Yeah, I was lucky you straightened me out. You straightened me out so good I live alone like a fucking animal in a cave. Scared

if I even bring a woman home I'll start beating the shit out of her."
His hands were shaking, and he stared at the table a long time.

He heard a rasping sound like laughter and looked up, but the
old man was crying, his hand spread across his face and the tears
squeezing out of the corners of his eyes.

"Don't hate me no more. It was the drink, Ray, the drink. I
wanted to be good, but I was weak. I couldn't handle it. Working
at that fucking quarry and breathing that shit all day and coming
home to the water heater's shot and the bills and you sick all
the time. And her wanting me to be something I couldn't. I
couldn't." He put his hand across the table and touched Ray's
arm. The old man's flesh was hot, and Ray wanted to pull away.
"Do you think this is what I wanted? You think I didn't want to
be going home at night? I was weak. I was weak. You can't be
better than you are."

"Yeah." Ray lined up the cigarette packs in front of him and
pulled back from the table. Nodding as if Bart had said something
wise. "That's what I was afraid of."

RAY DROVE BACK up 95, his head on fire. He had felt driven to
see his father again, to try to sort out what was him and what his
old man and the way he'd been raised. He had come up to the
edge of something standing in the store with that girl with the
glasses, and he wanted to know would he always come up to that
edge and look out and away at something he'd never really get to,
never live out. Now Bart was going to die, and he didn't know if
that mattered, if it meant he'd be free or stuck forever.

He remembered guys upstate drinking raisin jack, only the

guys he knew called it chalk. Older guys, mostly, who'd been in for a decade and more or were back for their third or fourth jolts. He remembered a guy named Long John keeping a plastic bag full of rotting fruit and dinner rolls under his bunk. He'd had a drink of thin, milky liquid from a glass jar and thought it tasted like orange-scented gasoline. He didn't get the point, with weed and meth around most of the time.

He'd hated every second of prison but saw guys at home there. Guys who'd get out with the couple of bucks they gave you, what the old cellies called shotgun money because that was all it was enough to buy. They'd blow the money in a couple of days, stick up a 7-Eleven or a gas station and be back inside. Get in bar fights still wearing the Kmart jackets they got when they were gated out. They'd talk like it was bad luck or people on the outside fucking with them that brought them back, but the truth was they couldn't make it outside.

One day upstate they took him off the laundry and sent him and a big convict named Merce outside to bury two guys who'd died within a couple of hours of each other in the infirmary. One from AIDS and one from old age. Merce spent the whole time telling him about the beef that got him locked up, killing a friend in the dope business.

"I went out to get my scratch tickets, I come back, the mother-fucker's drinking my last can of soda. You believe that shit?"

"Uh-huh." They were standing in a field in the snow, watching a trusty scratch a trough in the frozen ground with a green backhoe. Ray kept his hands in the pockets of his thin jacket, and

Merce smoked a cigarette, stabbing at Ray with the red end to make his points. Ray's arms ached where they had been broken.

"That wasn't Coke or Sprite, neither. That was Guarana, what my baby drinks."

"It was what?"

"Guarana. It's from Brazil. You can't get that shit at the Wawa. You got to go to a Brazilian store like all the way the fuck up in Norristown. I said, you did not just drink my last soda."

"Huh." The trusty was taking his time, smacking the ground over and over to break up the frozen clay. Ray felt the ground under him shudder every time the bucket on the backhoe hit the ground.

"He said you just go to the store. I said, bullshit you go to the store. I went to the closet, got my crossbow."

Ray looked at him, eyebrows up.

"You heard me. My baby didn't like guns in the house."

"Good compromise."

Merce gave him convict eyes, his head lowered, smoke from his Newport streaming from his nose. Then he gave a snort and started a deep laugh that shook his frame and started him coughing and made his eyes tear. "Yeah, I guess you got to laugh now."

There was a grinding snap, and the backhoe stuck fast in the frozen ground. The engine died, and they heard the trusty swear. Ray watched a thin film of frost materialize on the plywood coffins. Thought about it forming on the dead men inside the boxes. Merce's eyes fixed on the middle distance.

Ray said, "Lesson learned, huh?"

"Yeah." Merce bent to the stacked coffins, throwing the cigarette away in an arc of smoke like a plane going down in a war movie. "If only my baby had bought more soda, I wouldn't be in this fix."

CHAPTER FOUR

THE NIGHT MANNY picked him up it was raining, and they went for Rick, splashing through black streams covering the roads at every low intersection. Ray held the thickened bones in his arms, and under the dark clouds they sang to him, an eddying ache that made him wince and sigh. The van slewed in the water, and Manny cursed. "Christ, look at this. And it's still a thousand degrees out, how is that possible?"

"I figure it's good for us. Keeps the civilians indoors, watching TV."

They slowed in front of a white house in Horsham fronted with crumbling asbestos tiles. Rick limped out under a sheet of newspaper and climbed in. "Look at that rain. I thought maybe you'd call it off."

Ray shook his head. "Nah, neither rain nor dark of night. What happened to your leg?"

"Ah, I went around to my ex's to get my fucking stereo back, and her asshole boyfriend was there. Like to take my fucking knee off with a monkey wrench."

Manny put the van in gear. "Been there. You notice they always trade up for somebody with bigger shoulders than you?"

Ray watched Rick rubbing the knee. "You take something for that?"

"Ah, you know. I handled it." Manny looked over at Ray and shook his head.

"Rick, you high right now?"

"No, man. Just took the edge off, you know."

"If you aren't a hundred percent it's better you tell us now."

"No, no way. I'm cool, really. It was hours ago, and I'm in the pink."

Ray watched Rick, who looked out the window. He did seem all right. When he turned and saw Ray considering him, he smiled, held up his hands.

The car in front of them stopped short, and Manny stood on the brakes, the back of the van fishtailing. They all cursed, and Ray put a hand out to the dash. Rick slid forward and hit the back of Manny's seat; he screwed up his face and grabbed his knee. "Mother . . . fuck." He gritted his teeth and clenched his eyes shut.

After a minute they began to inch forward. Ray saw a cop, waving a flashlight, and a traffic barrier three cars ahead. They were being waved onto a side road. Far ahead a tree lay across the road, green leaves splayed out in the rain, pink shards of wood broken over the road looking like wet bone. Ray grabbed a map from the floor and began to try to orient himself.

Rick pointed at a road sign. "Left or right?"

"Left. No, right."

They turned onto a smaller side street. Dark water streamed in a ditch by the road, and lightning illuminated low clouds that looked to be a few feet above the trees. Ray called the turns. Once they ended up in a cul-de-sac and had to backtrack. Eventually they came out on the right road a few miles beyond the tweaker farm and pulled over.

Manny and Ray climbed into the rear, and Ray pulled a duffel bag out of the back and put it on the rear seat. He opened it and pulled out the DEA windbreakers and Manny's pump gun and handed them over. Next came a box of shells and a big Colt Python with a six-inch barrel. He held the gun out to Rick, opening the cylinder and spinning it to show him it was loaded. He pulled out three folded parkas and handed them around and then brought out two walkie-talkies and three heavy police flashlights. He flicked on one of the lights and pointed it at the walkie-talkies each in turn, tuning the dials to the same channel and then clicking them on. He adjusted the volume on both and handed one to Rick and clipped the other to his belt. He rummaged in the bag for a minute, pulling out items to show Rick and Manny and then dropping them back in the bag. Tape, the heavy wire wraps that they used as cuffs, a folding knife, a half pound of ground meat, bottles of water.

He took out his map and laid it on the seat and put the light on it.

"This side is me. I'm moving up from the street along these trees. You're on this side, and we're both moving parallel to the driveway in the middle. You two come to the side door here, I'm going to the front door. I'll take care of the dog, if it's out. Fucking thing barks nonstop anyway as far as I can tell, so it's not a big deal." He drew an arrow on the map.

"When you get to the side door here, key the button a couple of times. Don't fucking say anything, just key the button." He clicked it so they could hear the corresponding click and hiss on the other walkie-talkie. "I key you back and we go in." Manny, loading the shotgun, nodded and gave him a thumbs-up.

Ray pointed at Rick. "Just take it fucking easy. If you're clear when you get to the door, take off the parka so they can see the DEA jacket. They'll piss and moan, maybe they'll try to hide, but no one's going to draw down on a Fed unless he's fucking insane, and then we got a bigger problem."

Manny smiled. "Which is how to get the hell out fast."

"If they shoot, run. This—" Ray pointed at the Python in Rick's hands. "This is for show. You're not a Fed, you just play one on TV, get it? This ain't worth nobody getting a bullet in the brainpan. Not even those shitbirds up the hill. Plus the whole fucking place is liable to burn like a furnace you shoot off a gun in there. They're meth cookers. The fucking place is full of acetone and ether and Christ knows what-all."

Manny laid the shotgun down on the floor and went into his pocket for a glass vial. He pulled an old piece of rearview mirror out from under the seat and shook out three rocky lines of off-white powder. He took a flat piece of cardboard out of his pocket and pulled a single-edged razor blade out of it. He chopped the three lines into six. He rolled up a twenty and handed it to Rick.

"Oh, man, thanks." He did two lines and passed the twenty to Ray, who did the lines and then opened one of the water bottles and poured a little out into his palm and then snorted the water out of his hand.

"That is some nasty biker crank."

When they were set, Ray got behind the wheel and drove slowly past the property, pointing up the tree line he'd be walking. "I'll be heading straight up this way." He drove past the driveway to the fence on the other side of the property and stopped. Manny and Rick got out, guns out of sight under their parkas. They slammed the doors, and Ray angled the van over to turn around, awkwardly jockeying it back and forth until it was headed back up the road.

He parked again in the little turnoff and looked at his watch. Eleven o'clock. Grabbing the bag, he turned off the ignition and dropped the keys under the seat. After a minute of running through things in his head, he took a deep breath and stepped out of the van. He stuck the Colt in his windbreaker pocket and made his way up the hill, moving slowly in the black.

HE KEPT SLIPPING in the grass. He walked for what felt like forever and didn't seem to be moving far from the van. The night and rain turned him around, and he had to keep looking back down the hill to get his bearings. The line of trees seemed wider somehow and the ground more uneven than he remembered it. In a couple of minutes he was struggling, his own breath roaring in his ears under the parka and sweat pouring down his back. The bag weighed a ton, and he looped the strap over his shoulder.

After what seemed like an hour, he crested the hill and saw the lights of the house. He couldn't see the dog and thought that a good sign. He was panting now and dropped to one knee to catch his breath. There were lights in the house and one on upstairs in the barn, which he didn't expect. He had thought the building was a padlocked wreck and hadn't paid much attention to it. He took the binoculars out and put them on the barn window, but the dark made them about useless.

He put the binoculars away and moved toward the house along the driveway, then crouched behind the blue van, breathing hard. He felt exposed, the lights in the barn were throwing him off. His shaking hands were slick with sweat and rainwater and he kept sticking them under his parka and wiping them on his jeans. He moved around the van and then walked fast to the barn, keeping to the side away from the house. Now that he was close he could see the caved-in doors were open, and he swore to himself.

The black, empty doorway felt like a mouth waiting to close on him. He slowly crossed in front of the sagging doors and then edged around the building, stopping once to pull the Colt out of his pocket. When he came to stairs leading up inside the barn, he stood for a long time, listening, but heard nothing from inside. There was a hiss-click, loud in his ears from the walkie-talkie, and he jumped and almost pulled the trigger on the pistol.

He put his hand on his chest and willed his heart to stop racing, then moved quickly across the driveway to the side of the house away from Manny and Rick. He inched across the front, keeping low, ducking under a dark window to reach the porch. He pulled the parka off over his head and threw it behind him. He pulled the walkie-talkie out his bag, dropped the bag on the porch, and pointed the big Colt at the door. He keyed the mike twice and threw the walkie-talkie down and kicked the door in with a steel-toed boot.

THE HALLWAY WAS dark. There was a stink of ammonia and acetone and charcoal, the wet, catpiss reek of meth labs that made his eyes water. He heard Manny shouting that they were federal agents and did the same. He moved into the open space, wheeling left and right with the pistol. Somewhere in the house the dog barked, crazy to be let out. There were two dark and empty rooms on either side of the hallway and stairs leading up. He ran down the hallway screaming, "Down on the ground; get down!"

At the end of the hallway he turned right and saw Manny standing over Ponytail, who was on his knees with his hands behind his head.

Ray pointed at Rick with his empty hand. "Cuff him."

Rick stuck his pistol into his jeans and pulled a wire wrap from his belt. He pushed Ponytail onto the floor face first and jerked his hands up behind him, fumbling with the wire wrap. He rubbed his knee and winced. "Hold still, you dumb Piney fuck."

Ponytail screamed into the floor. "You got to read me my rights. You like to broke my nose."

Rick pulled the pistol out of his belt and smacked the barrel against the back of the prone tweaker's skull. "Shut the fuck up, hillbilly, or I'll break your head."

There was a piercing scream from the doorway, and the thick-waisted woman stood there in a yellow T-shirt and cutoffs pointing a long-barreled shotgun. Rick jumped up as Manny and Ray aimed their guns at her. The dog was going insane behind a door somewhere, the barking like a scream over and over.

"Drop the gun!"

"Federal agents!"

She swiveled the gun at Ray and Manny in turn, her eyes wild and full of tears.

"You leave him be!"

Ray pointed his pistol at the floor and held one hand out. "Calm down, for Christ's sake. No one's hurting anyone."

Ponytail tried to raise his head. "Charlene, go get my cell phone and call my brother!"

Ray bared his teeth, trying to smile. "Don't move, Charlene."

Ponytail's voice was hoarse, lisping through rotted teeth. "It's the Zionist occupying army. They come to put them chips in us."

"Chips? What?" Ray heard a loud metallic click and turned to see Rick pulling back the hammer on the big revolver, the gun at Ponytail's temple.

"Drop that—" was as far as Rick got before Charlene's shotgun went off, deafening Ray. The blast spattered Rick and Ponytail and a yellow refrigerator with buckshot. Ray dropped his pistol, and Manny pulled the trigger on his scattergun, knocking the woman back into the hallway. Rick howled on the floor, rolling in blood and brains from Ponytail's shattered head and what looked like milk leaking from a half-dozen holes in the refrigerator.

Ray felt like his skull was cracked, his ears ringing. He took two steps into the hallway to see Charlene's staring eyes and caved-in chest. Manny stepped to the side door and vomited into the rain.

Ray picked up his cold pistol and stuffed it into his belt. "Everyone be calm," he said to no one.

Rick moaned and turned in circles on the slick floor, trying to stand up. The air was full of blue smoke. Ray smelled burned gunpowder and the meaty tang of blood. He pulled a chair onto its feet and sat down in it. "Everyone just stay put." He felt insane.

There was a cracking somewhere and a rush of feet and the dog was in the room. Ray jerked at the pistol at his waist, but the animal careened through the kitchen and out the side door, knocking Manny off his feet and leaving a trail of bloody paw prints.

Rick sat back on his haunches, bleeding from his arms and his chest. "Jesus, my arm's broke." His eyes rolled back white and he fainted, falling into the corner against a pie safe. Urine splashed out of his pant leg as he breathed one last terrible, gargling breath, a sound like water emptying from a copper pipe. The dog's barking dwindled as it disappeared into the storm.

Manny lurched back into the room, wiping his mouth with the back of his hand. Ray shook his head, not believing any of it. He said, "We gotta go."

"Fuck that. I'm not doing this for free." Manny stepped across the kitchen, trying to avoid the mess on the floor.

Ray held his hand up. "I'll look. Let me look. Find something to get rid of this mess with." He looked around at the blood on the walls. "Jesus fucking Christ, what the fuck happened?"

They stood there for a minute, and then Manny put the shotgun on his shoulder and walked out into the rain. Ray got up and walked back out through the hallway, trying not to look at the woman and to stay out of the widening pool of blood. Neither plan worked. He saw that her T-shirt was a uniform red now. He forced himself to keep moving, scraping his shoes on the linoleum to get the blood off. At the end of the hallway he turned left and came back out to the landing. He went out to the porch and rummaged in the bag for his flashlight. When he got back inside he pushed the broken door back into place and pointed the light into the corners of the front room. He could see the cooker with its tubes and wires, dark and cold, and thanked the Tweaker Jesus for this little bit of mercy. There were Mason jars and empty two-liter soda bottles on a long table, a stack of coffee filters, a pile of charcoal briquettes. In the corner of the room was a yard-high pile of empty charcoal bags and ripped packages for cold medicine.

He made his way upstairs, forcing himself to move fast and trust that there was no one left in the house. He kept replaying the scene in the kitchen over and over, trying to make it happen right. He moved from room to room down the narrow hallway, finding each one empty. A wet, reeking bathroom, the tiles peeled from the wall; empty bedrooms, old bedsteads furred with black dust. In what had been the master bedroom there were clothes on the floor, bottles of water, and a box of surgical masks. Under the mattress on the floor was a paper bag with a few hundred bucks in it, and he picked it up. He rolled it tight and jammed it into the pocket of the windbreaker. He pushed open the closet doors, pointing the flashlight beam at stacks of wood, a pile of newspapers with headlines about Reagan.

Off the master bedroom was a padlocked room, and he lifted his leg and kicked the door twice hard with the sole of his boot. The cleats gave way in the rotted wood, and the door swung back with a banshee howl from the rusted hinges. He found a light switch on the wall and pushed it up with a hand covered by the sleeve of his parka.

A faint orange light set in a lamp shaped like a rocking horse showed a child's room, a room for a girl: white furniture, a pink plaid ruffle around a sagging bed. Everything was sunken in gray dust unmarked by fingerprints. A brush with a red handle was sitting on a white vanity, a Mariah Carey poster hung bowed out and sagging. Ray thought there was something wrong about his going into the padlocked room, and standing in the doorway he wished he hadn't forced the door. The closet stood open, empty, and he half-heartedly opened a couple of drawers, releasing a shower of dust onto his boots. He turned off the light and backed out.

He came back downstairs and pulled open more closets. Kicked over a low desk and dumped out the drawers. Retraced his steps back down the hallway and turned left. A door hung on its hinges, the edges clawed. They must have locked the dog in here. He stepped in and covered his nose with his hands and tried to breathe through his mouth. There were piles of shit on the floor, a rubber replica of a rolled-up newspaper with holes chewed in it, a dented metal bowl. There was a cracked window and deep claw marks on the sill. On a table was a stack of plastic bags. He picked one up and dumped it out, and a dozen smaller bags of powder rolled out onto the table and the floor. He swept them back in and looked around for something to carry them in. On the floor was a duffel, and he pulled it open and saw bundles of cash, tens and twenties and hundreds held together with rubber bands. There were more plastic bags jammed with foil packages. He stuck his pistol into his belt and swept the bags from the table messily into the duffel and then hefted the bag with both hands and hustled it out the door. He dragged it out the front door and dropped it on the porch.

Manny appeared near the porch carrying a can of acetone. He and Ray went back into the kitchen and began dragging the bodies down the hallway and into the front room by the cooker.

Ray pointed down the hill. "Get the van, I'll finish this."

Manny ran off the porch and down the drive. There was a flash of lightning that lit the whole world, and for one fraction of a second Ray saw everything in a flare of blue white light and black shadow: Manny halfway down the drive, running flat out, the dead man and woman and their horror-movie wounds, the tracks of blood and fluid leading out to the hallway, the footprints, the money, the discarded shotgun, and his own terrible face in an antique mirror over the fireplace. His eyes were huge and white, his hair matted, his mouth open as if he were screaming. Then it was dark again.

He went back into the kitchen and bent down over Rick. Ray put a finger on Rick's neck but wasn't sure what he should find. He felt nothing but cold skin, and Rick's staring eyes were dry and black. Ray looked into the dead and empty pupils, inches from his own but staring through him, as if reading something written on the wall behind Ray's head. He almost turned to look.

Finally he grabbed Rick's jacket and pulled him slowly toward the door. The body twisted and began to come out of the jacket, and Ray struggled to get a purchase with bloody hands. He began to be conscious of the stink of shit and blood and piss, and he

66

started to gag. How long had they been here? An hour? Three? Would it be light soon? He braced himself against the door jamb and pulled and got some momentum. He pumped his legs hard and didn't stop until he collapsed by the front door. Good enough.

He stepped out to the porch. He heard the van coming up the drive and grabbed Manny's shotgun off the bag and ran to take a position behind the ruined pickup in the grass. When Manny opened the door and jumped out, Ray stepped from behind the truck and showed himself.

Manny jumped. "Christ, you scared the shit out of me."

"Sorry. I was standing there listening to you come, and it just hit me that it might not really be you." He handed Manny the gun and ran to the porch and dragged the duffel, bumping, down the stairs.

Manny left the side door of the van open and came over to help him heft it. "Christ, is that all cash? How much is in here?"

"Whatever it is, it's not enough."

They policed up the house and the yard, doing a quick look for anything they had forgotten or dropped in the excitement. Finally Manny went to the van and Ray went back into the front room. He picked up the acetone and uncapped it, splashing it on the bodies and the floor and backing out to the door, choking on the stink. He spat into the grass and then dumped the last bit of the fluid on a snapped-off piece of dowel rod he found on the porch and lit it. He tossed the can underhand into the house and threw the lit stick in after it. There was a rush of air and a thump, and the front room glowed blue for a few seconds and then flashed over white and orange and the front windows blew out.

He stood back and watched it burn for a moment, then ran over and jumped in the passenger side of the van. Manny gunned the engine, throwing gravel and splashing through ruts filled with water.

AS THEY CRESTED the hill there was a flash of lightning, and they both saw a car turning into the driveway in front of them.

Manny jammed on the brakes. "Oh, Jesus Christ. You have got to be fucking kidding."

"Swing right, up on the grass. Go." Manny spun the wheel and the van skidded and slid, the back end fishtailing around. Ray tried to see behind them, but whatever was going on at the house was still out of sight behind the hill.

"Calm the fuck down." The car moved slowly toward them up the driveway, something long and wide across the ass—a Dodge Charger, an old one. Dark blue, maybe, or black. Manny hooked around them, and Ray caught a brief glimpse of a young guy behind the wheel, long hair and a neat goatee, smiling, and a dark figure beside him. Manny punched the gas and the wheels spun in place, burning a hole in the wet grass. The other car disappeared over the rise toward the house. Ray, breathing hard, put a hand on his chest and felt his heart hammering. Manny smacked the steering wheel with the heel of his hand and stomped on the gas. The back end of the van slid down the hill and the tires caught. The van popped forward about three feet and the engine stalled. Ray put his hands up and caught himself. Manny hit the steering wheel hard with his chest. "Motherfucking motherfucker."

There was a couple of seconds of silence in the van, and Ray could swear he heard shouting from somewhere. Manny grabbed the key and twisted. Ray's mind went completely blank, and he just watched Manny cranking the engine over and over. There was a glow over the rise behind them, and Ray began to see red light reflected on the tops of the wet trees. The starter growled and finally caught, and Manny hit the gas and spun the wheel to straighten them out. He got the van moving down the driveway and picked up speed as they moved down the last of the hill and thumped down onto the street. Manny twisted the wheel and the tires spun and whined, trying to find a grip on the wet asphalt. They shot down the road as the Charger's headlights disappeared over the rise, where now Ray could see flames cresting the hill.

"Oh, Jesus, get moving." They were almost out of sight of the driveway when the Dodge shot back down the driveway and took the corner. Ray could see it fishtailing, and it almost kept going across the road into the trees, but the driver got it under control and gunned it. Smoke formed around the rear wheels as the car gained traction and shot forward after them. They lost sight of it as the van rounded a corner and began to climb.

THEY WERE LOST, and Manny was moving too fast for them to get their bearings. Ray tried to keep him moving east toward the Delaware, and Manny made turns when he figured the van could make it without catapulting them across an intersection and into the trees that lined the dark country lanes. Ray climbed across the seats and tried to hold himself at the rear window with the shotgun. He jacked more shells into the breech and held on to a seat belt strap as the van banked from side to side. Manny jammed on the brakes to make a turn, and Ray smacked his head against the door. The car would be faster and handle better on the wet roads, but once they had made a couple of turns it didn't seem likely that the men following them would know where they were.

Ray climbed awkwardly into the front and dropped into the passenger seat, sweating and cursing under his breath. There were no lights and not many signs, and none of them meant anything to Ray. They passed farms and small developments with a few houses and crossed a creek swollen and black in the moonlight.

There was a hissing, clicking noise, and Ray jumped in his seat.

A voice, close by, said, "Ten-four, good buddy."

Ray looked at Manny, who looked at Ray's waist. The walkie-talkie. Christ, they must have dropped the other one in the yard. The cheap thing only carried a few miles, so that meant the Charger was still behind them and moving fast to stay close.

"Man, you guys know how to party." Ray unclipped the radio from his belt and held it up. "Come on, let's talk for a minute."

Manny shook his head. "Throw that thing the fuck out the window."

Ray held up his hand. There was something about the voice. Ray wondered if it was the young guy he had seen at the wheel of the Charger. It was deep, confident. Amused, maybe, at how fast things could get fucked up.

"Say something. I figured you left this one behind 'cause you wanted to talk things over, figure out how to resolve this thing." The guy had a soft accent, a New England burr that slightly opened the vowels with *r*'s and twisted others, like the way he said "resolve" with a throaty "aw" sound.

Ray clicked the handset twice, then, after a beat, twice again. Manny slowed at a five-way intersection, headed vaguely left.

The voice said, "Okay, that's better." There was a long pause. "I'm just trying to understand this. I'm willing to give you the benefit of the doubt. Old Randy was a crazy man. Maybe things just got out of hand? You were just going over there to cop and Charlene came on to you, shows you her stuff. Randy flips out, starts in with the black helicopters or some shit? Something like that?" The voice was calm, but in the background they could hear the Charger's engine racing, trying to catch up with them.

Manny shook his head, glaring. "Will you throw that fucking thing away? Suppose they can home in on the fucking thing or something."

"They're not the CIA, man. It's just a pissed-off dealer, and maybe he tells us something we can use to stay the fuck out of his way."

The voice said, "I guess there are two problems with that scenario, where it's all just a big misunderstanding. One is this here radio. Which I can't figure unless you were police, or miscreants, and this little dime store thing is not police issue. The other thing—and this is where things get real complicated—the other thing is you stole my fucking money and my dope." The voice had an edge now. "Now, I know you might think I want to avenge the deaths of those two hillbillies or some shit. I tell you sincerely I am only thinking about the money." The voice was fading, static building on the line.

"So here's a way out for everyone. You just tell me where you are, you drop the bag out the door and drive away. Then this becomes a funny story about how you almost ended up getting tortured to death for no good reason, instead of a sad story about two headless corpses found in the river." Riv-ah, the way the guy said it. Ray tried to think if the guy at the farmhouse, Randy, had an accent, or the woman. Rick had called him a Piney, and that's what Ray remembered, a backwoods kind of accent tinged with Philly.

They came to a stop sign, and Manny turned right. The road climbed and twisted, and the van slowed with the effort. The voice got louder and clearer. Ray stared into the rear window, eyes burning with the strain of trying to pick something meaningful out of the wet dark behind the van. "What do you think, that you'd be that tough to find? A couple of white guys ripping off dealers in a brown van? This walkie-talkie tells me you've been doing this a while. And that means there are a bunch of people out there who want me to catch you and put a bullet in your eye."

There was lightning, and the walkie-talkie hissed and popped with static. "You should think about this. You can still make it all go away. The fire, that'll probably keep the cops out of it. I love a good fire, it's like the fuckup's friend." Ahead, two yellow eyes appeared in the road, and Manny stood on the brakes. The van jerked and swiveled in the water, and Manny fought to hold the road. The van spun until it was sliding broadside down the road. Ray was thrown against the door, trying to grab at the dash, the seat, anything. The eyes in the road got huge, like some kind of monster bearing down on them. Finally the van stopped with a scream of rubber. They sat for a moment, watching the deer move daintily into the trees. Manny let a breath out like air escaping from a tire and cranked the wheel until the van pointed back down the road.

The voice said, "Don't make me do all the talking, pal. I'm patient, but you gotta start dealing with this situation or there are going to be serious fucking repercussions." There was hissing and a harsh click timed with a flash of lightning. "I need that fucking money, you hear me?"

Manny hit the roof of the van with his fist. "That's enough of that shit." He grabbed the radio out of Ray's hand and sailed it out the window into the trees.

Ray nodded. "Yeah, fuck it. Just go." But he had wanted to hear more. He wasn't learning anything, not really, and he probably wouldn't have. It would have been impossible to say why he wanted to keep hearing the deep voice, telling him he was going to be caught and die, but he did. He would have sat there all night with the walkie-talkie listening to the terrible shit that was going to happen, if Manny hadn't grabbed the thing and thrown it away.

THEY MADE A right and then a quick left again and passed an old Victorian house with a bed-and-breakfast sign and then came to a dead end.

Manny yelled at Ray, "Where am I going?"

Ray took in the yellow sign marked with arrows pointing north and south. "This is River Road. Turn right and haul ass."

Ray stowed the shotgun under the first row of passenger seats and covered it with a parka and then climbed into the passenger seat again. The road was narrow, and they began to see traffic going the other way. Ray stiffened every time a car passed them, thinking they were going to get a face full of windshield if it was the Charger.

What could they know? So they had gotten that there were two of them in a brown van. The guys in the Charger had been at the house for like five minutes before they came out after Ray and Manny. If they had looked at their faces, what could they have seen? Ray had barely registered the driver of the Charger, and it seemed to Ray that the guy had been staring straight ahead.

"Assume the worst, right?" He looked over at Manny, whose face was dripping, as if the rain were coming directly at them into the van.

"I'm way out ahead on that. I'm thinking they're already at my house with a blowtorch."

"I mean, how much trouble could we be in? What could they even find out?" Ray's mind raced and his head throbbed. "They saw the van, so what? The plates are from the junkyard, and we dump the thing tomorrow somewhere." He wanted a cigarette. "They ID Rick? Can they tie him to us? And why would they? Who knows our business?"

"Hoe Down." Hoe Down was Ho Dinh, a Vietnamese in Philly they downed drugs to from the dealers they took off. Ho was the one they ran all their scores by, the guy connected to the bikers and the organized guys running speed. They talked with Ho about everything they did, and Ho would warn them off dealers or cookers who were protected.

It made what they did a kind of public service for the established guys. Cleaning the little operations off the street, keeping things quiet and running smooth in ways Ray didn't even get. What Manny called *agita*, Philly Italian for heartburn, aggravation.

Ray said, "Yeah, but doesn't Ho have as much to lose as we do? If word got out he was taking the stuff we took off other dealers and putting it back out on the street?"

"Dude, some biker sticks a gun in his mouth he's only got one thing to lose."

"Yeah, I guess." Ray liked Ho, didn't like to think of the moment they couldn't trust him anymore.

"Then? At that minute? He's not thinking long term."

AFTER A FEW minutes they came to a bridge and crossed into Frenchtown on the Jersey side of the river. The houses were dark and nothing was open. When the road dead-ended again they turned south on 29, following the black coil of the river and passing through crossroad towns, most of them too small to have names. When they hit Lambertville, Ray told Manny to get off 29, and they drove through the town. Ray saw his first human being on the street, an old man walking a dog on George Street. As they passed under a streetlight Ray angled his watch and looked at the time. Twelve thirty-five. Everything had happened so fast. He tried to think about each thing but it all just unspooled in his head in a rush. The noise and fire and the stink of blood and ether and smoke. And those guys, those fucking guys in the Charger. At the south end of town they kept going, headed toward 95.

CHAPTER FIVE

THEY WERE TOO freaked to go home, so they rented a room at a no-name motel in Bordentown. Ray paid for the room, and Manny took the van off the street and parked it behind the hotel. When Ray got to the room, Manny was dragging the duffel bag up the curb. Ray unlocked the room and went back out and got the shotgun and wrapped it in his windbreaker and carried it in, locking the door behind him. He pulled the curtains tight, and Manny began dumping the contents of the bag out and sorting the plastic bags of dope from the cash. A fat black spider fell out of the bag, and Manny made a disgusted noise and stomped on it. Ray opened his knife and began cutting the rubber bands off the bundles of money and dumping more cash out of plastic bags. Manny found the remote and put the TV on, something to make noise and cover their conversation. The bag stank of dogshit, so when it was empty Ray took it outside and stuffed it in a trash can near the ice machine.

They developed a system, Manny making stacks of ones, five, and tens, and Ray organizing the twenties, fifties, and hundreds.

Ray fished in a drawer and came out with a pad and a green pen. After a while Manny went out and got them Cokes from the machine. Around two Manny stripped off his clothes and took a shower. When he came back Ray leaned back against the bed and shook his head.

"I can't fucking count any more. I'm fried."

"Where are we?"

"Right now, I'm at—" He added a column of figures on the pad. "One hundred and twenty seven thousand, six hundred, give or take. Not counting the dope. And there's still all this shit over here." He picked up a pile of loose bills and let it drop.

"Jesus Christ." Manny sat on the bed wrapped in a towel. "How do you figure Ma and Pa Kettle put together that much money? That's a shitload of eightballs."

"Unless it's not theirs."

"The guys in the Charger?"

Ray shrugged. The most they had taken off anyone had been twenty-two thousand, from a Salvadoran crack dealer in a housing project in Bensalem, and that had been dumb luck. The Salvadoran's crew of jugglers—underage kids who stood on the street and serviced the rockheads walking or driving by—had been sitting at the kitchen table emptying their pockets at the end of the day. One of them, who looked about nine, had actually started to cry when Ray and Manny came in with guns up, shouting. The kid had put his head on the table and started sobbing, yelling, "*No me mate,*" with his eyes clamped shut. Don't kill me. Which was a pretty useless thing to say, but Ray guessed you had to say something when the guns came out, and that was as good as anything.

RAY WALKED OVER to the sink and ran the water, dumping it over his head with his hands. Manny put his dirty clothes back on and sat on the edge of the bed, paralyzed by the pile of cash and drugs.

"Seriously, man, what the fuck do we do next?" Manny asked. "Do we just clean the fuck out and run? This is too much fucking money for these guys to be the kind of assholes Ho lets us take off. These guys are going to come after us to get this back."

"We could run. Between this and the shit we got stashed, we could stay gone awhile."

"But?"

"But I don't know. You and me can run, but what about Sherry, or her mom, or Theresa? It seems like all they have to do is get ahold of someone we know and go to work. So unless we're taking everyone we know and moving away, we have to figure out a way to deal with this."

Manny kept his voice low. "Deal with what? Are you fucking nuts? That was the most fucked-up situation I ever been in, and I don't want to get in another one like it. We're not shooters, Ray. What we mostly do is take candy from babies, like that kiddy crew last week."

Ray adjusted the curtains to cut down on the light coming through and snapped off the light. He walked over and threw himself on one of the beds and put his hands over his eyes. "I gotta sleep for an hour. Get my head straight, so I can think. The guy wasn't from around here. Did you hear his voice?"

"Where was he from?"

"New England somewhere. He had that 'pahk the cah' voice."

"So?"

"So I don't know, maybe it means something. If he's in a club from up north and he's going up against one of the local clubs or something?"

Ray heard Manny light a cigarette, blow the smoke out. He turned to see Manny pointing at him with it, the end glowing red.

Manny said, "Or working with them, so he's that much more plugged in. Or he moved here twenty years ago and the accent don't make a fucking difference."

Ray shook his head. "Yeah, maybe. But if anyone knew him down here, Ho would have told us to back the fuck off."

Manny jumped up and picked up a pistol from the low chest of drawers and stuck it under the pillow on the other bed, then stretched out again. He put the cigarette on the edge of the night-stand between the beds. "Man, what happened back there—"

"Yeah, I don't want to think about that for a while."

"Think about this, though, okay?" He held the cigarette in his hand without lighting it, then dropped it back on the table. "I know shit happens and you can only plan so much. It wasn't any-body's fault except maybe Rick, and he paid for it." They could hear cars hissing by on the wet highway. "But here's the thing, okay? Next time someone shoots at us? Fucking shoot back."

HE LAY IN bed a long time before drifting into a thin sleep bro-ken by sounds from the highway and the low, resonant rumble of

Dennis Tafoya

thunder that seemed to come from the ground beneath him as much as the sky.

He's sixteen and standing in a dark living room in Abington in December. It's late, maybe two in the morning, and Manny is climbing over the sill in the window behind him and trying not to laugh. The house is big, full of massive furniture looming in the dark rooms and throwing crazy shadows from the lights on the Christmas tree, the headlights of passing cars. Manny gets his boot caught in the curtains and goes over, jamming his hand in his teeth to keep from laughing out loud while Ray grabs his shoulders and drags him onto the carpet. He shakes his head at Manny, who finally pulls himself up and makes his way out to the kitchen, pulling sweat socks onto his long hands like gloves. The room is full of Christmas shit. Little houses with lights inside them. Holly wreaths set out on the tables.

Ray wanders down a hallway off the living room, passes a bathroom lit blue by a humming nightlight, pushes a door standing ajar with one elbow and finds himself in the master bedroom. A man and a woman are sleeping, two humped shapes under blankets. The room is darker than the rest of the house, and he stands a long time, his eyes adjusting. The woman is snoring slightly, her mouth open, blue-gray hair splayed out over the pillow, and the man is curled beside her, one slack white arm over hers. On a low dresser are pictures of kids he can barely make out. Grown kids and little ones that must be grandkids. On the table are the woman's glasses and a picture of a man and woman that Ray picks up and turns in his hands till he can see it's the woman and he guesses the man, too, only they're young and skinny and the man wears a white jacket that's too big for him and the woman is wearing dark lipstick and has a flower in a thing on her wrist like the girls wear to prom.

He wants to go get Marletta and bring her here. He has the crazy thought that she could explain it to him, act as a guide somehow to the kind of life where people get old together and have kids and grandkids. He reaches into his thin coat and brings out a pint of 151 and quietly unscrews the cap and takes a small sip and makes a face. Something about the way the man's arm touches the woman's arm makes him think he could wake them up and ask them if him and Marletta could live here until she graduates and he turns eighteen and can get a job somewhere.

Finally he walks back out, passing Manny standing on a chair trying to get the star off the tree, fishing drunkenly with a fireplace poker and making a tinny musical clinking noise every time he hits one of the ornaments. Ray doesn't say anything, just goes back to the window and is climbing out when Manny sees him caught in the yellow glare of headlights, and as Ray lets himself down onto a dead azalea bush, he can hear his friend whisper, "Man, what's wrong?"

Manny dropped him back at his house at about five. Ray jumped out of the van and kept his hand stuck in his pocket, the Colt rattling in his shaking fist. He tried not to run to the house, but he had an itch between his shoulder blades and couldn't keep himself from looking up and down the street over and over as he closed the distance to the door of his apartment. There was a bad moment when he realized his keys were in the gym bag over his arm and had to dig around in the bag while trying to look over his shoulder every other second. Finally he got the door open,

Dennis Tafoya

jumped inside, and slammed it behind him, turning the lock and dropping the bag on the landing. He ran up the stairs and pulled the pistol out of his pocket, pointing it into every corner of the living room. He checked the bedroom, the closets, and behind the couch, finally closing the curtains and sitting in the darkened room for a minute, waiting for his heart to slow.

He picked up the remote and turned on the stereo, clicking through the CDs in the changer until he settled on old Stan Ridgway. After a while he got a chair from the dining room and took it down the stairs to the front door. He wedged it under the doorknob and checked the dead bolt and chain, then carried the bag upstairs. He went into the closet, reached up, and knocked back a trapdoor in the ceiling. Balancing on a Rubbermaid storage box full of stuff from his father's house, he reached through the hole in the ceiling and brought down a shotgun wrapped in rags and a box of double-aught shells. The gun was dusty and smelled of oil and old metal, and he sat down on the bed and wiped it clean, then loaded it and racked the slide. Stan Ridgway was singing about a lonely town, and Ray wished he could get high and let the rest of the day go by. Instead he stripped off his clothes and threw them in the trash can in the kitchen and pulled out the bag and left it on the kitchen floor.

The shower felt good, and he kept making it hotter and hotter, standing under the nozzle and letting the water pulse on his head while he tried to figure angles and means and whether it was possible to run or if he had to stay and slug it out with whoever was out there wanting him dead. He had to fucking calm down, is what he had to do. No matter how bad the guy in the Charger wanted them, it would take days for him to get to someone who could give him their names. They could make some kind of rational decision about what to do and where to go and how long they could stay there with the money they had.

He couldn't help thinking, though, how did he think this was going to play out, anyway? Even before they fucked up at the farmhouse, where was it going? How did shit like this ever end? Either they stopped or they got killed or they got locked up. Upstate he had known guys who were stone thieves, and they had all of them spent more of their lives behind bars than on the street. Ray was thirty, and he felt like he had come to the end of the life he'd been leading. He just didn't know if that meant he was going to change or if he was going to die.

He got takeout from the Golden Palace on 611 and sat in the dark listening to music. He ran through his Stan Ridgway CDs, grabbed by the strange mood of songs about loners drifting on western highways and people on the run from big trouble or fucked over by the ones they loved. He wanted to get into the last of the heroin, but he had things to do, so he loaded up the one-hitter with some coke Ho had given him the last time he had been at the big stone house in Chestnut Hill where he lived with his wife, Tina, and three kids. Ray had brought coconut rum and pineapple juice, something they were drinking that summer, and Ho and Tina kept bringing dishes out of the kitchen that smelled of tamarind and lotus and laughing gently at Ray's attempt to pronounce them.

Manny pulled up in front of the house at about midnight. Ray was already in his car and blinked the headlights when Manny pulled up. He followed Manny up 611 and then north on 202 into Jersey. The night out here was black except for the lights of farmhouses and little developments far away. There was lightning in the clouds but no rain, and Ray put the window down and smelled wet grass and asphalt, the smell of country roads.

It reminded Ray of riding the back roads with Manny when they were kids. Alternating long sips of vodka from the bottle with swigs of orange soda. A girl with a black eye they had picked up in Bristol. White-blond hair and Kmart perfume. They had pulled into a turf farm somewhere off Swamp Road and run around, drunk and high, screaming and rolling in the grass. Manny turned the radio up, and they lay on the cooling hood of the car and passed a beer-can bong back and forth and talked about running away to California. He remembered that he couldn't stop looking at the girl's small hands, fixed on them moving white in the dark, in that way that you sometimes did when you were high.

Now they pulled off the road into a soybean field. Ray stopped just off the road, and Manny pulled the van about fifty yards in and got out. Ray killed the lights and waited, and after a couple of minutes he could see Manny's silhouette against the orange haze in the sky from the cities to the north. There was a yellow glow visible through the rear window of the Ford that grew until it filled the back of the van. As they backed onto the road, Ray saw the windows blow out. They headed back down 202. Halfway across the bridge, Manny cranked down the window and sailed the plates out over the Delaware.

They stopped at a diner in New Hope and had a cup of coffee.

They sat in silence, and Ray watched the young waitress come and go. She had a big ring on her left hand.

"Tell me about the guy who put you onto the house."

"Yeah, I been thinking about that. Danny Mullen, from down in Charlestown, over near Valley Forge. I saw him about three weeks ago down at the Neshaminy. He put us on the place in Marcus Hook, remember?"

"I remember. What did he say this time?"

Manny lifted his shoulders, spread his hands. "I don't know. He said he knew this place up north, a meth lab where some buddies of his had copped, and did I want it."

"Nothing weird?"

"He did say the guy was crazy, but I figured what the fuck did that mean? Who's in that business, you know? Sane people?" They watched the waitresses carrying plates of pie to a table of giggling teenagers at the front of the diner.

Ray tapped the table twice with his index finger, tried to look decisive. "Okay, we see Ho and we see Danny. Try to figure out if there's a way to know who we're dealing with. Did you talk to Sherry?"

"Yeah, I told her stay with her ma a few days. She was pissed, but she'll get over it."

"I figure I'll try to get Theresa out of town for a while."

"Yeah, good luck with that. When was the last time she was out of town?"

"She likes Atlantic City. She goes down on the bus with her girlfriends. I could stick her in a hotel down there for a couple days, I guess."

"How long do we do this? When is this, you know, over?"

Ray shrugged and looked out the window, trying to keep the feeling like he had a plan and it was going to lead somewhere. He kept dancing around the end of it in his mind. Could they talk to the guy? Scare the shit out of him? Get something on him that made it more of a pain in the ass to come after them than it was worth? It was like a chess game where all the other guy's pieces were invisible while his own sat out in plain sight, waiting to get taken off the board.

The deal with Ho was supposed to keep this kind of shit from happening. Some crazy fucker might blow up at them, but mostly they were closing down people who would slink away and never be heard from again, or pull up stakes for some place where any tweaker with some ambition and a few charcoal briquettes could go into business.

THE NEXT MORNING was Sunday, and Ray got up early, restless and fidgety. He took a shower and went out to his car and pulled out, not knowing where he was heading until he found himself on 611 going north toward Doylestown. He cranked the window down, and the warm air felt good after all the rain of the days before. When he reached the town he parked and sat for a minute. As soon as he stopped the car, the air inside began to heat up and he began to sweat. He thought about putting on his jacket anyway, the better to carry the little .32 he had with him, but in the end he just left the pistol in the jacket and the jacket in the car.

He walked by the bookstore again, but the dark-haired girl wasn't there. He prowled around the aisles for a while and bought himself a book on classic horror films, the kind of movie he hadn't been able to stay away from when he was a kid, even though thoughts of the monsters kept him awake at night.

He took his book and walked up the street, stopping at a Starbucks and buying a cup of coffee and then walking aimlessly past craft shops and jewelry stores. He liked the town. There were gaslights on the street and nice old buildings with a little character in the details. He walked and sipped at the coffee and sweated till he came to a bench in the shade of a tree and sat down and paged through the book. He was trying to find a reference to the movie the girl had recommended when he looked up and there she was. She was walking along with a paper cup of coffee and stopped to sip out of it, wearing a blue oxford shirt with long sleeves and what he thought of as a peasant skirt that hung almost to her ankles, some kind of reddish-brown print from India or someplace. He smiled and watched her walk toward him and almost didn't say anything as she got closer, until she was right beside him, looking distracted.

"Hey," he said, and held a hand up. She looked at him for a minute with a frown, and he began to feel nervous and maybe a little disreputable, and then her faced changed and she cocked her head and gave him that crooked smile again.

"Hey, *Night of the Demon*." She laughed and shook her head. "I'm sorry! I don't remember your name."

"No, I've been called worse. Anyway, I don't think I ever said it."

"No, but still. I could have said the cute guy who was looking for a movie, or something." Her teeth were white and even, and he felt the levers moving in him again, wheels spinning and metal balls dropping and rolling through the hollow pipes inside him.

"I'm Ray."

"Michelle." She shook her head. "This is wild. Do you live nearby?" She looked away, and then back at him.

"No, actually down near Willow Grove. This is the second time I've been here, and I've seen you both times. Are you like the mayor or something?"

"The official greeter. How are you enjoying your stay in our little town?"

"Swell. You should have a sash and a top hat for a job like that." He should have been nervous and distracted, with his head on a swivel for trouble and unfamiliar faces, but he was relaxed and warm inside, and he let himself focus on the girl. On Michelle. She laughed and sat down next to him, and he moved over to make room. She reached over and put her hand in the book, took glimpses of him out of the corner of her eye. He could smell that sweet, fruity smell again.

"Horror movies, I love it."

"Not just any horror movies." He opened the page to show her the entry he had been reading, on *Night of the Demon*. "Also called *Curse of the Demon*, 1957. Dana Andrews."

"I'm impressed. You know your stuff."

"Ah, that's all I know, and I just read it. Anyway, everyone looks smart holding a book. I should carry one around all the time." She looked directly into his eyes, and he made himself look back. It was like looking at the sun, and he had to get used to it. "So, you must live around here, then."

She pointed up the street. "Right around the corner, on Mary Street. I was just on my way to Meeting."

"A meeting? For work?"

"Not *a* meeting, just Meeting. Quaker Meeting, the Society of Friends?"

"Oh, right." He had known a few Quakers. One of his social workers had been a Quaker, and one of his public defender lawyers, and there were plenty of old meetinghouses around the county, but he didn't really know anything about what it meant to be a Quaker. It was a religion, he got that, but what they believed or what went on inside the meetinghouses, he couldn't say.

"I'm not a member, just an attender." She said it like it had capital letters. "I'm not really religious, that's not my thing. It's just, I don't know. It's just nice. There's no priest or minister or anything. You just sit in silence, and if someone wants to say something, they do. Sometimes the whole hour goes by and nobody says anything, but usually someone'll say something about, you know, the war or how they're trying to work something out for themselves. It's like antichurch, you know? Church without all the bullshit."

He laughed a little. "That would be something to see. I grew up Catholic. All my friends are Catholic. I stopped going when I was eight. I had an argument with the nuns about pagan babies going to hell."

"Me, too! I love it." He picked up that this was something she said, that she loved things. Of all the ways you could go through life, was looking for things to love all that bad?

She shook her head. "They'd make these ridiculous sweeping

statements about who was going to hell, which was pretty much everybody, and I'd sit there thinking about special circumstances where it didn't make any sense to me to send somebody to hell just because they were gay or had an abortion or were mad at God or had just never gotten the word about Catholicism before they, you know. Shuffled off this mortal coil." She moved her arms when she talked, making arcs and swoops in the air with her hands.

Ray said, "I never got the religion thing at all, to be honest. I've been, you know, around some pretty bad guys, and everyone always talks about God, or has to have some special diet or something because of their religion and meanwhile they're fucking everyone over for—" He almost said for a pack of cigarettes. Why not just roll up his sleeves and start showing her the tats? "For a nickel."

He had to be careful, but he didn't want to be. "Being in a church seems like, I don't know. Like just painting everything a certain color. You're still a, you know, a jerk, you do whatever the hell you want, because everyone does. But if you're a Catholic you paint everything red, if you're a Jew everything gets a coat of yellow, if you're Muslim it's something else. Does that make sense?"

"I think so. Like the fact of being in a religion means something more than it really does. Like you don't have to do the right thing or help anyone or think about your actions. As long as you say the right prayer."

He nodded but then shook his head. "Like I know shit from Shinola. Like I'm in the deep thinking business."

"I have to ask." He braced himself, waiting for the just-what-is-your-business question, and his mind raced for the right thing to say. "I've heard that expression a million times, but what the hell is Shinola, anyway?"

He breathed out. "Shoe polish."

She looked up at the sky, waggled her head. "Okay, I can buy that. But I think you do."

"I do?"

"Know shit from Shinola." She got up. "And with that, she headed off to church."

"Have dinner with me." He didn't know where that had come from. He felt like he was in some twilight zone, off from his real life, and he could go back and forth between the world where girls wore peasant dresses and he sat on the street drinking coffee and the world where he was being hunted for money and dope. Was he out of his fucking mind?

"I can't do dinner, but how about coffee? Tomorrow night, like seven?"

"Okay." He smiled. "At Starbucks?" He pointed back up the street.

She lowered her voice. "Fuck no. I hate their coffee. There's a little place around the corner, Coffee and Cream. They have great homemade ice cream, too."

"Tomorrow night." He stuck out his hand, and she took it. Her fingers were long and cool to the touch.

"Seven." And she moved away, waving over her shoulder.

He thought, if I still have my head.

AT TWO HE woke himself up trying to scream. A man with a misshapen head had been standing over him, staring down at him, eyes dark and hard. He opened his mouth and couldn't force anything out. No sound, no breath. When he opened his eyes he forced out a croak and started coughing. He got up and moved around the apartment with the Colt in his hand checking locks. Put the TV on and fell asleep to muted infomercials about no-money-down real estate.

CHAPTER SIX

MANNY PICKED HIM up the next morning in a black Toyota 4Runner he had picked up in Trenton, and they headed down 309 toward Chestnut Hill and Ho Dinh's. Ray had met Ho upstate when Ho was doing six months on a stolen merchandise beef and Ray was in for boosting cars, taking them down to a guy in Aston who moved them overseas in a complex deal that seemed like more work than work. Ho told him he could do better, and when Ray'd gotten out he began to move the cars through him and got a couple more points. Plus, Ho was easy to deal with, and Ray just liked the guy. Manny would always make jokes about eating cats and shit, and Ho just grinned and shook his head, as he had when the Rockview yardbirds began calling him Hoe Down about ten minutes after he got there.

When he had first told Ho what he and Manny were onto, taking down small-time dealers, Ho told him he'd help them when he could. Keep them from stumbling into something bigger than they could handle. Warn them off dealers and labs run by guys who were connected to the local clubs or gangs Ho did business with. Nothing was guaranteed, but up till now nothing had gone wrong and no one had come after them. Of course, they hadn't stolen a hundred thousand bucks off anyone before, either.

The meth business around Philly was run mostly by biker gangs, and they fought and jostled each other for territory. They'd rent farmhouses in rural counties and cook up for a few weeks, then shut them down and move on. Once in a while a club from some other part of the country would come into the area and get beaten back, or some small-timer would appear and begin to get noticed, and he'd get smacked down or warned off, or they'd let Ray put him out of business, at least for a while.

Manny had a baseball cap jammed on his head and sunglasses on. They pulled to the curb in front of Ho's gray stone house in a quiet residential neighborhood off of Germantown Avenue. Ray got out with a gym bag, and Manny took a pistol from beneath the seat and stuck it under his thigh.

Ray moved up the walk. In a second-floor window he saw a man with binoculars around his neck and wraparound sunglasses that made his face unreadable. It was Ho's cousin, Bao, a wordless, stone-faced killer as broad and muscular as Ho was thin and frail. Bao had done serious time for killing two Chinese guys in some kind of scrape over the massage parlor business. Ray had seen him working out in Ho's yard, massive shoulders painted with stalking tigers and smiling demons. Now he nodded to Bao, and Bao nodded back and pointed to the door.

Ray knocked, and Ho's wife, Tina, let him in. There were three kids sitting at the breakfast table and an old woman standing at the kitchen counter and some kind of wild exchange going on. The smallest girl had a cereal bowl on her head and was bang-

96

ing it with a spoon. The old woman was making angry faces and talking a mile a minute in Vietnamese. Ray guessed it had something to do with how kids should act at the table. Tina led him out into an enclosed porch looking out at a neatly trimmed lawn. She pointed outside to where Ho stood over an older man Ray took to be Ho's father, kneeling in a patch of garden.

"There he is, arguing with his father about bitter melon." Ray shrugged and smiled. Tina threw her hands up. "Don't ask." She gestured to a recliner. "Want some coffee, Ray?"

"No, I'm good, Tina, thanks." She went back inside.

Ho was short and rail thin, with glasses that gave him a studious look. He nodded his head toward Ray and smiled. He exchanged some more words with the man in the garden and came around to the outside door of the porch. He waved to Ray to follow him, and they walked back to the kitchen, where there was now a high-pitched argument about breakfast foods going on. Ray figured Grandma was pushing for something healthy, holding a heavy frying pan and pointing it at the kids, who were pouring cereal with a wild abandon. Two dogs scrambled to get the cereal that hit the floor. Ray thought it was funny how much you could get without knowing the words at all.

Ho let Ray go ahead of him down the stairs and locked the door behind them. He clicked on the light, and Ray settled on a leather couch. The room was furnished tastefully, with a slate bar and dark furniture, muted prints of Chester County on the walls. There was a massive safe on one side of the room and a locked metal gun cabinet next to it. Ray figured this was the safest room in Philly and felt some tension go out of the muscles in his shoulder.

He put the bag on the table and waited for Ho, who grabbed a bottled water from a minibar and offered Ray one.

Ho pointed to the bag with his bottle. "How's business?"

Ray raised his eyebrows. "That's an interesting question. I'm hoping you can help there."

Ho sat down and opened the bag. His eyes got wide. "Christ." Ho had been in the country since he was two and had only the ghost of an accent that surfaced in clipped consonants when he was agitated.

"Yeah, wow is right. Plus a nice haul of cash."

"But?"

"But, there was a mess, and someone put their eyes on me and Manny."

"This was that thing in Upper Bucks, right? It was on the news."

"Somebody with an interest in the place shows up just as we're leaving. We see him, he sees us. Plus, he finds a walkie-talkie we left on the ground, starts talking to us. Telling us how easy it's going to be to find us. Two guys ripping off dealers."

"He got a good look?"

Ray shook his head. "I don't think so. It was dark, it was raining. But man . . ."

Ho took the bag off the table and knelt by the safe.

"He said something?"

"He was just so fucking sure of himself. Like it was a matter of time."

"That's our game, though, isn't it?" Ho turned the dial on the safe with small, precise movements, then pulled the steel handle and opened it. He took a canvas sack out of the safe and began transferring the dope from the bag Ray had brought to the sack. "What we do, how we make money. In what I do, in what you do. It's the image you project. You play a role, right? It's what keeps people from doing something stupid, at least most of the time." He put the canvas sack in the safe next to some neat stacks of currency from different countries. "But it's all an illusion. The illusion of reputation, the illusion of control." He pulled a colorful bill from the stack and put it on the table between them. "Even this, when you think about it."

Ray bent over and looked at the bill closely. It was beautiful in the way foreign money was often beautiful next to the monochromatic green of U.S. bills. He picked it up and turned it over. One side was a subtle pink and showed some kind of government building and had "1000" printed on it, the only thing Ray understood. The other side, a soft blue, showed men riding elephants.

"Where's it from? Looks like Asia?"

Ho smiled ruefully. "Vietnam. Actually South Vietnam, about 1975." Ray held it out to Ho, who waved it away. "Keep it."

"What's it worth?"

"About five bucks, to a collector. Which is my point. Even money is just a note from the government saying, 'We promise this piece of paper is worth something.' It's just a bet, right? On that illusion, or projection or whatever it is." Ray folded the note and put it carefully in his shirt pocket. Ho pointed back up the stairs. "My old man left South Vietnam with a couple million dong. That's what the note is, it's a thousand South Vietnamese dong. By the time he got to the States the money wasn't worth the paper it was printed on. He talked to a guy from the State Department and the guy told him to wipe his ass with it."

"But he kept it."

"I guess it's a reminder. At the end of the day you can't depend on anything. Everything changes, everything ends. All you got is what you got up here." He pointed to his head. The sound of high voices in argument bled through the ceiling. Ho smiled. "And family."

Ray knew how Ho felt about family. He remembered Ho telling him about his parents taking him out of Vietnam right after the war, when he was barely a year old, his mother and father carrying him in their arms in a leaky boat across the China Sea. His father had been a colonel in the army, and they were on a boat with about fifty people who wanted him dead. The army and navy dissolved, and deserters were cruising around in stolen patrol boats and one of them attacked the boat and machine-gunned everyone. Ho's parents hid with him among the dead. They drifted around the ocean for days with no water until a Taiwanese trawler picked them up.

Ray tried to picture the ferocity of that kind of love, and he thought about his father and mother and about how maybe family could be one of those things that just ends. Maybe it was all six kinds of bullshit, and you just made a choice about what illusion to believe.

RAY ASKED IF Ho had any idea who the guys were, running a dope lab in a farmhouse in Bucks County. Ho shook his head.

"I have two guys I ask about that shit. It's not an exact sci-

ence, I just ask them what you ask me, if you go to a certain corner on a certain street, does anyone have a problem with that?
They tell me no, or yes, and if it happens I down some of the
money I take off you to them. Usually, they're happy to have less
competition." Ray described what he had seen of the guy and the
car, the New England accent. Ho nodded and said he'd quietly
ask around.

Ray put his hand up. "For Christ's sake don't let this get back
to you. Maybe it was all talk, but this guy sounded crazy. All I
need is enough information to get to this guy before he can get to
me and Manny."

"You need anything? Guns, ammunition?"

"Guns I got. My old man used to say you didn't need more
guns than you got hands, and I got more than that."

Ho looked thoughtful for a minute, then held a finger in the air.
He went to a closet with a steel door and pulled a ring of keys out
of his pockets. After a second he found the right one and snapped
open the door, stepped inside, and was gone for a minute. When
he came out he had what looked like two dark blue sleeveless
sweaters, each wrapped in plastic. He handed them to Ray, and he
felt how heavy they were. Bulletproof vests.

"Yikes. I don't know, man. If it comes to this . . ."

"If you're not going to run, then you're going to find him or
he's going to find you. What else could it come to?"

RAY WENT OUT to the 4Runner and put the vests in the back and
covered them with a gray blanket. Manny was smoking and keeping his eyes on the street.

"Ho will pull the money together in a few days. If he moves it first there's more for us than if he has to front it."

"Is that Kevlar vests?" Ray nodded, and Manny sighed. "Great. Well, at least we know Ho's on our side. That's something."

"He's going to ask around, see if he can find anything out about these guys."

"Where to now?"

"Let's swing by and see Theresa and keep trying to get ahold of Danny, or someone who knows him."

Manny started up the car, and they moved down the street. Manny looked at Ray and then back at the street.

Ray watched him. "What?"

"He had a black eye."

"Who?"

"Danny. He had a black eye when I saw him. It just came into my head. I didn't think of it before."

Ray looked away, thinking. "So maybe . . ."

"Maybe he had a beef with the guys he put us onto. Maybe he thought why not make a few bucks putting me onto them 'cause he was in some kind of scrape with them. They ripped him off and threw him a beating or something. Or they just pushed him around 'cause he's kind of a punk, Danny."

Ray put his hands over his eyes, suddenly tired. "Maybe. Or maybe he just fell down 'cause he's a stone junkie and a thorough-going dipshit."

"Maybe." Manny laughed and shook his head. "You know, I'm starting to have more respect for the police. This is some Sherlock Holmes shit."

* * *

THERESA WAS SITTING in the living room talking on the phone when Ray came in carrying a plastic bag under his arm. Manny was sitting in the backseat of the 4Runner, trying on the vest and watching the street.

"How long will that take?" she was saying, making notes on a yellow pad. She had a cigarette going and had the phone book open and papers spread out on the coffee table. When she noticed him come in, she waved and made a motion with her hand, opening and closing like a mouth flapping. "And how much will that cost?" She made more notes and shook her head. After another minute of listening she hung up the phone.

"What gives, Ma? Looks like big business."

"The fucking government and fucking lawyers." She picked up her cigarette and squinted at him through the smoke. "I'm about ready to unscrew somebody's head."

"What is it? You got tax problems?" She made a small motion with her head, like she didn't want to talk about it. "You need more money, Ma? You just gotta ask."

"Well, yeah, I'm going to need more money, but it's not for me."

His face darkened. "I can see where this is going, and I won't fucking have it." He stood up.

"Raymond, hon." He stood at the stairs with his back to her.

"Theresa, there's nothing I don't owe you. For you, whatever you need, you know you got it. For that prick, I got nothing. He can die right where he is."

She said, "He told me you went to see him." Ray nodded and

went into the kitchen, rummaged around in the fridge. "Then you know," she called from the living room. "You know he's got just a couple good months left." She got up and moved into the kitchen and stood over him. He took out a beer and sat down at the table, and she sat across from him. He looked at the bottle, taking a dollop of foam off the mouth of the bottle with his tongue.

She spoke quietly, with no force in her voice. It was tougher to take than if she had been screaming. "The first time you got locked up, who was there for you?"

"You."

"Me. And the second time, when you went to Lima, and the time after that when you went to the penitentiary. I never asked nothing from you and I never will. Not for myself."

Ray took a long pull on the beer and then played with the label, peeling a corner up and plastering it back down. The dog sighed under the table. Ray put his hand over his face, talked through his splayed fingers. "You know, for a long time I just figured he killed her, my mother. One day she was gone, and he said she ran off, but I just figured he got so juiced and crazy he split her skull and dumped her in a ditch. Then that postcard came, and at least I knew she was alive somewhere."

"He loved your mother, and he loved you. He still does."

"Maybe. I don't know. But what the fuck good did it ever do any of us? Even you?"

"It's not about what people do for you or to you. This is what I think: You just never give up. That's what family means. He's your family and I'm your family, and you're ours. And that's that."

Theresa went to the cabinet and got out a glass. She took the bottle from Ray and poured the beer into it. "I'm not stupid, Ray. You got a duffel bag full of money and no job. You and that dopehead Manny are stealing or dealing drugs or something—"

"Ma—"

She held up a hand. "Don't even start." She sat across from him at the table and picked up her lighter. "Just grit your teeth and give it up."

Ray blew out a long breath and held his hands against his temples. It was like every cell of his brain was firing at once. Too many wants and fears were crowding each other in his head, and he couldn't sort them out or figure which were the important ones. He couldn't pick anything new up without dropping something. He felt like he had run a hundred miles in the last few days and he hadn't gotten anywhere, had no idea what direction to move. He had the feeling again that he wanted to cry but that if he did he would lose control of himself completely. His eyes burned.

"Okay, I'll make you a deal." He combed his fingers through his mustache and made calculations in his head. "I'll finance the great escape if you go down the shore for a few days, on me." Her eyes narrowed, and she chewed her lip thoughtfully. He held up his hands. "Don't blow a head pipe trying to figure my angle. Just do what I say and we all get what we want. Though from what Bart said when I seen him inside, I don't know that he wants what you want here."

"Okay, okay, but I got calls in to the lawyer and the DOC. I'm at the shore they won't be able to get me."

Ray opened the plastic bag and pulled out a throwaway cell

phone. He grabbed a pair of scissors off the counter and cut the package open. He booted up the phone and waited for a signal, pulling a pen and a pad of Post-its from a caddy near the wall phone. "I got you covered." He watched the readout and scribbled down some numbers, then handed her the phone and the Post-it. "For the next few days this is your phone number. Call everybody back and give them this number. Keep it with you all the time, and I'll check in with you every day or so. After you talk to the lawyer and whoever, pack a bag and I'll take you down to the limo."

"You're in some kind of trouble, Raymond. Don't think after all these years I can't read you like a comic book, you little pissant."

He dialed his own cell phone number, and the phone in his pocket buzzed. "Nah, I'm trying to stay out of trouble, and I'm trying to keep you out of trouble, too. So do what I say for once in your life. I'm taking you out of here in half an hour. So do what you have to do."

"I'm an old lady, Raymond, it takes me a while to—"

He held up his hands. "Ma. Don't talk, pack."

"What about Shermie?"

Christ, the fucking dog. "I'll get him to that kennel up on County Line."

While Theresa got her things together and kept a running complaint going about being rushed out of her own goddamn house, Ray went back into his bedroom and pulled the duffel out from under the bed. He had to assume at some point they'd be here, and he didn't want to leave anything for them to find. The bag was heavy, so he hefted it in two hands and lugged it out to the Toyota and set it on the open hatchback. He took out money in short stacks and put two in his pockets, handed two to Manny, and held two aside for Theresa. Down the street, two kids crept around their yard with water pistols, angling for position from behind bushes and skinny trees and then popping out to squirt each other, shrieking. He went back into his room and stood on the bed, pushing aside a ceiling tile and bringing down a tape-wrapped square of bills and throwing it on the bed and then reaching up for a short-barreled police-issue shotgun and a box of shells. He wrapped the money and the gun in his bedspread and carried it to the car.

He kept hearing a voice in his head telling him to leave it all, the money and the guns and the whole thing, and just get in the car and drive away. Was it Marletta's voice? Maybe it was, trying to propel him away from the terrible things he had done and the terrible things he might do now. Was he really trying to get to some kind of safety or just so far down this road he couldn't see any other place to go? He had been thinking so much he'd like to talk to her again, to ask what he should do. To explain he wasn't trying to hurt anyone, not really. He'd just fucked up so many times that every move seemed wrong, every way he could go seemed to lead down into a hole.

Manny was dialing the cell again, and he snapped his fingers to get Ray's attention. Ray looked up, and Manny mouthed *Danny* and handed the phone to Ray.

"Hello?" The voice sounded whiny, young. Something else, agitated.

"Danny?"

"Who is this?" Fear. That was the something else he heard.

There was a tremor in Danny's voice, and Ray heard him breathing hard.

"Danny, it's Ray. Manny and Ray."

"You fucking guys, what did you do?"

"We did what you told us to do, Danny."

"No, no way. I never told you to kill nobody. You fucking guys." Whining, like a kid, Ray thought. Jesus, and this junkie dipshit knew who they were.

"Danny, don't be an idiot. We're on a cell phone."

"You think that fucking matters now? You fucking guys, honest to Christ."

"Tell me what's going on."

"What's going on? They know me, that's what's going on. You got to get me money and I mean right fucking now today, got me?"

"Danny, what did you get us into?"

"What did I get *you* into? Are you high? Manny never told me nothing about killing nobody."

"What do you mean, they know you?"

"These guys from New Hampshire. They stayed at my fucking house, they know where I live."

"Jesus Christ, Danny, why would you put us on to something that could get back to you?"

"I need money. I got bills and shit. I got a dependency problem and I owe people and I had no idea you two fuckups would get somebody killed."

"Danny, they don't care about that, which you should please stop saying on the fucking phone. They want their money back."

"I need my money. You come here and gimme my money so I can get gone."

"Why did they for Christ's sake stay at your house?"

"My cousin, Ronnie, he knows these guys from being inside up there."

"Jesus, Danny."

"And they gave me money and I got dependency problems. I seen they were trying to get established down here. And I thought you guys weren't going to fuck this up so bad. Ronnie called me."

"Danny."

"You better fucking hurry up. Those fuckers come back I am giving you two assholes up, you hear me?" There was a click and the line went dead. Ray tried calling back, kept hitting the SEND button, but Danny never picked up again.

Manny raised his eyebrows at him, and Ray shook his head. He couldn't believe he had given his life to a junkie for safekeeping.

THEY WENT TO Theresa's bank, and Ray gave her money to pay lawyers and whatever expenses she thought might come up, then dropped her at a hotel in Willow Grove where she could meet a limo to take her to Atlantic City.

He went into the lobby and got a ticket for the limo and a schedule while Manny took her little paisley suitcase out and extended the handle. When Ray handed her the tickets she held him close and kissed his cheek.

"I know you're pissed. I know it. But I did the same for you and I have to do this for him."

He held up his hands in surrender and shook his head, smiling, and backed up toward the car. Out of her kitchen she looked tiny, frail, but her chin was up and her eyes bright.

She said, "Family's got to come for you when no one else will."

He took out his cell phone and waved it at her to remind her to keep it near her and on, and Manny put the Toyota in gear and they drove up to the Wal-Mart at Jacksonville Road. Manny pulled the Toyota up to the door when Ray came out, and he piled the things he had bought in the back. Manny drove up to a U-Store-It around the corner. They rented a narrow, cinder-block storage unit for a couple of months and paid a hundred and eighty bucks.

They drove down the long, empty rows of doors and found the unit they had rented, number 181. They angled the car in and got out, and Manny mouthed the number to himself. Ray laughed, and Manny said, "What?"

"You're going to play that number?"

Manny said fuck you and laughed and hauled the door open and went inside. Ray took some flashlights and batteries out of a plastic bag. They closed the door and turned on the flashlights and sat on the cement floor with the bags, the guns, and the money. Ray sorted out his cash from the money he'd been holding for Manny and the money they owed Danny, splitting everything between two imitation leather suitcases with the tags from the Wal-Mart still on them. Manny loaded and checked their guns and put them into the olive duffel. Ray had bought them some bottles of water, a couple of T-shirts, and candy bars, and Manny put them into a new knapsack.

When they were done they shared a bottle of water, their faces lined with sweat. Manny opened the door a crack to let some air in.

Ray put one of the flashlights up against his chin and made a moaning noise like a ghost in an old radio program. "It is *later* than you think."

Manny made a face. "What's that?"

"Something my old man used to do."

"Christ, what, to help you sleep?"

Ray turned the light on the floor. "Yeah, he was a charmer. It was something from an old TV show. Used to scare the shit out of me."

Manny lit a cigarette, waved the match out.

Ray said, "Guess we can't stay here forever."

"Nah. It's too fucking hot, for one thing."

"We had it sewed for a while there, huh? Set 'em up and knock 'em down. How did things get so fucked up?"

Manny flexed his skinny biceps, his tattoos sliding and puckering on his arms. "Things are what they are. The thing I don't get is why you think they should be any different."

"We had it under control before. If it wasn't for that fucking Rick, or that moron Danny . . ."

"Oh, will you please? If it wasn't those two it would have been one of the tweakers. Somebody was going to go for a gun eventually. Somebody was going to dime us to the cops or just come to our houses in the middle of the night." He stabbed the air with his cigarette. "You think, what? Shit can't go wrong cause you're smarter than they are? Cause you got a plan?"

"I used to think that. I used to be one smart motherfucker." He watched a bee hover in the light from under the door, jinking back and forth, looking for an angle on something it wanted. "Now I don't know shit." He took the keys to the padlock out of his pocket and gave one to Manny.

"Listen, I got to say this out loud. You think there's any point in giving the money back?"

"Only if you want to be standing still when they kill you."

"Yeah."

"You heard that fucking guy's voice. What do you think he's going to do? Say thanks and no hard feelings?"

Ray shook his head. He couldn't say he saw it any different. He shifted on the cement. "If anything happens, we . . . split up or you don't know what happened to me, just leave my bag here for a month and then come back and give the rest to Theresa."

"You don't have to say it."

"I know. See, I'm making the possibility that you could lose track of me but I could still be alive. Just by saying it out loud."

"You think that's how it works?" Manny smiled and shook his head. "So, we go into this fucking hornet's nest and I don't come out. And if I don't come back and get my hundred and fifty thousand dollars, it's not because someone stuck a gun in my mouth and punched my ticket."

"No, not necessarily. You could've just gotten real busy doing something else and the money just slipped your mind."

"I think you slipped your mind. Look, Ray, we're just a couple of lowlifes. Guys like us, we make our run and we go out. We get locked up, we get killed." *Kilt,* the way Manny said it. "We knew it going in."

"Did we? I don't remember going in, is the thing. It was like I was born in."

"Yeah, well, I never got what you were doing anyway." Manny scratched his neck. "I mean, you were smart enough not to get caught up in this shit."

"I was? Why didn't someone tell me before?"

Manny tipped a bottle of water over his hair and shook his head like a dog coming in out of the rain. "I don't know. I figure it's some kind of fuck-you to your old man. Something like that."

"Maybe."

"Anyway, you were always good company, and who wants to do this shit alone?"

CHAPTER SEVEN

AN HOUR AND a half later they were coming off of 202 in Malvern. The sky was full of clouds, white and dark blue moving across the sun. Things could go either way, more rain or more sun. There was a breeze, but it was just hot air moving. Ray kept trying Danny's cell phone number but got nothing. It didn't mean much. Danny used, and he could've lost the phone or had his service turned off or just been bingeing on dope and ignoring the ring. They turned onto a narrow country lane, and Ray began looking at the numbers on mailboxes. Finally they turned into a driveway that wasn't much more than a trail into the woods.

The house where Danny lived with his mother was speckled with green—some kind of mold or fungus that made it seem as if the house were being reclaimed by the forest. There was a washing machine rusting in the yard and cracked and rotted asbestos tiles on the walls. A pickup truck sat in the carport with blue plastic covering a missing passenger side window. Manny turned off the engine, and they sat for a minute, watching the house. Somewhere far away a dog barked and birds moved in the trees. Ray began to open the door, and Manny put a hand on his arm and reached into the backseat for the vests. They struggled into them, sweat pouring down their backs, and then stretched and shrugged, trying to get used to the bulk. Manny lifted a hip and awkwardly dug a one-hitter out of his jeans, and they both did jolts of brown meth. Ray smacked his forehead while the dope burned in his sinuses like he'd fired a flare gun into his head.

They both got out and left the doors of the 4Runner open. Ray held up his hand for Manny to stay at the car. He nodded to Ray and pulled his shotgun from under the seat and stood with the open door between him and the house. Ray reached over the seat and got his Colt semiauto and worked the slide, putting a round in the chamber. Maybe it was all for nothing, maybe Danny was okay and they could give him some money and send him packing, but the house sat there closed and quiet in the woods, and Manny and Ray looked at each other, feeling wrong.

Manny wiped sweat from his face with the heel of his hand. He flexed his shoulders and whispered, "Christ, I can barely move in this thing. I feel like a fucking astronaut."

Ray held the Colt behind his leg and walked to the front door. He looked back at Manny and then knocked on the door with his fist. "Danny!"

They stood for a minute. Ray blotted at the sweat at his temple with the back of his free hand. He knocked again, this time banging the butt of the pistol against the door. After a minute he tried the door and found it unlocked. He looked back at Manny, who put the shotgun sight on the door. Ray stood clear and pushed the door open, flattening himself against the outside wall. There was no sound except the door creaking as it opened. Manny shook his head.

Ray moved inside, pointing the gun into the hallway ahead of him. He called Danny's name again and waited. After a minute with no sound but the birds in the trees and the faraway dog, he moved down the hallway into the kitchen. He circled through the first floor, checking the empty rooms. The place was a mess, and there was a stink of unemptied garbage and mildew. In the living room there was a big new flat-screen TV standing next to the box it came in. This was Danny spending his end of the score he had put Manny and Ray onto before he even got his hands on it. In the living room a few steps from the front door, a suitcase was open on the floor. Clothes were pulled out and heaped on the dirty carpet.

He went to the front door and shrugged at Manny, who came out from behind the car door and moved around the back of the house. Ray went up the stairs, and the garbage smell got stronger. All the doors were open except one, and Ray moved to it and stood in front of it for a moment, adjusting the pistol in his sweaty hand. Finally he pushed the door open and looked for a minute before stepping away and breathing through his mouth, gasping and spitting to keep from throwing up.

He forced himself to look again. An old woman was in the tub. There was blood and vomit on her chin and down the front of her robe. One eye stared, a milky blue. There was a hole in her chest and her throat was open. There were flies walking in the blood on her mouth and a terrible buzzing noise that filled the small room.

Ray used the sleeve of his coat to grab the door handle and pulled it closed, wiping it again after it was shut. He didn't want to see what might be in the other rooms and ran down the stairs and out the front door. He heard Manny calling his name as he wiped the doorknob and pulled the door shut.

He moved cautiously around the house, the gun out and pointing down. He came around the corner into a junk-strewn backyard. Manny passed him going the other way, back out to the car. In the back a Plymouth Fury was up on blocks, the exposed wheels rusted through. There was a woodpile with spiderwebs running down one side and an ancient deflated football stuck in the mud. There was a clothesline strung from the house to a pole stuck in cracked cement. And there was Danny, staring at the sky. Thinning red hair showing white scalp, pale blue eyes. His right arm was broken over a flat tree stump, and there was an axe separating his right hand from his fingers.

Ray heard the car starting and looked around the yard, rubbing his own right arm. He looked everywhere but at Danny. After a minute, he went back to the front of the house.

Manny was on the cell phone when he got in the car. Manny started it up and began to back the car around, pointing the nose down the driveway.

"Sherry? Yeah, hon, it's me. How you doing?"

Ray looked in the glove compartment, thinking there must be something to drink in this fucking car.

"Good. That's good." Manny stopped the car and reached into a green sport bag. He pulled out a pint of something wrapped in a paper bag and handed it to Ray. "Nothing, just wanted to hear your voice." Ray took a long drink of what he thought was some kind of sickly sweet schnapps. "Listen, Sherry? I want you to take your mom and drive to Atlantic City. Yeah, I know. I know. Yeah, I know but just do it right now. Don't pack, don't fuck around or call anyone. Just go." Ray could hear a shrill voice on the other end, but not the words. "Don't worry about money or anything. Sherry, you can scream at me later. You can scream at me all night long, I promise. Sherry. Sherry. Just hang up the fucking phone and get your fucking mother into a car and go to the Trop. Use the card I gave you for emergencies and get a nice room and take a bath." Manny put the car back in gear. "I'm hanging up now, Sherry. I love you. I know. I'll see you in a few hours." The voice on the other end was still going when Manny folded the phone and dropped it on the floor.

"Will she go?"

"She'll go. She's a pain in the ass, but she's not stupid."

Ray looked back at the house. His hands were shaking, and he watched Manny's head swivel, looking around them into the trees. "Why did they do that?"

"Who knows?"

"I mean, you know he gave us up the second they walked through the door."

"I know."

"So why do that?"

"They're animals."

The windshield shattered with the first gunshot, then a man stepped from the trees with a shotgun raised and the glass went white and blew in. Ray felt shards of glass hit his face and upraised arms. Manny pushed his door open and jumped out with the Remington in his hands, screaming something unintelligible, the 4Runner still moving. Ray threw himself over the backseat, wondering how bad he was cut. They moved fast, amped by the crank and adrenaline, and Ray was more afraid than he could ever remember being in his life.

There was a loud pop and more glass breaking. He flattened himself in the bed of the trunk, yanking the pistol out of his waistband and shooting wildly toward the front of the car at nothing he could see. The SUV smacked into a thin tree trunk and stopped moving, and he cracked his head against the wall. Ray heard the heavy bang of Manny's pump gun and the cracking sound of the slide working, and he flailed at the hatchback door handle. He pushed it open and let himself fall out onto the driveway. More shots rang off the metal and starred the glass over his head.

He could hear Manny racking the shotgun and firing and the hollow plastic chime of the expended shells hitting the ground. He stuck his head under the car and saw two sets of legs in front of the car, one moving left and one right. He put the front sights of the pistol on the set of legs on the right and pulled the trigger twice while Manny screamed something, burning off the fear and dope. The recoil of the gun stung his hand, and the shells ejected up and pinged off the tailpipe of the 4Runner. Someone screamed, and a guy wearing a black leather jacket fell heavily onto the driveway, grabbing his ankle. Ray fired again and hit the front tire on the right side.

Ray pulled himself out from under the car as it lowered on the flattening tire. He pointed the gun to his left, waiting for the other one to come out into view. The barrel of a long gun appeared at the left, and Ray tried not to breathe, wondering how many shots were left in the pistol. He held himself rigid and watched more of the gun barrel appear as the shooter slowly made his way down the side of the Toyota. Finally the guy made a quick move into the open, raising the shotgun and swiveling to put the front sight on Ray. He was wearing black leather, like the big man down in the driveway, and wraparound sunglasses. Ray could see tattoos on his hands and spiking up his neck from inside his shirt. There was a bang that Ray felt in his chest, and the guy folded up, blood haloing his head. Ray pulled the trigger involuntarily, and the shot pushed the biker onto his back, his eyes open. Ray could hear the other, bigger guy down in the driveway moaning and calling them motherfuckers.

Manny moved out of the woods to the left. He gestured with the shotgun toward the front of the car, and Ray wheeled and pointed the pistol down the passenger side of the 4Runner. The big guy was pulling himself along the driveway, leaving a trail of blood in the wet grass and gravel. Ray ran to the front of the car and pulled the door open. He thumbed the magazine catch, dropping the clip. He pulled another clip from the sport bag and pushed it into the Colt and racked the slide, his hands shaking and blood dripping from his face onto his hands. He closed the door as the big biker pushed himself to his feet and began to limp down the driveway.

Manny said, "Hey!" and the big man pointed the gun clumsily behind him as he tried to hobble faster down the trail. Ray pulled the trigger, holding the gun low, and the biker's legs went out from under him and he screamed again. He dropped his pistol and kept moving, crawling hand over hand and moaning into the dirt.

Ray ran over and kicked the guy hard in the ribs. The guy put one arm around his stomach and puked into the grass. Ray dropped onto his hands and knees and smacked the guy in the head with the butt of the pistol again and again. He saw the dead woman in the bathroom and Danny's staring eyes. He was aware of an animal sound, a snarling wail that was coming out of his own throat but that he had no more control over than if it had been coming from someone else. Manny grabbed him under the arms and pulled him off the guy and threw him into the grass, and Ray lay there, breathing like he'd run a mile. He lifted his pistol and saw that his hands were bathed in red and there was blood and matted hairs on the butt of the gun. He could feel a pounding in his ears and blood ran into his eyes.

He flipped over onto his stomach and put the pistol down. He could hear Manny rummaging around in the car and then his footsteps coming closer. Somewhere insects started a reedy hymn, one note rising and falling.

"Hold out your hands."

He did as he was told and he felt tepid water being poured over his bloody fingers. He splashed the water into his eyes and blinked, and gradually his vision cleared and he sat back on his haunches. He took the bottle from Manny and poured more of it over his head before he gave it back. Manny upended the bottle and finished the last of it, then threw the bottle back into the open door of the Toyota. Somewhere crows made terrible noises, like someone coughing out a last few choking breaths. Ray looked over at

Dennis Tafoya

the biker, who was staring at something in the grass, his pupils black.

He was wearing colors, a black vest with the name of a club Ray didn't know and FRANCONIA, NH embroidered on it in red, and BLOOD IN, BLOOD OUT. There were skulls and lightning bolts tattooed on his neck and the exposed parts of his arms. On the back of one hand was a spidery jailhouse tat of the words LIGHTS OUT.

"Look in his pockets." Manny called over his shoulder as he went around the Toyota to the other body. Ray got up stiffly and went over the big man, turning out the pockets. He pulled a clip for the pistol, a lighter, a lock knife, a pack of cigarettes, and a set of keys out of the leather jacket and threw them into a pile in the grass. In a back pocket of the greasy black jeans he found an envelope with names scrawled on the back. Danny Mullen, Hoe Down, Manny's name, and his. His name was underlined.

When he came back around the SUV, Ray saw now that Manny was moving stiffly and he watched as Manny painfully shucked off the vest. He held it up to Ray, and Ray could see a dull slug stuck to the jacket on the right side of the chest. Manny slowly pulled his shirt open, and there was a red welt over his rib cage. He shook his head in a gesture that might have meant anything.

The Toyota started, and Manny pointed it off the road into the trees. He threw their bags and as many of the spent shells from Ray's gun as he could find out onto the grass and then stuffed everything into one of the bags. Ray got a shoulder under the smaller of the two bodies and pushed him into the back and slammed the door. They each grabbed an arm of the bigger biker and dragged him to the passenger door of the front seat and clumsily dumped him in. He looked at their faces one last time. Neither of them was the young guy with a black goatee. Which meant he was still out there, still looking for them. Ray got behind the wheel of the SUV and began to pull forward again into the trees, leaning forward to look through the hole smashed through the cracked windshield.

He drove as far as he could away from the rutted track and into the woods, maneuvering around trees and over stumps and rocks that crunched against the undercarriage, occasionally stopping to wipe sweat and blood out of his eyes. Finally he got out and went around wiping down surfaces in the car with the gray blanket from the trunk. He took the flask out of his pocket and stuffed one end of the blanket into the gas tank and dumped some of the schnapps onto it. He dumped the rest over the bodies, stinking of shit and meat already starting to turn in the heat.

Christ, when things happened they moved fast. Both events, the farmhouse and now in the woods with the bikers—it was like they were over before they began. Before he could make rational decisions or some kind of plan. Standing there looking at two dead men in a wrecked car, he tried to think how long it had all taken. Three minutes, five? He played things over and over in his head, but all he got was a kind of faulty instant replay that came out different every time.

In the movies they showed gunplay in slow motion, but that wasn't it, really. It was more like everything was speeded up except you. Everyone was moving fast, coming at you with deliberation and purpose, and you couldn't finish a thought or get ready for the next thing. He thought maybe it was like being in a hurricane or a tornado, something fast and out of control.

He flicked the lighter he had taken from the biker and lit up the blanket and walked away through the trees. When he reached the drive again, Manny was waiting with a bag over his shoulder and the other one in his hands. He was looking down the rutted trail toward the house and chewing on his lip. His face was stained with dirt cut by lines of sweat from his hairline, and there were bits of broken glass on his shirt and in his hair. Ray turned and looked into the woods, but he couldn't see the SUV anymore.

"Did it catch?"

"I don't know. It did or it didn't and either way we got to go."

"You have keys?"

Ray held up the set of keys he took off the biker and jangled them. Somewhere nearby was another car. There was a distant smell of smoke, and somewhere the dog started up again, a remote, impotent sound of rage. Ray thought that if there was a God, that was his voice, just a distant complaint that didn't make anything come out any different.

Flies buzzed, and a fat black bee made a machinelike rumble as it passed by his head. He stumbled down the drive toward the road and thought about the flies in the bathroom and the man he had just killed, his head open in the dirt. He realized this was what he had been waiting for his whole life. All of the beatings he took, every night his father had lunged at his mother or stood at the bottom of the stairs smacking a leather belt into his hand. All the times in Juvie when some hulking lump of shit smacked him down or some guard in a county jail popped him across the knuckles with a stick because he could, because Ray was inside a cage and the guard was outside and he just fucking could. Ray had taken it and stored it up like a battery, all of it, every fucking thing. All for this day, when it would come pouring out of his heart and into his hands. It was something electric, something that gave off an ozone smell and made him dizzy and blind, like being electrocuted by crossed wires in his own brain.

THEY HEADED NORTH again in a black van they found parked in the woods near the end of the drive.

When they got in, Manny handed Ray a cell phone. "I took it off the little guy."

Ray thumbed through the memory, looking at calls that had come in and gone out and stored numbers. One of these, Ray thought, was probably the guy in the Charger.

They stopped at a pharmacy in Malvern, and Ray stayed in the car while Manny went in and bought a bunch of bottled water, alcohol, and Band-Aids. Ray looked at the cut on his forehead, glued over with dried blood and bits of grass and dirt. When Manny came back they drove to a remote corner of a shopping center parking lot, and Ray sat on the edge of the seat, pouring water over the cut to get the dried blood and dirt off and then dabbing at it with the alcohol. Cleaned up, it wasn't that bad. Deep, but not wide. He put a Band-Aid on and smoothed it down clumsily, looking into the side mirror. With his hair pushed forward it was pretty much invisible. Manny had torn his jeans and had a scrape on one elbow where the shirt was ripped away. Ray dabbed at it with alcohol, and Manny made a fist and swore. He kept touching the tender place on his rib cage and pulling his shirt back to look at the welt.

The cell phone rang. They both looked at it on the seat for a minute, then Ray picked it up and held it a few inches from his face.

"Yeah," he said, trying to sound indistinct.

"What happened? You said you were going to call or come back in an hour." The voice was different than the young guy in the Charger. The voice on the phone was another New Englander, but he sounded older and rougher-edged than the young guy from the car at the farmhouse.

Ray moved the phone away from his mouth again to talk, trying out an imitation of the accent. "I'm all turned around out here. How do I get back there?"

"Did they show up?"

"No, but we can't stay here."

"Well, the man here needs his money. You come back here and get cleaned up, you're going right back out to work, got it?"

"Yeah."

"Okay. Tell the truth, I don't know where the good Christ I am down here either." There was a hoarse laugh, a sound like someone gargling stones. "Let me ask Scott." *Scawt.* There was shouting and calls for Scott and music in the background. A bar, maybe, or a party going on. He heard the older guy saying that the knuckleheads were lost and needed directions back, and then the noise of the phone being passed around, and then the Voice. The guy from the Charger.

"Which one is this?" Ray was about to speak when he heard the question answered at the other end of the line. It's Eldon, the older guy said, and called him Knucklehead One.

"Eldon?"

"Yeah," Ray said, trying to keep it quiet.

"Can you find 202?"

"Yeah."

"Just come up 202 to 422, keep going north." *Nahth*. Ray was making mental notes in case he was called on to say more. The young guy gave them directions to a place in the woods between Kulpsville and Lansdale. A place with a long driveway, probably another farmhouse meth lab.

"Got it, knucklehead?" said the Voice, and laughed.

"Fuck off. Later." He hung up.

MANNY DROPPED RAY off at his apartment. He showered, put his clothes in a plastic bag and threw them away, and then opened the new things he had bought himself at Wal-Mart. He was still alert, unsure, kept jumping up at every slammed door on the street and looking out the window at the traffic. He looked around and realized he'd have to stop coming back here, find some other place to be. When he looked at the clock he realized it was almost seven, and he sat on his bed in his underwear and thought for a minute if it was smart to put everything on hold while he went to meet Michelle. Thinking of her name knocked it over in his mind, and he quickly got dressed. He pulled the dirty Band-Aid off his head and put on a smaller one, a round dot that was almost covered by his hair.

Dennis Tafoya

Outside, the sky ran from bright blue in the east to dark clouds and flashes of lightning in the west, but he couldn't tell if things were going to get better or worse. Going north toward Doylestown he felt weirdly relaxed again, his guard down, as if it were possible to take a time-out from his game and just be a normal human being. He put the radio on and found a station playing a Matt Pond PA song, upbeat music that reminded him of old Moody Blues. The wind picked up, trying to pull the car out his hands and rolling leaves and bits of paper across 611.

It was almost seven twenty when he reached the little coffee shop. He stood outside and watched her through the glass, sitting at a small table, reading a newspaper with a mug of coffee in front of her. The shop was tiny, just a few tables, a counter with ice cream. It looked cool and quiet, and he wanted to go inside, but he just stood and watched her. He could see the lines by her eyes. What could he have been thinking, coming here? Maybe it was just that she looked a little like Marletta. Some quality in her face. The same honey-colored skin, familiar brown and sympathetic eyes. But who was she? He was falling from the top of a building, and she was someone who looked out a window, catching a glimpse of him on his way to the sidewalk.

He put his hands up in front of him. They were mottled with bruises and traced with old scars. He stuck them in his pockets, but he could still feel them, swollen from what he had done. He watched her for a long time. She sipped at the coffee and looked at her watch, but she never looked up. There was something about the way she looked around her, something he recognized. Stealing glances at people and avoiding eye contact. He had taken it for flirtatiousness, but it was something else. He became conscious of the sun going down, of the street darkening. He willed her to look up and wave to him, wave him in so he could go inside and sit down, but she kept her eyes on the paper.

A couple with a baby sat down at the table next to her in a shower of pastel-colored toys and diaper bags, and she turned to look at the back of the baby's white head. Michelle's eyes were blank and unreadable, and Ray got that she was seeing things that weren't in the room.

He looked up the street to his left, and when he swung his head right there was a young guy wearing sunglasses just past his elbow. He had one of those complicated-looking goatees with skinny lines of hair running alongside his mouth and down along his jaw. Ray could see a pimple under the kid's ear and could smell his breath, fruity and sour from whatever he'd been drinking. The guy was smiling, his head cocked, and he had a jacket on and his hand in his pocket. Ray stepped back, away from the window, hoping that now wasn't the moment Michelle would finally look up. The guy leaned into him and shook his head, and Ray turned toward him. He sensed someone move behind him, then felt a big hand on his left shoulder and heard breathing close to his ear. The kid raised his eyebrows and nodded as if Ray had asked a question.

"I seen a lot of stupid people, but you're right up there." The kid looked up and down the street and kept his voice low. "Man, you walk around like you got no cares. Are you really brave, is that it?" The kid moved the bulge in his jacket where his right hand lay and nodded toward the street. "You Bruce Willis, is that the thing?" The hand on his shoulder squeezed, and Ray flinched. They got closer to the curb, and Sunglasses put a hand up and gestured to someone down the street. Ray heard a throaty engine. He watched a van creep along the curb toward them.

Ray looked up and down the street. There were people around, but no one was closer than a half block away, and it was almost dark. He saw a young couple standing in front of the movie theater, the boy with curly brown hair, the girl gesturing toward a poster. They began to sort money out in front of the ticket booth, and Ray thought that by the time they got out of the movie he'd be in a hole in the woods somewhere and this kid would be kicking dirt and leaves over his face.

"You're like a goldfish in a bowl, you know it?" The kid shook his head at Ray. "You don't even hide from us? Come right back to your house, drive around in your own car?" The van pulled up, and Sunglasses put his free hand on Ray's arm. He was conscious of the big man behind him moving, and then the guy stepped into view, reaching for the sliding side door of the van. He was big across the shoulders and had a shaved head, a black T-shirt, a shelf of gut over his jeans. The kid was still talking. "Eldon called me, told me your name, I figured we'd never see you again." He started to laugh and swung his head up and down the street. "Is this, like, your job? Nine to five you're a scumbag thief, then what? You like, punch out, go home, go see a movie?"

The big guy was turned to the door, standing in a gap between two parked cars. The kid was crowding Ray into the gap, trying to jab him with the gun hidden in his coat. There was a buzzing noise and the streetlights came on. The kid reached up and grabbed his sunglasses and began to lift them off his eyes. Ray dropped almost to his knees and then snapped up straight, cracking the top of his head against the kid's chin and knocking him off balance. The big guy with the bald head was still turned to the van, and Ray pushed with both hands against the kid's head, smacking it against the hood of the car behind him. The sunglasses rattled onto the car's hood, the kid blinking, stunned.

Then he ran. He didn't turn to look behind him, he just took off running as fast as he could down the street, past the theater. He heard the kid's high voice, yelling something, a low grumble from someone else, and then the squealing of the van's tires as the driver gunned the engine. He felt like his back was a target a mile wide under the lights. He saw the faces of people down the street and wanted to call to them, signal them somehow, but his throat was frozen and he couldn't force any sound out of it.

He saw a gap between the stores on his right that resolved into an alley as he got closer, and he pivoted as he reached it and poured on as much speed as he could as he made the corner. He was a few steps down the alley when the van screeched its brakes and stopped on the street behind him. Then he could hear it bumping over the curb, trying to jockey into the alley. He could hear the footsteps, too, the kid's lighter ones and the heavy clomp of the big guy's boots farther back.

Ahead of him the alley emptied into a small parking lot with meters. Past the lot the town was dark and he tried to move faster. He was about five yards from a white Lexus SUV trying to make up his mind which way to break at the end of the alley, the van's engine getting louder, when he heard a popping sound and the side window of the Lexus blew in. Two more shots smacked into the car, leaving black holes the size of quarters, and he involuntarily jumped left, away from the shots, and cut between a Mercedes and another SUV, a Lincoln Navigator big enough to give him some cover as he kept going, the air burning in his mouth and lungs.

He heard a roar behind him, and he looked over his shoulder in time to see the van two feet behind him hit the massive Lincoln dead on the rear end with a popping noise of breaking glass and grinding metal. The Navigator rocked on its springs, and Ray dropped and clawed his way under the Mercedes. He could smell oil and metal and fried food from the kitchens of restaurants. There was shouting now and the sound of feet scraping along the asphalt, a civilian getting into it with whoever was driving the van.

"What the fuck?" he heard a raspy voice say, a man, maybe in his fifties. "That's my fucking *car*." Ray shimmied back and forth, trying to see what he could from under the Mercedes. It was a tight squeeze. His hair caught on something; flecks of rust drizzled into his eyes. The older man was loud, and his voice echoed from different points around the small, boxed-in lot.

"What the fuck are you doing?" To his right he saw oily black boots and then a pair of white bucks, probably the guy with the raspy voice. He heard someone hitting the buttons on a cell phone. "Don't go anywhere," he heard the guy say. He heard two low voices conferring, then a pop and a scuffling noise. The white bucks tilted, and a face slapped the ground, inches away from his, and Ray almost shouted. It was a man with white hair slicked back from his face. The face was tan, freckled, the eyes blue. The features were empty and slack, and a red arc of blood poured out of his temple and hit the ground. Ray had to cover his mouth with his hands to keep from making some kind of sound.

"Dumb fuck!" He heard a young voice, out of breath, probably the kid with the sunglasses. "You are the dumbest dumb fuck I ever saw." There was more of the other voice, low, and then running steps and the van engine roared. He saw the van tires backing up and heard a sound of tearing metal and plastic, and the rear bumper of the Navigator hit the ground. There were sirens now and more running feet and screaming somewhere away to his left.

He could see the van tires arcing away to his right, and then it vanished from view. He began shimmying again, pushing with his feet against the tires of the Mercedes and slowly extracting himself from under the car on the driver's side, away from the body of the man with white hair and his terrible blank eyes. He got free and lay there for a second, his chest scraped raw, his heart hammering.

There was a guy in a white apron holding a meat cleaver standing a few feet away who jumped a little when he saw Ray trying to pull himself upright. "Jesus Christ, are you all right?"

Ray made a dismissive wave with his right hand. "Okay," he finally got out.

"Did you see them shoot that guy? Jesus Christ. They just shot him."

"I, uh." Ray was suddenly dizzy, out of breath, the words hanging somewhere in his brain he couldn't get to. "I just . . ." He made a diving motion with his hand: himself crawling under the car. "When I heard the shots."

"No shit." The cook nodded; he'd have done the same thing. "Who needs that shit? That big fuck must be crazy." A crowd was starting to form, people coming out of a restaurant, a bar, a candy store and taking tentative steps toward whatever was going on in the lot.

Ray moved toward them, bending over, trying to look as stricken as possible. "I have to . . ." He pointed vaguely toward the bar door he could see open.

"Sure," the guy in the apron said. He waved with the knife. "The cops are on their way. Fucking shot, over a fender bender. Christ."

Ray walked through the crowd. The first few people he passed looked at his face, but farther back in the crowd people were just trying to see past him, craning their necks, moving around him. He picked up the pace as he reached a sidewalk, a path between some shops that led toward the street. He walked faster, then began to jog. Where was his car?

He moved north along a tree-lined street, looking for a way to cut back toward where he had left the Camaro. He walked a long block and turned left and there was a police car, its lights on, stopped at the curb. Ray's breath caught in his throat. A young kid with long hair was bent over, hands in his pockets, talking to the cops through the open window. Ray tried not to react, walking purposefully, trying to look as interested as any passerby would be in a cop car with its lights on, slowly blowing through his nose to keep his breathing under control. The block was short, and he kept moving up a hill as if he knew where he was going. He kept his eyes straight ahead and resisted the urge to turn and look at the cops. He passed a low building, some kind of club or lodge or something. One of those places that Ray imagined was full of dark paneling and leather chairs where men smoked cigars and talked about business. Past that he came to where another small alley opened out to the street. He turned left and saw the cop car coming out of a three-point turn and then heading up the hill toward him. No siren, but the lights going; blue, red, white.

When he was out of sight of the cops Ray began to run, his steps echoing between the close-set houses, and he looked for a place to disappear. He passed two low stone houses and jogged left and pushed through a waist-high wood gate and followed a cement path green with mildew into the dark behind a three-story Victorian haunted house, the windows dark and empty. He stopped and listened but didn't hear the cop car or see its lights. They might not even be looking for him, might not know he was involved in what had happened in the parking lot. He stood for a while in the dark, listening to faint sounds from other parts of town. Sirens, kids shouting, music from a house somewhere nearby. A party maybe. He took his time threading his way through an abandoned garden of flattened tomato plants, gray and dead in the heat. He stepped over a low fence of iron bars and came out into a small space between two massive hedges. It was full dark, the street in front of him lit orange-white by a streetlight.

He was standing in the shadow, trying to orient himself to the street he had parked on, when Michelle appeared two feet away. She was walking uphill, a book under her arm. Her head was down, and she looked lost in thought, her lips moving silently. He put his hand out but didn't touch her or speak, just watched her pass slowly, inches away. If she had raised her eyes, turned her head, anything. If he had made a sound, cleared his throat, moved suddenly . . .

Then she was past, and he stepped out. He watched her move up the street and turn a corner, the light catching in her hair, her face in silhouette for a moment. Then she was gone.

CHAPTER EIGHT

RAY SLIPPED OUT from the darkness and moved back down to the busy street where he had parked. There were cops out on the sidewalks, an ambulance at the head of the alley where the bikers had shot the man with white hair. He could hear voices from police radios, and he struggled to stay calm and look like he belonged. He got his keys out and held them in his fist, tried to keep them from rattling. He passed the ambulance crew, young kids in blue jumpsuits carrying metal clipboards and leaning against a parked car, and a cop carrying a shotgun at port arms who looked at Ray hard when he passed.

Back in the Camaro, he cranked the ignition with shaking hands and felt around on the seat for his cell phone, grabbed it, and started to dial before realizing it was the one they had taken off the dead biker out in Delaware County. He tossed it away and snapped open the glove compartment, pulled the black automatic, and sat for a minute, looking compulsively up and down the street and breathing fast. Finally he decided it was better to be in motion, and he put his car in gear and pulled down the street, turned south, and picked up speed.

He dialed Manny and told him what had happened. The telling was out of order, distorted by his fear and adrenaline. He kept touching his chest and feeling his heart beat, touching his temple reflexively at the place where the hole had been in the man's head. That man, someone's father or grandfather was dead, and wasn't it his fault? He hadn't wanted any of it to happen, but if it wasn't his doing, whose fault was it? Was everything that had happened just his fucked-up life spilling out over everyone he came across?

"How the fuck?" Manny wanted to know. "Did they follow you, or what?"

"They picked me up at my house. One of them said. Those guys at Danny's must have called them." He kept checking the rearview, looking for the van or anyone trying to get to close to his bumper. So taking the piece of paper with their names on it hadn't stopped anything. How stupid, how fucking stupid could he be? The guys had called Scott, and everyone knew who they were. And who was everyone? Were there ten guys, twenty, a hundred? He was sweating but felt cold. "Fucking motherfuckers."

It came to him that it could have been Michelle standing with him when they pulled the guns, and that put more terrible pictures in his head that crowded his thinking and made his heart race. He pulled over to the side of the road, and it dawned on him they knew his car, had in fact followed him to Doylestown. The kid had said it. Jesus. He wasn't thinking, wasn't planning. He needed to slow down, get right in his head. He was on 611, near a big shopping center at Street Road, and he pulled in and told Manny to get away from his own car, find another one, and come for him.

He cruised through the lot, pulling behind a Genuardi's and

nosing toward a Dumpster. He switched off the car and looked around him, grabbing his small duffel and checking the Colt. He pulled the slide back to put a round in the chamber, then slowly let the hammer down and stuck it into his belt, an awkward move sitting down.

On the dark floor, something flashed green. He stopped and watched. After maybe thirty seconds, he saw it flash again. He leaned toward the pool of darkness in front of the passenger seat and put his hand on the dead biker's cell. He flipped it open and looked at it. The display had bars for battery life, a little graph for signal strength. There was a symbol, a 1 and an *X*, which meant nothing to him, but then he noticed a flashing letter *G* in the lower left hand corner. Was that for GPS? Did that matter? Did these guys have some kind of software that could track the cell phone or something? Were they right now boxing him in again?

He jumped out of the car and looked around. Two kids in green aprons sat smoking on overturned milk crates. One of them, a big kid with red hair, waved with his cigarette. Behind the car, Ray saw a slight grassy rise, a driveway leading away toward an exit; across the driveway the ground sloped down to what looked like a creek, a black line in the dark sketched through a stand of trees. He took two steps and fired the cell phone hard over the road and down toward the creek.

The kid with red hair pumped his cigarette hand in the air. "Fuck, yah."

The other kid laughed, nodding his head. "Toss that bitch."

Ray jumped back into the car and sat with his head in his hand for a minute, thinking.

The red-haired kid took a few steps closer, eyeing the Camaro and Ray. "Nice ride," the boy said, and the silent one sitting on the crate shook his head in agreement. "Want to get wasted?"

"Yes," said Ray and put the car in gear.

HE LEFT HIS car in another shopping center farther east down County Line, by a dark and empty Dunkin' Donuts. He got out and locked the car under feeble lights that left the parking lot the dull green of a lake bottom. He called Ho and told him what had happened while he walked across the dark lot to stand in the shadow of a Sunoco station. It had all happened fast, he told Ho, and chances were the guys they killed hadn't told Scott about Ho, but he should take whatever steps he thought were right. Ho thanked him and hung up, and Ray watched the street and kept his hand in his pocket, on his pistol, clicking the safety off and on, off and on.

He thought about Ho's kids, and Tina, and that made it tougher to think straight, but Jesus, was everything bad that could happen his fault? Ho was in the life, ran massage parlors and dope houses, and had a cousin who sat at an upstairs window with an AK, so there was already the possibility hanging out there for Ho, and Ho knew it. But Ray knew even as he had those thoughts that it didn't get him off the hook. This shit had gotten away from him, and he had to make it right somehow.

Manny took him by his own place, and Ray took Sherry's old Honda and drove it slowly home, taking a long route around Warminster and through Horsham. Later he sat in the dark car by his building and watched the traffic go by, the headlights throwing twisted silhouettes of trees onto the fronts of the houses, tangles of shadow that moved and broke apart into nothing.

He tried to see into the cars going past, caught glimpses of dark figures going home, going out. He thought about regular life, tried to think of people he knew who just went to work and came home, went to sleep, got up, and did it again. Just about everybody he knew was in the life except Theresa and her retired friends from the neighborhood who got together at the Ukrainian church to play Bingo on Wednesdays. Tough old broads who had raised kids and buried husbands, worked at Acme or the post office or Warminster General.

He had worked straight jobs, but never for very long. He had worked in pizza joints when he was a kid, liked the smell of the dough and flirting with the waitresses and the girls who came in for a slice and a Coke. But then he'd just blow it off; he'd go get high with his friends, and the next thing he knew, he'd be driving someone else's car to the Oxford Mall, or sneaking around a dark house, high, drunk, banging into things and trying not to laugh, or running through black yards at night with a pillowcase full of cheap costume jewelry he took off someone's bureau while Manny took cold cuts from the fridge.

Could he stop being who he was? He thought about Marletta, about the last time he saw her. What had they said? She wanted a normal life for him. If things had gone different with her, would that have been his way out? She was in his thoughts more and more now, working on his head. The way she loved him and thought he could be more. Gone all this time until that picture brought her back, the picture in the house on Jefferson Avenue of the young girl in the cap and gown.

Marletta had died, and they'd sent him up for it, and he'd let them. He'd picked her up from graduation and they'd driven around, went to a park, gone to his house and made love, and when he was driving her home a drunk had crossed the center line and she'd been killed. Thrown from the car into a field full of tiny white flowers whose name he couldn't remember. Her old man was a state trooper, and he'd hated Ray even before that day. They'd taken Ray to St. Mary's with a concussion, and her old man would sit in the parking lot in his car. Every time Ray had gone to the window, her old man would be there. At night, he'd see his cigarette going in the dark, a slow red pulse as her father breathed.

Her old man had pushed the case about the stolen car, and they'd locked him up. He sat in Juvie for months, waiting, and one night her old man came for him and took him out and beat him with a tire iron and took him back with a thin story about Ray falling in the dark. So when they finally convicted him, sent him upstate as an adult, he'd had two busted arms. Ray had let it happen, let it all come, and none of it, no matter how bad it got, was as bad as he thought he deserved for losing Marletta.

After a few minutes he gave up the idea of going back for his shit. Instead he drove west to Montgomeryville to get more clothes, toiletries, and a couple of CDs to calm him down and help him think. It was late when he finally pulled into a motel on 611 near the turnpike. Standing in the bright lobby by the highway brought his paranoia on hard again, and he drummed his fingers

Dennis Tafoya

and hunched his shoulders waiting for the sleepy clerk to appear from the back. He checked in, then drove around the back of the place, twitching with fear. He ran upstairs, his insides turning to water, and then sat in the dark with the pistol in his lap.

What would Marletta think of him now? What would she say? He was so far from the things he had let himself want when they were together, but he felt like he wanted something like a normal life now more than ever. Was it just that things were so fucked up? That he was afraid and looking for a way out?

He rummaged in his bag and pulled out some CDs and threw them on the bed, then chose one and put in the CD player on the bed table. Henryk Górecki. Classical music. What he called it, anyway. It had been playing when he walked into a Tower Records in King of Prussia, and he asked the girl behind the counter what it was, and she pointed to a stack of CDs near the counter.

He had looked up the music online and knew that the words were from a prayer, and they sounded that way. Someone pleading or crying, he guessed in Polish. He thought all pleading was the same in whatever language. Help me. Forgive me. Don't leave me. Don't kill me. He thought about the white-haired man and the terrible red arc streaming out of him, and Rick Staley slipping around in his own blood on the floor of the dope lab in Ottsville. He wanted to let himself go, start screaming and breaking things. He wanted to get high. After a while, he fell asleep.

HE GOT UP at eight and had coffee in front of the window, watching the street. A woman jogged by; a man in one of those spandex outfits he didn't get rode by on an expensive-looking bike. He got awkwardly to the floor of the room and did a few sit-ups and wanted to puke. He thought about being in Juvie, where he met Manny, and work details hauling trash and clearing brush.

They had been tough little fuckers then, tanned and fit, ready for anything. They got out six days apart and started boosting cars and stereos together. They shaved their heads, and Manny gave Ray his first tattoo, SS lightning bolts on his right arm done with a homemade gun with the motor from an electric razor and a guitar string. They'd split the money from stealing and get high and go to the movies. They watched *Predator*, he remembered, over and over, doing Arnold Schwarzenegger and Jesse Ventura to each other, capping bad guys in the jungle. "If it bleeds, we can kill it." How different was his life now, when you broke it down? He had stopped spending money on candy and soda but still bought movies and CDs and books compulsively. Didn't understand savings plans or IRAs, hadn't worked forty hours in years. The year before, he had gotten his last tattoo, DOPE THIEF in heavy black Germanic letters high on his left arm. At the time maybe committing himself, or maybe just letting go of every wish he ever had for a normal life.

Ho Dinh called Ray around ten, told him to come by. He took a shower, got dressed, and put on a sweatshirt and a sport coat to help hide the automatic. He spent a last ten minutes watching the street, his face tight, before he finally jogged to Sherry's Honda and took off.

WHEN RAY PULLED up, Ho came out of the house and jumped in alongside him.

"Keep going, down to Green Street."

"Where we headed?"

"West. We're going to see a guy I know about your problem."

"What's he know?"

"So far, nothing. And we should talk about what you're going to tell him. He doesn't have to know your business, just the part about the guys from New Hampshire." Ho took a piece of paper from his pocket and called the turns. They made their way along Kelly Drive, slaloming along the edge of Fairmount Park toward the Schuylkill River. Ho wore a light jacket even though it was in the eighties and expensive-looking sunglasses that he pushed up on his head whenever he consulted the paper.

Ray asked him if the guy they were going to see was with one of the clubs that controlled the meth business in the Delaware Valley.

Ho waggled his head back and forth. "I don't know that he's with any of the biker clubs, exactly, but he knows them and does business with them. They have some kind of deal together. I think he cooks for them and they distribute his product." Ho took his glasses and cleaned them, which made him look momentarily even younger. "So if we've got guys from up north pushing into his area, he might care enough about that to make your fight his fight."

"You think?"

Ho looked at him out of the corner of his eye. "You got a gun with you?"

"Under the seat. And in the glove compartment. I got more in the trunk, it comes to that. We going to need them?"

"I hope not. This guy's a little nuts, is all I know. You can't hang around that shit as much as he does and not be a little cooked yourself." Ho opened the glove compartment and pulled out the Colt. He worked the slide to see that it was loaded and put it at his feet.

THEY CROSSED THE river and made their way down Route 1 for a while, finally turning off and heading north. Ray stopped recognizing things as soon as they were out of Philly. The houses got more spread out, the yards big and green. He saw a sign for Blue Hill, and they made some more turns and came to a dirt road. When they pulled in, Ho told Ray to stop and handed him the pistol. He wedged it in his belt and pulled his sweatshirt over it.

He put the car in gear again and rolled down the rutted track that led to what looked like an abandoned shack. There was a new-looking red pickup truck pulled in next to the house and a big guy with a shaved head sitting in the bed. He had wraparound shades, and his hands were under a blanket that covered his lap. He worked a toothpick in his mouth and stared at them as they turned the car off and sat, listening to the engine tick.

Ray raised his eyebrows at Ho. "Should I have worn the vest?"

"Think bulletproof thoughts."

Ray shook his head.

Ho looked at the big guy in the pickup. "Tell me, what's with the shaved heads? Too much to look tough and comb your hair, too?"

"I did it once. Me and Manny, when we were young."

"Remember why?"

"No. If I had a nickel for every stupid thing we did when we were kids." He considered this for a minute. "Wait, I probably do."

Ho sighed and opened the door. He kept his hands in plain sight and nodded to the guy in the truck, who inclined his head toward the open door of the house, his own hands still under the blanket.

Ho disappeared into the house for a minute, then came back to the front door and waved to Ray. He slowly pulled himself out of the car and stretched, Pickup Truck Man watching him intently. Ray wished he had a toothpick to push around in his mouth; it would keep his mind off wanting to scratch himself and causing an accidental bloodbath.

It took a long time to reach the door, but eventually Ray closed the distance and made his way in past Ho and let his eyes adjust to the darkened interior for a minute. It was hot inside, airless, as if the house had stood empty a long time. Ray took in yellowed wallpaper, a dusty coffee table, a crumbling piano, keys going brown with age.

There was a tall, thin guy folded into a chair at the table and wearing a leather jacket. He had wiry gray hair pulled back in a ponytail, and his eyes looked cloudy to Ray, like the eyes of something that lived underground. His face was long and thin, and he had his hands flat on the table. The left hand was scarred, mottled with pink lines, and his left ear looked slightly melted. A woman stood behind him cradling a Remington pump gun. She was tall, too, and probably had been beautiful once. She had tattoos on her hands, yellow sun and bright clouds on one hand, stars and a smiling blue moon on the other. There were deeply etched lines running back from her hooded eyes, which were a brilliant green. The guy outside might be paid help, Ray thought, but this one was here for love. She was the one to watch if things got weird.

Ho moved a hand between Ray and the table. "This is Cyrus." The man nodded at Ray, who nodded back. There was one chair, and Ray stepped forward and sat in it.

Cyrus tilted his head at the wall. "My grandfather built this place in the thirties. He built it himself from plans he saw in a Sears, Roebuck catalog. In them days you could order a house from Sears and they'd build it for you." Cyrus had a deep, cracked voice to go with the lined face. Years of breathing chemicals.

"It's real nice."

"It's all beat to shit now, but it was a good house to grow up in. My pop got killed in some rice paddy in 1963." He nodded at Ho. "Probably by your uncle." He put his eyes back on Ray, tilted his head. "Where'd you do your time?"

Ray thought for a minute about how much to say to someone he didn't know. "Rockwood. Some other places."

"I figured you for a yardbird. That where you met Luke the Gook here?" Ho chuckled and shook his head. Cyrus was quiet and intense, and Ray was on edge. He couldn't figure whether the guy was going to blow up or if this was just how he was.

Ray shook his head. "You been inside?"

"Nope. I figure that's what separates me from you retards. I'm ready to die to stay free."

"That's one way to go."

"You should die proud when you can't live proud."

"Nietzsche. You're into Nietzsche, you'd love the joint. It's all psychos who figure they got permission from a dead German to skip on their child support and shoot their girlfriend's dog. I don't get it myself. I figure you want to rob a fucking gas station, go nuts. Why do you need quotes from *Twilight of the Idols* to make it cool?" Ray looked at Ho.

"Cyrus, my friend has a story to tell we thought you'd want to know."

"I'm all ears."

Well, Ray thought, an ear and a half, but he let it go. "There's a guy cooking dope in farmhouses in Bucks County and Montgomery County." Suddenly, Ray wasn't sure what he wanted from this guy.

"There's a lot of guys cooking dope around there. What, you want a cookie?" Cyrus stood up, his left eye twitching, and Ray put his hands on the arms of the chair, closer to the pistol. "This is costing me money, parlaying with some yardbird thinks he knows shit."

Ho said, "This guy's got people from New England clubs with him."

Cyrus was still and his face went slack. "And?"

Ray held up a hand, but Ho went on. "He's got guys down here from Massachusetts and New Hampshire."

"Who's moving his shit?"

"That we don't know."

Cyrus sighed and looked up like they were exhausting his infinite patience.

Ho pushed his glasses up on his sweat-slick forehead. "Tell him the last bit, Ray."

"I don't know. I want to think about this." Things were moving fast, and he couldn't think. What did it mean to tell this guy everything?

Ho looked at him but kept going. "We can draw you a map."

"You can fucking take me there."

"Yeah, screw that." Ray made a wiping gesture with his left hand. He was having trouble keeping it together, the guy's hard stare working on his head. "I already seen enough of these fuckers to last me a lifetime."

"So you want me to take care of some shit for you. You owe these guys money?"

Ray sat up straight. "That's none of your business, Merlin."

Cyrus slapped the table with his hand. The woman behind him pulled the shotgun down from port arms, ready to go to work.

Ho put his hands up. "Okay, let's all take a breath." After a long moment, Ray and Cyrus sank back into their chairs. Ho looked at Ray, who nodded. "We'll take you there. You can look things over, see what you think."

Cyrus breathed through his mouth. Was thinking, maybe, or just short of breath. "I'll call you in a day or two." Ray stood up slowly. Cyrus raised a finger. "You're fucking with me, or you get me hung up or waste my time, you're going to find your way to a deep hole in the dirt."

ON THE WAY back Ho looked at him. "Man, what the fuck was that?"

"Ah. I just can't stand that shit. Guys like that who think they're in charge of shit and like to lay down the law." Like his old man, he almost said.

"Shit, Ray."

"Yeah, I know. Sorry." He had almost lost control of things, pushed the crazy fucker too hard and made something bad happen. Something was happening to him, he could feel it. Old feelings and resentments were just beneath the surface of his skin, like barbs he couldn't get out.

Ho looked over at him. "Ray, this guy might be our ticket out of this thing."

Ray thought about that, about the fact that Ho's name was on the paper he had taken off the dead biker and what that might mean. He thought about Tina and the kids and got a sick feeling. He knew there was no ticket out, but a chance, maybe, and he'd have to take it or other people would pay for his stupidity.

He decided that whatever happened, he'd try to keep Ho and Manny at a distance. As they drove, he and Ho talked about what Cyrus might do and about other characters they had known in their business, most of them locked up or dead. Ho told Ray about his cousins who lived in Thailand and worked protection for Thai warlords moving meth from Burma.

Ray frowned. "Meth? Really? I think of opium or heroin coming out of there."

"Who knew? Turns out they can make it and move it here and it's still cheaper than the stuff made by those hillbillies you take off."

"The invisible hand, huh? I guess if it works for sneakers and T-shirts it works for dope."

Ho said, "Still, it's kind of depressing, isn't it? Another line of work for high school dropouts closed off by foreign competition." They laughed.

"It's the same everywhere, isn't it? You've been overseas."

"Yeah, I guess in most places it's only worse. It's a crappy deal for people with nothing no matter where you are."

Ray looked up as they got back into the city, and he saw a row of tired-looking people waiting for a SEPTA bus on Roosevelt Boulevard. He thought about how the fact that he was outside of the law and straight life didn't control his reaction to the way the world worked. His father had started off a working man, and Ray still thought of himself as working class, distrusted the rich, still thought there was something worse about Enron and country club crime than what he did.

He tried to put it into words, couldn't get it straight in his head, but said, "I mean, you got thousands of years of human history, people thinking about how to get organized, how to distribute work and money, and what? This is it? This is the best we can do?"

He made a gesture that took in everything around them. The Korean dry cleaners and the Mexican kids standing outside the car wash, the lined and anxious faces of the women at the bus stop. Maybe the fix he was in, too.

"Every man for himself?"

"Worse. Worse than that." What his mother had always said, bent over the unpaid bills like a galley slave over an oar, her face bruised with worry: "Dog eat dog."

CHAPTER NINE

FOR TWO NIGHTS Ray stayed in a motel in Marlton across the river in Jersey. Clean, but the towels were like sandpaper and the bed sagged in the middle. He called Theresa on the cell phone the first morning. She'd won eight hundred dollars playing nickel slots.

"Christ, Ma, that's like sixteen thousand nickels. What do they bring, a wheelbarrow?"

"They pay in cash, smart-ass."

"Keep it somewhere safe, that's all."

"Don't worry about my money, dope fiend. I'm saving it to spend on my grandchildren."

"Okay, I can see where this is going. I'll check in later."

"I talked to the lawyer about your father."

"That's great. I'll talk to you later."

She started to tell him something else, and he hung up.

AT NIGHT HE cruised up and down 73 in Sherry's Honda. He'd stop and get a drink at an empty bar, then get antsy and leave. He ordered from the drive-through at the Taco Bell. He felt like a shark circling in black water. Moving up and down from Marlton to Berlin, restless, jumpy, watching his rearview mirror and not knowing what to expect. The stations on Sherry's radio were tuned to Jesus and teenage-girl pop, and he dialed around until he found a black gospel station promising hell but offering full-throated music against the Day of Judgment. He went around the circle at 70 and followed it west. He passed dark industrial parks and convenience stores, finally pulled in at a strip joint in Pennsauken that billed itself as an International Gentlemen's Club. He sat in the car and pulled a one-hitter from under the seat and filled his nostrils with coke. He felt his pulse begin to race and his gums went numb. The car began to get hot, and when he opened the door he could smell the tar from the parking lot and the exhaust from passing trucks.

He sat at the bar and ordered a vodka and tonic and then turned to watch a short, wiry girl in a half-T move languorously up and down along the pole, her back arched. Her hair was a sooty, unnatural black, and all he could think about was how different she was from Michelle. Her eyes were half-closed, her movements as slow as if she were a sleepwalker, or moving against a current in a dark sea. Waitresses with hair tortured blond moved from table to table under dim red and blue spotlights that made it look as if they were being alternately frozen and then roasted alive. He finished the first drink fast and took another to a table in a corner. There was a black light overhead that made his shirt an unnatural white. He had more drinks and went to the men's room to do more blow, navigating the tables of gray-haired businessmen and kids with baseball caps doing a frantic pantomime of desire for their friends.

The girl from the stage came down and stood by him, her teeth brilliant in the ultraviolet light. He leaned into her, and she whispered to him. He took money out and gave it to her. She stood closer to him, and he felt heat in his face and along his arms. She smelled like perfume, something sharp and astringent, and beneath that sweat and cigarettes. She moved between his legs and breathed into his neck and somehow kept from touching him. Ray moved his hand along her leg, and she smiled and moved back a few inches. He held out a twenty, and she rolled a hip toward him so that he could put it beneath the band of the G-string.

"I know the rules," he said.

"Do you?"

"I just don't want to follow them." He opened his fist and began counting off hundred-dollar bills. She closed her hand over his and told him she'd be done at eleven thirty.

HE WALKED OUT, crouching to hide his insistent erection until he reached the car. He did another hit and rubbed his cramping jaw, blinking under the lights, which now looked ringed with purple motes from the dope in his blood. He drove back out to 73 and went into a package store. He walked up and down the aisles, conscious of being high. The aisles tilted away from him; the labels were too small to read. He walked up and down with a basket, eventually getting the layout. In the end he took a bottle of vodka and two bottles of tonic to the front and also bought pretzels and a handful of lottery tickets to give to Theresa, who saw tickets from another state as exotic: unfamiliar fruit from another continent.

Back out on the road, he drifted again, killing time. At the last minute he caught the sign for a used-book store and cut the wheel fast to catch the driveway. He killed the engine and took a pull from the bottle and washed it down with a long swig from the tonic water, which fizzed hot in his mouth and dribbled down his shirt. He wiped his hand over his mouth and blotted at his beard.

Inside it was quiet. A young woman with her lip and nose pierced stood at the counter talking on a red cell phone. He walked up and down the aisles, hunched over and trying to read the flaked and broken spines of westerns, mysteries with culinary themes, horror novels with titles that seemed to leak blood. He settled on Louis L'Amour, one of the Sackett books he knew but hadn't read in a while.

Next to the counter was a stand of cheap DVDs like the one in the store where Michelle worked. While the girl rang him up, the cell phone stuck between her ear and her raised shoulder, he flipped through the movies, looking for something he knew.

"Do you have *Night of the Demon?*"

She held out his change, shook her head, turned her back to finish her call. He felt the chemical thunderbolt of the cocaine in his blood and a flash of loneliness and shame that made his shoulders cave in on themselves, and he went to the car and pawed around for the vodka.

He went back to the club and waited for the black-haired dancer, who came out with a bouncer and turned and said a few words to him before he went back inside. He waited, then got out and gave a nervous half-wave, and she pointed to her car. He pulled out, and she followed in a black Jetta.

IN HIS ROOM, she said she didn't have much time; her mother was watching her son and expected her home at midnight.

"He's nine." She held up a cigarette and raised her black eyebrows, and he nodded. She fished in her purse and brought out a Zippo and a scuffed photo of a tiny kid with a mass of black curls in an oversized football jersey and shoulder pads. He smiled at the picture, and she looked at it, and when she put it away Ray could see her hands were shaking. He watched her light the cigarette, her full lips pursed and her eyes watching his.

He sat on the edge of the bed, and she came over and sat in his lap fully clothed. He put one arm around her but thought of a small, black-haired kid in a messy living room watching TV, the grandmother asleep in the blue wash of light, mouth open, dentures loose. A smell of unwashed laundry and old cigarette smoke.

He could feel a tremor in her arm across his chest. At the club he had wanted her with an ache that seemed to run through him, carried in his blood. Under the yellow light from the cheap bed-table lamp, it all fell out of him and he could see she was afraid that he might be a cop, that he might beat her. She wanted him to know about her son. She wanted the money for her rent, or maybe to get high. He had always known this about the massage parlor women, the strippers he had briefly dated or just fucked for money. Something about killing a man with his hands, or almost getting killed himself, or turning thirty, or talking to his father had changed the way he saw things. The way he saw himself, moving through the world. Maybe it had just been the house on Jefferson Avenue, the picture of the girl in her cap and gown looking so much like Marletta, and her voice in his head again. The way she had looked at him and the things he had let himself want when he held her.

People were weak and stupid, and he had used that knowledge to get over on them. The things they needed, the people they loved, made them vulnerable. This special knowledge he had spent his lifetime accumulating he realized now was absolutely obvious to anyone alive in the world, and it made him ashamed to see it so plain. Anyone who wasn't crazy or greedy or stupid knew it. He shifted to get his hand in his pocket and took out his money and handed it to the girl. He lifted his head and told her to go home, and she unfolded herself from his lap and got up and was gone in a few seconds. He had wished for a moment that she would stay and talk to him. The smell of cigarette smoke and perfume hung in the air for a minute. He had wanted to tell her something, but whatever he had to say she already knew it.

When he closed his eyes he could get glimpses of Marletta, and of Michelle, the two of them sometimes getting mixed up in his head. They were like two lights on a dark horizon, and if he could stay fixed on them, move toward them, he thought he could get away from all of this. Not just out from under this trouble but away from everything he knew, be something different, do something with his life, maybe.

He stayed up through the night, drinking vodka and tonic to

Dennis Tafoya

bring himself down off the coke and reading the book he'd bought. He thought, not for the first time, about the land in the westerns he read, the way the men in the stories found their way by the colors and shapes of rocks and canyons. Everywhere he had been in ten years had looked the same to him. The Philly suburbs were hills rolling out monotonously, every inch covered with weedy industrial lots, Wal-Marts and Kmarts and malls, and you couldn't fix yourself in them. The stars were lost in a milky sky lit orange by sodium lamps. Sometimes he dreamed of himself on a horse in the desert, navigating dry wash canyons by the color of the sand and riding in the blue shadows of massive rock formations like pyramids grown from the earth.

He lay with Marletta in his small bed, naked on the covers, heads close. He pulled a pillow from the floor and put it under her head, and she smiled at him. She was larger somehow out of her clothes, the fact of her working on his head, his need for her moving in the muscles of his arms and legs. Her eyes were shining and wide as if desire were a drug moving in her blood.

She touched him, and he closed his eyes, moving his hips against her hand, and she kissed him and rolled onto her back. She caught his hand and guided his fingers to her, and he felt where she was wet and his breath came harder and he moved over her and balanced there.

She put her hands on the small of his back and, lifting herself, drew him down onto her. He watched her eyes close, and fat tears rolled from the corners and she bared her teeth, and he stopped moving. Her eyes opened, and she saw there was something frantic and afraid in his face and put her hand on his cheek.

"I don't want to."

"No," she said. "It's okay."

"I don't want to hurt you. I can't hurt you."

"No, I love you."

"I don't know what to do." His voice was horse.

She drew his head down and put her lips to his ear. "I need you to be with me. I love you. Everything beautiful is on the other side of this. Everything is coming for us."

At dusk the next evening Ray went to a small strip mall in Trooper and waited for Cyrus. He got out of the Honda and paced, drinking Dunkin' Donuts coffee and wanting a cigarette. At eight thirty it was still hot, and he wiped at his eyes with the heel of his hand. The phone buzzed in his pocket, and he looked at it. Manny again, wanting him to relent and let him be there to watch Ray's back. He turned it off.

He watched people go in and out of a convenience store, watched a man with tattoos and one wandering eye come out of a thrift store carrying an armload of scuffed toys. Moths and mosquitoes came out of the dark and thrashed against the green lights overhead. The man got into a worn El Camino and two small girls lunged at him, clutching at the toys with wide smiles.

Cyrus showed in the huge red pickup, the kid with the shaved head riding shotgun. Ray made eye contact with Cyrus, and the older man took his hand off the wheel and pointed down the road. Ray got back in the Honda and headed out. They snaked over low hills, the pickup hanging back. Ray kept it slow, keeping them in his rearview. After a few turns he noticed there were more cars behind them and Cyrus was talking into a cell phone as they made the turns, his big head silhouetted against the slewing lights of trucks and SUVs.

On Forty Foot Road Ray slowed and then pulled over. He got out and walked back to the pickup, kicking gravel and empty plastic soda bottles.

The skinhead jumped out and moved out front. He had big, wired-looking eyes and thick rings on his knuckles. "What's up?"

"What is this? I thought I was taking him to look it over."

"Mister, you and me just do what we're told." He stepped back, pointing ahead.

"You don't need me. To look it over."

"You're the one called this deal. You're done when he says you're done." The big skinhead pointed back at the cab, where Cyrus cocked his head and pointed his red hand down the road.

Ray shook his head but got back in the car and started away. Two vans and another pickup stayed close behind Cyrus. He turned down a long dirt road leading around a hill and watched the moon slide between clouds. At the bend he stopped. The road led into a copse of trees, and ahead he could see the lights on the pointed roof of a tall old farmhouse and the blank side of a white barn. He opened his window and heard music and a loud, rough laugh. Cyrus pulled up and got out, and Ray watched as the two vans and the truck pulled into the grass. A dark Taurus made the turn from the road and parked behind the other cars. Ray went under the passenger seat and retrieved the Colt and put it under his jacket at the small of his back. His breath was coming harder, and he put a hand on his chest. He got out of the car but left it running.

To the north he could see heat lightning flash soundlessly. There was a din of crickets; a hot wind pulled at his shirt and hair, and sweat began to run on his neck and chest. Men came out of the vans wearing embroidered colors. They crowded around the trunk of the Taurus and talked to each other in low voices. Ray wanted to jump back in the car and get out.

Cyrus moved over and put his ruined hand on Ray's back, moved him forward away from the car. He closed the door and reached in through the open window and pulled the keys out of the ignition and pushed them into Ray's hand. "Let's go see what's going on." He nodded down the road toward the farmhouse.

Ray looked behind him and got a glimpse of men carrying long guns and someone hefting a cardboard box. "This isn't what I thought." He made a gesture at the crowd of men filling the road now, kicking up dust that looked blue in the moonlight.

"What did you think?" Cyrus leaned into him in the dark, and Ray backed up.

"I thought you were just . . ." Ray licked his lips.

"Bullshit." In the dark, Ray could only see the liquid whites of the older man's eyes. "You knew exactly what I was going to do." Ray shook his head, and Cyrus pushed him hard against the car door with a rigid arm that compressed Ray's chest and stopped his breathing. "Don't lie to me, yardbird. You knew. You knew the minute you looked in my eyes." The other men crowded around them, their eyes reflecting the blue glow of a distant light pole.

Ray's voice was thin and breathless. "I can pay them the money."

Cyrus reached into the skinhead's jacket and came out with a pistol, a fast move like a magic trick in the half-light. He stuck the gun under Ray's chin. He saw the skinhead wince a little, as if he were expecting to hear the flat, detonating pop and to see Ray's head come apart. After a long moment, Cyrus pulled Ray off the car by his shirt and pushed him down the road.

"Now fucking move."

Ray began to walk, pulling weakly at his clothing to recover himself, keeping the low hill on his left, between him and the house and barn. He left the gravel road and went into the grass, followed by Cyrus, the rest strung out in a line leading back to the cars. It was impossible to know how many there were in the dark. As they moved around the hill the music got fainter. His eyes adjusted to the darkness, and he could begin to make out junked farm equipment shrouded by tall grass, broken bottles catching the flashes of lightning. A pile of tires loomed and then retreated, and then they were walking through the trees.

The music and party noise grew clearer as they made their way past the hill and into another stand of trees closer to the house. The men with Cyrus spread out as they came to the edge of the overgrown lawn, and everyone slowed. Ray dropped to his knees next to a scarred dogwood that bowed over to almost touch the ground. There was a clink of glass behind him, but when he turned all he could see was Cyrus carrying a double-barreled shotgun and some indistinct shapes of men among the trees. Ray's own harsh breathing filled his head, and his heart hammered.

Ahead was the house, and beyond that the white barn. Men were sitting on the steps of the house and wandering in and out of the barn. There was a row of parked bikes, a white pickup. He could see more cars out on the other side of the barn and tried to pick out the Charger. The inside of the barn was bright with lights, and the music threw clattering echoes off the house and trees. A song about skinheads. Women danced in cut-off shirts that showed pouched bellies and waved plastic cups in thick hands studded with rings. A man threw a bottle out into the darkness, and it broke against the trees nearby. There was a fire in a barrel, and a shirtless man staggered out of the barn and fell hard in the gravel. Someone kicked him and he rolled. Ray could smell dope and wood smoke and gasoline.

Ray turned his head and caught Cyrus striding out of the woods to stand in the sharp white glare from the floodlights on the side of the barn. The old man laid the shotgun down and stripped off his leather jacket and a dark T-shirt and bared his wiry torso, crossed with ropy veins and vivid tattoos: crossed swords, a helmeted Viking with a battle-ax, pit bulls on chains, and the words CRY HAVOC, inked liked a headline across his narrow chest. He picked up the shotgun, broke it open and checked the loads, and then stood unnoticed in the wash of sound and light from the party.

No sign of anyone who might be Scott. A man came out of the barn, turned his back to Ray, and sat on a bike. He had long gray hair and wore colors. Ray looked right and saw Cyrus turn to call something to the men in the trees. One of the other men was pointing off into the dark near the house and cradling what looked like an AK-47. A fat, sweating man hunched in the shadows and reached into the cardboard box Ray had seen earlier. He pulled out a bottle and handed it to someone behind him.

Ray was breathing hard, his mouth dry. He thought about Ho and Tina and Manny and the man who wanted him dead. Who might right now be one of the indistinct figures moving in the barn, obscured by the haze from cigarettes and dope.

The man on the bike stood on the starter, and the engine bucked and roared. At that instant a bottle arced from behind Ray, a flaming rag tied around the neck. Everyone looked up, the bikers, the dancers, the man on the ground, his mouth bleeding. The bottle seemed to hang in the air a long time and then hit the barn and broke over the wide doors, showering flame on two men drinking beer in the open doorway. The man on the bike tried to get off, the bike toppling and taking him down with it, pinning his right leg. Another bottle broke on the side of the barn, there were screams inside, and Ray turned to see Cyrus shoulder the shotgun and unload both barrels toward the men on the steps of the house.

There were more shots from the trees, and men and women were screaming and running. A Molotov hit the porch, and a man in a black T-shirt was engulfed in flames and ran out into the night. Someone in the barn began to fire a big revolver wildly into the trees, and the slugs splattered against the bark. Cyrus was pounding his chest and bellowing, his cracked voice rumbling and breaking, screaming that all these fuckers had to get out of his yard, his voice sometimes lost under the screaming of women, the ragged popping of the guns, and the strangled cough of motorcycle starters.

Ray dropped low and began to claw his way back toward the hill. He heard two more booming shots from the shotgun, answering fire from the barn and the house. When he reached a wide oak he stood in the lee of the massive trunk and looked back at the farmhouse. The men Cyrus had brought stood behind trees and along the side of the house. One of them threw something at an open window, and it broke open against the sill, dumping flaming liquid inside and outside of the house. The barn was already burning hard, and the guy with the AK was firing into the flames. Even hidden back in the trees, Ray could feel on his face the heat from the fire.

Cyrus was standing out in the clearing over the guy pinned under the bike. The meth cooker's eyes reflected the yellow light from the burning barn as he brought the butt of the gun down on the man's head hard and fast while the trapped biker feebly tried to protect himself with one curled arm. Some of the people from the barn had reached the cars, and Ray heard more engines cranking and the guttural blat of motorcycles firing up. He hadn't seen the Charger yet, but he wanted to get away. There was a terrible, shattered screaming from somewhere inside the house and sobs echoing from the dark. He saw pale figures disappearing into the darkness on the far side of the barn. The music was still playing somehow inside the barn, a wailing solo guitar that sounded as if a blowtorch had been turned on it.

Dennis Tafoya

He ran bent over, as if through rain. The moon had come out of the clouds, and he could see the grass as a dim blue and the black lines of trees. The sounds of the shots and the fire and screaming faded, and for a while all he could hear was his breathing and the sounds of his boots in the grass. When he broke out of the trees he turned to look behind him, and the low mass of the hill blocked his view. The sky was bright with firelight as if the hill were a volcano erupting, bleeding fire and smoke into the night sky.

He heard something moving through the grass and lifted his head just in time for a massive body to collide with him. The air was knocked from his lungs, and he tumbled over onto his side and scraped his arm open against a stiff bush bristling with thorns. The other man was sobbing, his eyes black and unreadable in the darkness. Ray lurched up onto his knees, and the man swung at him with a knife that caught the blue light of the moon so that Ray fell back again trying to stay out of his way. The other man had silver hair and a long face, and he pushed off a tree stump to stand over Ray with the knife. He feinted as Ray held an arm up, making short stabbing motions like a man looking for an opening to harpoon a fish. Ray fell back again, trying to work his arm behind him to free his pistol from his waistband, but the man stepped on his leg, and Ray cried out with the pain and pulled forward with an involuntary jerk.

"Hey!"

They both turned to see Cyrus, his gun leveled. Ray let himself drop back, and the old double-barrel lit up the clearing for an instant so that Ray could see the man, the trees standing spaced like pickets in the dark, the broken stump and the bush he was tangled in, each leaf standing out for a millisecond before the it was dark again and Ray was night-blind. He could feel blood and flesh hit his chest and arms, and the biker with the silver hair fell back, his legs jerking.

Cyrus walked over, breaking open the gun and jacking the spent rounds out, the brass ends catching the moonlight. He pulled two more rounds out of his jeans and snapped the gun together and stuck the barrel in Ray's ribs and leaned on the stock. The pain shot across Ray's stomach and down his legs and made him sick to his stomach.

"Run away." Cyrus leaned down. "And don't think about telling nobody what you seen here. You called this deal, and you and your gook buddy got just as much to lose as we do." He straightened up and walked back toward the house, disappearing into the dark.

What was all this for? he kept thinking. How much money was in it? There must be millions somewhere, right? Was all of this about the kind of money stuffed in the duffel bag? It wasn't enough. Not for all this. There wasn't even enough money to buy a decent house.

Laying there spattered with blood under the white moon like a hull of bone, he saw that there was almost nothing in it and that all around him were the dogs that slinked under the table and chewed each other's throats for scraps. These men, Scott and Cyrus, and him, too. Ray and Manny and their friends. Ripping at each other with teeth and black claws and the whole time dying themselves, worn thin and bleeding. Wandering away to die alone or killed for their weakness.

Ray pulled himself up painfully and ran without looking back. He could see men back by the line of cars, some carrying guns. He made for the Honda and had just reached it when the dark Charger rocketed up the drive and spun off the driveway at the turn, throwing gravel. Two men who had stayed back with the cars started firing shotguns at the long car as it missed the turn. Ray could hear the hard crack of glass shattering as whoever was inside stomped the accelerator and the big Dodge fishtailed and the tires whined and spun uselessly in the wet grass.

A third man ran close and threw one of the firebombs hard against the rear windshield. Already starred from the shotgun pellets, the glass bowed in, and the interior of the car filled with yellow light as the gasoline spilled across the rear seats. More shots hit the front windshield, and the wheels stopped spinning. Ray stood, transfixed by the sight of the car burning. It was blue, he could see now. Dark blue, midnight blue. The men who had been firing the shotguns ran back to the Taurus and slammed the doors. They pulled out, and the third man jumped into the rear seat while the car was still moving. It shot down the driveway, gravel spitting from under the wheels and clattering against the other cars.

Ray could hear sirens now and far away could see the red and white lights of fire trucks making their way up Forty Foot Road. There were distant pops and cracks from the direction of the farmhouse. Ray finally started jogging back toward the car, pulling his keys out of his pocket. When he got the Honda moving down the driveway, picking up speed, he kept looking back toward the Charger. The inside of the car filled with flame, and smoke spiraled out from under the hood. The doors never opened, and no one got out.

CHAPTER TEN

RAY CALLED MANNY and started telling him everything that happened, his hands vibrating like broken machines. Manny stopped him, told him to meet him at the place where he was staying, in a room over a bar where they sometimes hung out in Warrington, a place owned by a guy who'd sold them guns a couple of times.

Ray parked in the dark reaches of the parking lot and walked across the asphalt, feeling a bass beat from inside that resonated in his chest before he even opened the door. Inside, the noise was deafening, the place packed with kids. Young guys with ball caps on at angles and gold chains around their necks, shoulders hunched, going for some kind of effect that eluded Ray. Did they think, with their freckled skin and wide eyes, to be taken for dangerous? He elbowed his way to the bar and asked for a beer and a shot. He downed the shot and carried the beer back out to the entrance to get to the stairs, waved to the bouncer, a friend of Harlan Maximuck named Edgy.

At the top of the stairs he knocked, and Manny let him in with his right hand held behind him, poking his head through the door and looking up and down the hall. When Ray went by him Manny threw a baseball bat onto a mattress on the floor and dropped down beside it. The floor vibrated with the pulse of the beat from downstairs. Ray could feel it through his boots.

The place was a mess, a big empty space with extra tables for the bar, chairs stacked, cardboard cutouts of girls in swimsuits and cartoon pirates selling rum and beer. There was a little plastic fan sitting on the floor pointed at Manny, the box it had come in put into service as an end table holding Manny's works, a bottle of peppermint schnapps, a package of bright orange peanut butter crackers. There was scattered trash, empty bags from Yum Yum Donuts down the street, empty green beer bottles, an ashtray and a pack of Marlboros.

Ray told as much of what had happened as he could remember, though he knew things were already getting confused, his memory distorted by intensity and his own fear. "They went fucking crazy. They burned the fucking place down, shot people. I never saw anything like that."

Manny's head bobbed. "Good. I hope they killed that fucker and his dog. I hope they killed everyone who ever met him or knew his name." He scratched at a sore in the crook of his arm.

Ray said, "You're high."

"Fucking A, I am high." He went to the peanut butter crackers, took one out with exaggerated care, and made large, approximate movements of his arm to get it to his mouth. "Why are they orange? 'Cause of the cheese?"

"Fuck, man."

"I mean, is cheese really orange? Isn't it white, or blue or something? I mean, it's basically moldy milk."

"Manny."

"I'm just saying, why orange? I can't have an opinion about orange?"

Ray squatted by the box and picked up the bottle of schnapps and swigged it.

"That is some nasty shit."

"It's sweet. I got a sweet tooth."

"You got like three teeth, and you're going to be losing them soon." Ray went to the window and looked out through a hole in the shades. The lights in the parking lot glinted from pickup trucks and SUVs. He watched a boy kissing a girl sitting on the hood of a parked car. She was wearing a white top that stopped a few inches from her jeans.

"Where did you score?"

"Monk on Bristol Road. You going to give me shit about that, too?" Manny got to his feet, swaying. He pulled the bat off the bed and swung it wildly, losing his balance and backing into a wall, leaving a dimple in the wallboard where his elbow connected.

Ray waved his hand in front of his face. "Oh, fuck off. I just want to keep a low profile." He shook his head. "Like I give a shit if you get high."

"I know, I just . . ." Manny bobbed his head. "I can't handle this shit. Sitting around. I'd rather get out in it than sit and wait."

"Well, what the hell? Aren't I out there trying to handle it?

Rolling around in the fucking tumbleweeds with these hillbillies?"

"Okay."

"I don't need shit from you."

"Okay, okay." Manny held up his long arms and dropped his head, making peace, then went back to pacing, swinging the bat at flies. "Life goes on," he said, his voice low. "A man becomes preeminent; he's expected to have . . . enthusiasms." This was a favorite of Manny's, *The Untouchables*. De Niro a hulking animal in a gray suit. "Enthusiasms. Enthusiasms. What is that which gives me joy?"

"Smack?"

Manny dropped the bat and it bounced and knocked over some empty green beer bottles. "Not just that." He looked around as if seeing the place new and rubbed his eyes with both hands, like a child. "Stealing shit. Money. Sherry." He stared into the middle distance. "I gotta sleep."

"Go ahead, man. I'll keep an eye out."

Manny dropped to his knees and crawled to the mattress and dropped onto it, his black hair splayed around his head, his body long and white but for the tattoos aging green. Frankenstein on his right arm, Al Pacino as Scarface on his left. His junkie mother, from a photograph he used to keep with him all the time, across the small of his back. Blond hair in curls and a shy smile. She was long dead, cut to pieces and left in garbage bags by the side of the road in Bristol Township.

Manny didn't lift his head. "So, did we win?"

Ray thought about that. "I don't know. Maybe."

"When will we know?" Manny's voice was muffled by the mattress.

Ray shrugged, realized Manny couldn't see it but figured he took the meaning from his silence.

AT NINE THE next morning Manny was still asleep, so Ray left a note and went down to pick up a paper and took it to the Yum Yum Donuts at County Line and sat on a stool bolted to the floor. He hadn't slept, and his eyes were cinders in his head. He skimmed through the accounts of what had happened at the barn. Two dead, names unreleased, with three more in critical condition, a dozen more treated and released. The cops knew it was bikers fighting over turf, and there were sidebars on the motorcycle clubs, the Pagans and the Outlaws, and the meth trade. He would have to look at later editions to see the names of the dead.

He was edgy and his mind skittered from one thing to the next. He took out his cell a few times and looked at it, finally shoved it in his pocket and went to the car. His arms and legs twitched from lack of sleep, and a kind of strange electricity pulsed in him. When he got back to the bar he took the stairs two at a time, shouldered in the door to grab Manny's works, and then tied himself off using the cord from the fan. Manny was a freak about not sharing needles and kept spares still in their cellophane and paper covers. The noise of unwrapping them woke Manny, who sat up and watched him cook the heroin in his blackened spoon and bang his arm to bring up the vein.

Ray let the blood back up in the needle and shot it into his arm.

"Christ, Ray." Manny licked his lips. "When was the last time you fired up?" Ray untied the cord from his arm and smiled, but Manny shook his head. "Dude, I know you been chipping, but shit."

"So bill me."

"Fuck you, I don't care about the money."

Ray put a finger to his lips. "Don't talk. Go get more dope."

A wasp was buzzing, hitting the glass of the window with a rhythmic tick. Ray lay back and the buzzing filled his head. The hot light from the morning sun hammered his skin, and sweat rolled from his hair and into the hollows of his eyes. The bed was a raft on a sea of lava, and the air wrinkled with heat and fire. He heard Manny go through the door, but the sound was distant, tinny, as if it were on the radio in another room. Someone downstairs started up the sound system, and there was a resonant hum he could feel in his jaw and then long guitar notes. The room vibrated, and the beer bottles rolled, throwing green light onto the walls. The wasp hung in the air over his head. He focused on it, a perfect engine of rage beating the air with tiny wings in a relentless semaphore he could not follow.

RAY JERKED AWAKE. Manny was sitting on the floor, flexing his arm to bang up the vein and holding the needle. The sun was lower in the sky, and there was noise from downstairs communicated by vibration through the floor. They couldn't stay in this room much longer.

He'd had a dream about the accident that sent him away, when Marletta died. He was standing in the road with blood coming out of his hair and looking at a man asleep in the road, only of course he wasn't really asleep, and there were tracks leading off into the weeds where the car Ray had been driving was on its side, and he couldn't find Marletta anywhere. It was the most he had remembered about the accident that had sent him to prison. The most that he had let himself see, maybe. He knew there was more. It was like reading a terrible book and not wanting to turn more pages because you knew the story just got worse.

Ray got up and started policing up the mess into the plastic bag from the donut shop. He could smell himself, a rank tang of smoke and dope sweat and dust. He heard doors slamming and went to the window and watched guys come in from their trucks. Guys getting a beer after a day of work, three guys in jeans and T-shirts with a logo he couldn't make out. Landscapers or delivery men or warehouse guys. Something where they hauled shit or built shit or something that you got a righteous thirst from and at the end of the day you had a beer and bitched about, and then the married guys went home and the single guys stayed and chatted up the girls who would come in later. A life he didn't know, that he felt a million miles away from. Like the Plimsouls said, he was on the wrong end of the looking glass.

Ray had sat in bars with guys and listened to them talk, and when the subject came up he just said he worked for a painting crew, but things broke down when somebody knew somebody in the business, and his lies would become tenuous and elaborate, which gave him a bad feeling, like he was pretending to be tall by balancing on stilts. He would get tense and defiant, and the people around him would slip away.

He went around the room and began picking up Manny's

clothes and stuffing them into his bag, impatient to be on the move. Manny himself lay back, his eyes rolling, and Ray knew it was going to be a little while before he could get him out of the room and into the car. He dug through his jacket and found the one-hitter and gave himself a jolt so he could focus, formulate a plan of action. He wanted his car back, wanted to go home and get a shower and listen to his own music.

Loaded up with bags and bits of clothing, he moved down to the car, edging past drinkers in the dim bar and pushing out into the sunlight slanting through the trees behind the crumbling asphalt lot. Outside he became aware of his clothes, stiff and foul-smelling, and he caught sight of himself in the long side mirror of a pickup. His hair was wild, his face streaked, and there were dark stains on his clothing and he remembered where they were from and he shuddered and had to resist the urge to crawl out of his clothes right there in the parking lot. He looked and felt like someone who had been living rough in the open and thought if he had seen a guy looking like this in a parking lot he'd have figured him for a guy on the bum. He dumped everything in the back of Sherry's car and got in and drove up to County Line and cut left toward the Dunkin' Donuts. When he got there he drove to where his Camaro had been and found an empty square of blackened asphalt surrounded by yellow tape.

Ray parked and got out and stood looking down at the place where someone had burned his car. There were greasy stripes of black where the tires had been and pools of melted plastic set with bits of broken glass fogged white. He tried to think about the sequence of events and tried to dope out if it had been before or after the barn, which was two nights ago. Maybe. His head hurt and his thinking was furred and had a lot of broken lines and gaps. He felt like he had been in the room getting high for a week, but that was junk for you.

He got back in the car and drove back down Easton Road. When he got to his street he slowed and began looking into each parked car for someone who didn't look like he belonged there. Not that he would know. From half a block away he could make out the broad back and white-blond head of his landlord, Mrs. Gawelko, and a tall kid in his early twenties with big shoulders and a buzz cut. She was pacing and making broad motions with her arms, acting out some kind of opera for the kid, who Ray thought was her son.

He considered just driving on and coming back to deal with whatever it was later, but the urge to find out what was going on won out over what he felt was the more commonsense plan of action, to just keep going down to 611, get on the turnpike, and drive west until he saw red rocks and tumbleweeds. He parked the car and walked slowly across the lawn, flashes of muscle pain lighting up his arms and legs, bright spots and clouds in his eyes.

When she saw him crossing to her, she started shaking her head and pointing at him and then the door of the little apartment over her garage. "Men came for you. I told them no."

"It's okay, Mrs. G."

"No, it's not okay. These men are big, they have . . ." She brushed her hand down her arms. Tattoos. Yeah, he thought. I bet they had tattoos.

"I thought police, but they're not police. I can't have this." She turned and gave a stream of Ukrainian to her son, who nodded and looked sage, not wanting a part of this now that he had gotten a closer look at Ray. She paced and ranted while Ray smiled and edged closer to the door, his hands up.

"I know, Mrs. G. They won't be back."

"No! It's you. You won't be back." Then there was more Ukrainian and she poked her kid hard in the stomach and pointed at Ray.

"Okay, Ma. Okay. Jesus," the kid said. She wandered off muttering, and Ray stood looking at the kid, who shrugged. "You see how it is? She wants you gone."

"I see it."

"Whoever those guys were, they scared the shit out of her."

"Ah, just some . . . friends. It's nothing."

"Yeah, but she's an old lady."

Ray said, "Let me just get some shit and I'll get out of here." He moved up the short flight of stairs and turned around. "Tell Mrs. G," he said, but then shook his head. There it was again, his face burning, his breath coming short, not enough air to inflate his lungs. He put his hand on his chest, and the bits of light through the trees danced in his head. He watched the big kid cock his head.

"Man, you okay?"

Ray grabbed the banister, held up a hand. "I'm fine. Just tell your mom I'm sorry, and thanks for putting up with . . . You know."

He turned back up the stairs and saw boot prints on the door, but the lock had held, and he let himself in. Everything looked the same, all his stuff was untouched, but it all looked shabby and unfamiliar in the hard sunlight. He stood for a while, then went into the bedroom and got his duffel and threw it onto the bed. He packed his clothes and looked around. What did he want? His music, some DVDs. On the wall were movie posters he had gotten from the mall. Nothing he couldn't replace in ten minutes. There was nothing of him here. He flashed on standing in a cell upstate on the day they were gating him out, a CO watching him while he looked at a couple of pictures stuck to the wall with the tacky bits of putty they made you use.

There was almost no one who would look for him here and no one who would realize he was gone. His money and his guns were all he had, and that was in the car or locked away. He threw a handful of CDs and movies in with the jeans and underwear and T-shirts and left quickly, without looking back.

He drove aimlessly around for a few hours. Over to the river, down to Oxford Valley. Across the bridge at Trenton and back up 29. Looking for a place to be.

AT DUSK HE collected Manny, and they went back to Monk's and got more junk. They spent the night in another motel, this one in Lahaska. In another room somewhere a man and woman made lovemaking sounds that were like a terrible anguish. They paid for three days in advance and stayed high as much of the time as they could, breaking the fall off the heroin with coconut rum and hash. Ray would do coke out of the one-hitter to get straight enough for runs to a Wawa to get Tastykakes and soda and hoagies they'd pick at and then throw away.

It reminded Ray of when they were young and boosting cars and they'd get four or five hundred bucks for a car and blow it all in a few days on CDs and movies and dope and clothes and buying girls drinks. Seeing the same movie over and over. *Terminator 2* and *Predator 2* and a long list of crap they watched back to back for the explosions and the guns, the sounds echoing around inside their dope-hollowed brains.

But events kept going, even if the two of them were stuck in a groove. Sherry and Theresa came home from the shore. Sherry needed her car, so Ray told Manny to buy her something and take it out of the money at the U-Store It place in Warrington and he kept the Honda. One of the bikers burned at the barn died, and the story faded off the news. No one seemed to be looking for them. Whatever it was that had happened didn't seem to be ongoing.

On the fourth day Manny went home to Sherry's, and Ray called Ho Dinh.

"Man, how the hell are you doing?" *How da hell.* Ho's accent was more pronounced when he was agitated, and his words were clipped short now.

"I'm good, you know. I'm cool."

"Yeah? We were worried. Tina showed me the paper, all that shit that happened up there."

"Yeah, I'm good."

"You sound high."

"Well, good and high."

"Well."

"No, man, I wanted to say thanks."

"I didn't do anything."

"For hooking me up with, you know."

"I thought maybe you had a problem, Ray."

"No, no. I guess it all worked out."

"Man, are you all right?"

"Really, I'm good. Really, Ho."

There was a long pause on Ho's end. "If you say so."

Ray wanted to tell him the truth, but what point was there? He wanted to say his head was full of death and fire and he couldn't close his eyes without being drunk or high and he wanted to start screaming and never stop. He wanted to tell him that one night while Manny was fixing in the bathroom he'd taken out the old army Colt and dry-fired it into his mouth. But there would be something in there that Ho might see as aimed at him for setting him up with Cyrus. He didn't want that. Whatever Ho had done had been to help him out and protect Tina and the kids.

"No, I'm just taking a little vacation, really. I'll call you in a few days."

"Yeah?"

"Yeah, I'll come over, bring some wine. Tell Tina."

"Okay." Ho didn't hang up. "Just so, you know."

"Thanks, man. I owe you big on all of this."

"Ray."

"Really, man. I'll talk to you soon."

AFTER MANNY WENT home Ray moved to a cheaper motel, one of those places that used to be a real motor hotel back in the forties, with little cabins set apart down a short drive. He was stuck somewhere. He sat and watched the tiny TV in the room, flipping through dozens of programs about life on another planet. He would go to the car, stand there juggling his keys, not knowing where to go.

Ray called Manny's guy Monk again for dope, but he said he was short and gave him a name in Fairless Hills. Ray drove down around dusk into a neighborhood of close-set houses, pickups and cars showing Bondo and rust. Sprawling neighborhoods of postwar homes elbowing each other for a little sun, a little air. He sat outside, watching the house while it grew dark. There were kids' toys in the yard and a blue plastic turtle filled with sand and empty beer bottles. After a while he walked up and knocked. An older guy with prison-yard eyes answered and stood holding the door between them. Ray had the feeling he had something in his hands behind the door.

"What?"

"Monk gave me your name."

"Yeah?"

"Yeah. Was he wrong?"

"Monk is always wrong. He's a punk."

"I don't want to get into anything, man. I just want to get what I'm looking for."

The guy shook his head and slammed the door. Ray had started walking back up the cracked walk when the door popped open again. A small woman in shorts was standing there showing tattoos snaking up under a tube top. Her hair was a colorless brown, and there were lines etched around her mouth, but she seemed hopeful.

"Come on, get off the street."

He stood for a minute, thinking it wasn't a great idea, then finally walked back in. The yardbird was in a seat watching a Phillies game, a green bottle clenched in his fist as if he expected somebody to make a grab for it. There were more toys around, which Ray tried to see as a good sign. Though he knew better. The house stank of mold and stale beer and cigarette smoke.

The woman smiled at him and nodded, like a helpful clerk in a pharmacy. "What you need, doll?"

"I'll take what you got. Black tar, china, whatever."

"Okay, hon. How much?"

"A gram, two."

"You make small talk with Heston. I'll be right back."

The man, Heston, looked over his shoulder at him, then back at the TV. "You get your shit and keep moving, got it?" On the walls Ray saw swords, throwing stars, and pictures that looked like they had been cut out of magazines of women tied with ropes. Somewhere a baby started crying. Heston moved in his chair and turned up the sound on the game with a remote. Ray saw that what looked like a heap of wool blankets on a couch was a young obese woman with a black eye and a fixed stare. The noise from the baby was a resonant whine that pried at Ray's head like somebody was trying to get it open with a screwdriver. Heston banged on the arm of his chair.

"Goddammit, Rina."

The woman came back in carrying the baby, a wet rag of a kid with brown stains on its jumper, its face contorted in a now silent howl. Ray dug at his jeans and pulled money out, his body jerking with the need to get out and on the road. He saw Heston turn and throw the remote hard at the woman on the couch. She made no move to block the throw, and the remote hit her in the temple with a hard clatter.

The woman with the baby scooted Ray outside with her body, his hand with the money still extended. Her eyes were wild and full of something Ray couldn't imagine, fear or hate or something, so amped that it became something else, a wounded animal vulnerability leaking out of her eyes.

She held the baby out to him. "Take her."

"What? Do what?"

"Take this baby. You got to."

"Lady, what? I'm, uh, I use dope. I can't—"

"Take this baby and get her away from here. Give her away, do something. He don't let me out of his sight, and she's going to end up dead or in the hospital. Mister, these people are crazy."

Ray held his hands up and shook his head. "I don't understand." The woman shrieked and shook, and he retreated another step, waving the money like a flag of surrender.

The woman hit herself on the forehead with an open palm. "Oh, for Christ's sake, won't nobody help me?" She turned the baby to stare into its startled eyes and it was silent, and for a long and terrible moment Ray thought she was going to throw it away from her onto the walk. Finally she lowered the child back to her chest, where it folded itself against her. She turned away, her eyes unfocused, and slowly moved back inside and shut the door.

CHAPTER ELEVEN

RAY DROVE AWAY and got lost in Fairless Hills in the new dark, the endless developments leading one to the other, and he kept making aimless turns to try to find Route 1. He thought about the woman and the baby, and his heart knocked in his chest. He felt a hot hand on his neck, his conscience working on him in some way he couldn't understand. He couldn't take the baby. It couldn't be wrong to turn the woman down, but he did get a flash of himself as he often did, heading west on the turnpike, the dying sun filling his windshield and maps of the western states fanned out on the seat. Only this time there was a bundle beside him on the seat and he wasn't alone, and couldn't there be something good in that?

When he was back heading north, the moon was just beginning to show. His cell rang, and he picked it up.

"Raymond?"

"Hey, Ma."

"I'm home."

"Good, did you have fun?"

Theresa's voice got quiet. "You sound tired."

His eyes clouded over, and his breath hitched in his chest like it was caught on the bones of his ribs. "I am, Ma. I'm so tired."

"Why are you out?"

"I was just, I don't know."

"Come home. Come on home for a night and just rest, hon."

"I want to."

"Ray, I have to tell you something."

"What? Is something wrong?"

"No. No, nothing's wrong. Your father's here."

Ray didn't know what to say. The rage he had felt for so long was as burned out of him as everything else.

"He's sick, Ray, and he's just lying down. He wants to see you."

"Yeah."

"You know he's going to be gone soon."

"Yeah."

"Listen, just come over and have a meal with me and you can sleep in your room. He's all doped up anyway, and you don't have to see him until you want to."

"I, uh. I don't know."

"You don't have to see him if you don't want to."

"I'll see."

"Okay, hon. I love you. He loves you, too."

"Don't. Don't say that."

"Okay."

HE STOPPED AT a CVS on Old York Road and bought himself a toothbrush and toothpaste and a bottle of seltzer, and he brushed his teeth sitting half out of his car in the lot behind the store. He spat and swigged from the bottle and threw it back onto the seat and got out to throw away the toothbrush. He stood for a minute, looking at the traffic going by on York and rattling the change in his pocket, and finally went back into the store and bought a box of candy and a tiny spray of flowers and threw them onto the seat. The clerk was a young girl, maybe Spanish, and her skin was caramel colored and smooth. Ray smiled at her when she gave him his change, and she smiled, too.

When he finally pulled up to the house it was full dark, and for the first time since the spring he could feel the slightest cooling when he got out. Ray did math in his head, trying to remember the date. He got out and started to close the door but then remembered and reached back in for the flowers and candy. He wanted a cigarette for the first time in a while. He stood and looked at the house and listened to the motor on the Honda ticking and heard dogs barking up the street and then Shermie started up inside. The sky was full of stars and roaming clouds and the blinking lights of airplanes. Ray walked up the sidewalk. The cell he had left in the car began to ring again and he turned to see if it would keep ringing and should he get it or just let it go and a shape unfolded itself from the dark yew at the border of the yard and stepped into Ray and stuck a knife in him and he went down.

FROM A DISTANCE it must have looked like they were in an embrace. Old friends finally meeting. The man leaning into him and Ray clutching at the moving arms. Ray made a sound, something like a scream, and then he couldn't catch his breath. He had a flash of the face, the goatee and long hair, and he knew it was the guy from the midnight blue Charger, and the guy was saying something but Ray couldn't make it out. It wasn't important. Ray had heard it all before, about how he had it coming and that he needed to pay, and he had heard it and he had said it even about himself and now it was prophecy coming to pass.

The pain was like a note so high it passed out of hearing. The only thing that hurt after the first seconds was his left leg, though that didn't make sense. The guy must be swinging wild with that knife, he thought. He heard Shermie, louder now, and the door opened and there he was, the old dog moving faster than Ray had ever seen before. Shermie tore into the guy and Ray wanted to laugh but he couldn't make sounds anymore and then there was Theresa and she began to scream and stuck her hand into her mouth and there was more he couldn't follow, but the guy stopped to look at her. Scott, that was his name, he wanted to say it. They were both looking back at the door, at Theresa, and Ray wanted to tell her to go back inside, to get away, and the young guy had hold of Ray's shirt with one hand and when he turned he turned Ray, too, and he saw Theresa take a step back and say something about the police and then look back into the house.

And here was Bart. His old man, looking tired and small and weird in one of Ray's T-shirts and pants turned up at the cuff. The old man, out of prison a day, maybe, and he came through the door and the glass in the door broke and Theresa gave a little shout again from the fright of it. Bart moved right over to where Ray was on the ground and Scott crouched over him, turning back to raise the knife when Bart jerked back the kid's head by the hair and raised Theresa's cast-iron frying pan and brought it down hard with a hollow noise like two rocks cracking against each other. Ray dropped back and lost sight of the kid but saw Bart's arm going up and down twice more with a harsh energy like Ray'd seen him use to kill a spider in the basement once when Ray was young.

A car door slammed, and Manny ran up. Come to see the show. He was tall and gaunt as always, and he had his shades on even though it was full dark because that was Manny, man, he lived the part every minute of the day. He was cursing, and Ray saw Manny and Bart pull the kid by his feet into the garage and close the door, looking both ways down the street to see if anyone was out, doing that heads-up check that he had done himself a thousand felonious times, nothing to see here, nothing at all.

Manny was pulling him to his feet now and that was when it was bad, the blood gone from his head and he was fainting and waking up again while the three shouted in whispers to each other and Theresa kept putting her hand out to the house and saying ambulance and Manny was saying no and that's when Ray got what it was all about and said what he could say, maybe his last chance to weigh in on things.

"No ambulance. Get inside."

Bart got it and knew it was the right thing even as he wanted to come with them and balled his hands and cried at the sight of Manny half-carrying Ray to the car and screamed a sound of rage that made Ray smile and try to lift his hand and wave. The last he saw of them was Theresa folding her arms around his old man and moving back into the house. Flowers, he wanted to say, and chocolates. Lottery tickets for everyone.

IT WAS A long ride to the emergency room, hours and days of watching the streetlights flash by like flying saucers tethered to wires, each radiating an orange sodium glare that felt like sand in his eyes. Manny was babbling and kept pushing Ray's arms down onto his stomach and telling him to hold things together, but Ray didn't want to feel the ragged edges of himself under his hands, he wanted to feel the wind cooling his hot, wet arms and watch the lights. Manny was telling him a story about Scott coming to his house, but he was busy in his head and couldn't follow things. There was so much to say and no point in saying it. No one to hear. Manny knew all about it, knew all his secrets.

At the hospital Manny went in shouting and they got him onto a gurney and people with serious expressions gathered around him and he caught Manny's eyes and tried to wave him off and however it happened Manny was gone and Ray could relax, finally, and let go. It was bright and there were people everywhere, and he was tired but didn't sleep. There were people he knew, he thought. There were bikers with long hair and their hands on fire, Rick Staley looking apologetic, shaking his head like *don't blame me, man.* Danny Mullen with his one hand and Danny's mom with a bandage on her throat, and they all looked very concerned. There were other people that he felt he should know, guys from prison and cops, and it made him feel guilty that he couldn't remember their names. And there was the girl from the picture, in her cap and gown, only it wasn't the girl from the dealer house, it wasn't a stranger from Bristol. It was another girl, one he did know. A girl he had loved. Who loved him.

"HE'S DYING?" AN older guy's voice, clipped and precise. A cop. They all sounded military nowadays.

"Yeah, Gene." A young woman. A doctor, a low voice in case Ray was listening.

"Does he know it?"

"That I can't tell you. He's lost a lot of blood? He's got major organs compromised?" Her voice making questions out of statements. Meaning she didn't really know what to tell the cop.

"If he knows he's dying he can give us the name and we can use it in court."

"I don't know his mental state."

"Can I talk to him?" There was an insistent beeping and electronic whirring noises, nurses conferring and someone being sent for an X-ray cart.

"You can try."

"Raymond?"

"Yeah." His own voice, strange and hoarse.

"Raymond, do you understand you're dying?" The older guy, the cop, his voice raised over the murmur of patients and nurses and machines hissing. Someone was talking loudly into a phone, spelling Ray's name.

"I got shot at."

"Did he get shot?"

"No, he was stabbed, according to that kid who dumped him

here. Erin, were there gunshot wounds?" There was a sound of paper flipping, a metal clipboard clattering on a desk.

"No, Doctor. Just the penetrating stab wounds, abdomen, left thigh, medial, right arm, left arm. We have . . . heroin on a tox screen. Cocaine. Methamphetamine. Blood alcohol, negative."

"Christ."

"No GSW."

The raised voice again. "Raymond, you were stabbed, do you remember?"

"Shermie's out." He was trying to help, but he couldn't see anything under the bright lights. He wanted to shield his eyes but couldn't lift his arms.

"Shermie?"

"Shermie, he's out! Tell Theresa. I call her Mom."

"Raymond, did Shermie stab you?" Quieter, "Do we know who he's talking about? Do we have known associates?"

Another voice, deeper, another cop. More paper flipping. "I don't have a Theresa. Mother's name is . . . Caroline. According to the fax we got from Lower Makefield. Father's name Bartram."

"Tell her to get Shermie."

"What did Shermie do, Raymond?"

"He was biting."

"He bit you?"

"No, he's too old." There was a long pause, paper rustling, machines going, and the lights so bright it was like a humming in his head. Near his ear a nurse complained that the veins were all blown.

"Doc?"

Dennis Tafoya

"He's going. It's just . . . random connections, synapses firing. His blood pressure's down. The surgeon's on his way, but . . ."

"Shit."

There was a beeping, loud and close. A woman said, "Oh, there we go."

"Yeah, this is going nowhere. Who's on call for anesthesia?"

"Raymond, can you hear me?"

"What's her name? That girl. Look in the car. I knew her name. Marletta."

"He's out."

"That's V-fib."

"Yeah, he's . . ."

"Lidocaine? Ringer's lactate?"

"Is anesthesia here?"

"There he goes."

"Doc?"

"Start compressions."

"Doc?"

"Sorry, Dectective. He's going. He's got too many holes."

"So that's that?"

"That's it."

He pulled off County Line Road in Perry March's Lincoln, the lot packed, cars pulled up on the lawns of houses for graduation. He remembered how hot it was and the radio full of Nirvana because of Kurt Cobain.

Through his open windows he could hear a voice through a loudspeaker and distant cheering, and already people were leaving, moving in small knots clustered around beaming kids in black and white caps and gowns. And he did feel something, a pang in his chest seeing kids he knew, their arms around each other or being squeezed by parents and grandparents.

He drove slowly, looking at faces, a tall girl he'd had a crush on in junior high whose name he couldn't remember now; a kid he'd had English with who'd always said "president" during roll call. Then there she was coming across the lot from the gym, her gown lifted and showing jeans on her short, muscular legs as she ran toward the street and her cap under her arm. A smile stretched to the point of breaking, waving over her shoulder at friends, hitting the curb and juking right to run alongside his car. He slowed and she yanked the car door open and they were gone down Centennial Road like a bank heist.

She looked at him a long time without saying anything, and he'd steal glances at her until she smiled and hit his arm.

He said, "Put the cap on, I need the whole effect."

She did, and moved over to the door to pose, her hand under her cheek. He shook his head.

"So, how was graduation?"

"Fun. How was Juvie?"

"Oh, you know. There was one boy who I liked, but I couldn't tell if he liked me back."

"Jesus, Ray," but smiling when she shook her head. "You kill me."

"I could always make you laugh."

"Really, how was it?"

"Oh, it was fine. I cleared some brush, cleaned up some litter off 611." She made a move toward him, bringing in her hand like she was socking him in the jaw, touched his cheek instead.

Dennis Tafoya

"*I couldn't sleep, thinking about you in there.*"

"*Mars, it was fine, really. There are always some retards, but I just give them the eyes and they keep moving.*"

"*The eyes?*"

They pulled up at the stop sign at County Line, and he turned toward her and lowered his head, his eyes hooded and empty, and she turned her head.

"*Great. There's a skill. Honest to God, you scare me sometimes.*"

"*I don't want to fight, Marletta.*" *He put his hand on her leg. She kept looking away but covered his hand with hers.*

He said, "I would never hurt you, you know that."

"*Oh, stop. I'm not frightened of you, I'm frightened for you, dipshit.*"

"*Well, listen to the mouth on Stanard Hicks's daughter.*"

"*Yeah, well, my boyfriend is a bad influence.*"

They drove for a while, the windows open, music low. There was a blare of horns and Ray swerved, fought for a second to hold the road.

"*Shit!*" *A car loomed on the left, shot past. They heard the kids inside shriek; saw the soap on the windows.* GOOD LUCK! CLASS OF *1994. He lifted his fist. "Goddamn kids today.*"

"*Careful, hon. You just stole this car you and don't want to crack it up already.*"

He shook his head. "You think you're superbad?"

She looked at him out of the corner of her eye, shook her head.

"*So,*" *he said, "Cornell, full ride?*"

"*Yes, and you know who got me in?*"

"*You got you in. You worked hard for that.*"

"*I did, but it was Farah Haddad who wrote this absolutely incredible letter for me.*"

"Huh."

"I know you didn't think much of her, Ray, but she really stuck it out for me."

"Well, that's good. Not that you didn't deserve it."

"You know, she also told me she thought you were the brightest boy she had in years."

He made a noise. "Really? A C or something would have been a good way to show it. She failed me."

"'Cause you didn't give a shit, pardon my French."

"Yeah, well, what the fuck."

"Exactly." She shook her head. "And you practically wrote that paper for me on Vonnegut. Out of your head."

"It was easy."

"Not for everyone, Ray, for you. Because you're smart. You think. All I did was add punctuation to what you told me and I got an A off McGlone. And he doesn't give A's."

"Then why are you mad at me?"

"It should have been yours! You should have kept it together and stayed in school and gotten your own damn A's."

"Hon, we can't just fight when we're together. All we got is what? A month or two and you'll be off to school?"

"And then what? For you, I mean? What are you going to do?"

"I don't know. A buddy of my dad's said he might be able to get me something down the quarry."

They came to a light, and she moved across the wide seat of the Lincoln and put his arm over her shoulder and laid her head against him.

"You can be more, Ray. Everyone knows it."

Dennis Tafoya

"No, no one knows it. I'll be okay. And you'll be off to see the world. Get that degree, man, there'll be no stopping you."

"Why don't you come with me?"

"Is there a quarry in Ithaca?"

"Raymond, will you please?"

"Oh, Marletta, this is the way it is. Guys like me knock around, get work at the filling station or a factory shop. And the brilliant girls they fall for go off to Cornell and become doctors and lawyers."

"Oh, I am leaving. Do you know why?" She lifted her head and poked him hard under the ribs.

"Shit! That hurt. Anyway, why wouldn't you?"

"I would stay for you, Ray. I love you, you . . . dumb-ass."

"Now you sound like Bart. The dumb-ass part, not the love part."

"Is that who screwed you up so bad?" She watched his eyes. "Was it Bart beating you and your mom, or going to jail? Or your mom leaving?"

"Now you sound like the social worker at the Youth Authority."

"Well? What did you say to the social worker?"

"I don't know, Mars, I'm not the kind likes to dwell on the past. You know me, I'm more of an accentuate-the-positive sort of guy."

"Yeah, that's you all over."

"What? I do nothing but smile when I'm with you. I think sometimes I must look like I'm retarded."

"You say that, but what good does it do, Ray?"

"It does me all the good in the world."

"Really? 'Cause to me it looks like a waste of time." She slid across the seat and put her hand on the door.

He sat up and his voice was low in his throat. "A waste?"

They turned into the parking lot at Lake Galena, and he had barely pulled into a spot when she got out and slammed the door. She walked down the short hill without looking back, and he got out and closed the door and trailed after her, his hands stuffed in his jeans.

He got close to where she was picking stones out of the dirt and trying to skim them, the loose sleeves of the gown flapping. The first one shot in at a hard angle and splashed her. He sat on the grass a few yards behind her. "You got to lean, hon. Get your arm parallel to the water."

"I know how to skim rocks, thanks. I need to know how to steal a car you'll be the first one I call."

"Mars."

The next rock she threw hard, and it arced out over the lake, a long high course that ended with a small splash. "You told me you thought I was beautiful."

"You are. The most beautiful girl I've ever seen."

She turned to him and sighed. "See? You say that and I am beautiful. I feel beautiful." She lifted her arms. "And smart and capable and all the things you ever said to me, they . . ." She shrugged. "They helped me to be all those things. They made me see myself differently."

"I did that."

"Not just you. Farah Haddad, too. And Mrs. Cross, from the gym. Even Stanard Hicks, in his way." She sat down facing him in the grass. "But when I say what I see in you, when I tell you that you can do things, can be things, it's just, I don't know. Wasted breath."

"It's not—"

204

"Yeah, it is." She dropped her head. "I tell you you're smart, you break into a house and nearly get shot. I tell you I love you and you steal a car and get sent away for three months."

"That's not your fault, Mars. You can't think that."

"I know it's not, Ray. It's something in you. I don't know how it got there, though God knows enough crappy stuff happened to you."

"Oh, my life isn't that bad."

Her eyes flashed and she smacked the ground with her hand. "Will you stop! Will you please for one blessed minute stop and listen to me?"

She stood up and stomped over to him, and he thought for a minute she was going to slug him for real, her fists balled and her face taut and red.

"You're throwing your life away so fast I can't . . . I can't even keep up with it. I tell you I love you, I love you so much it takes my breath away, and it's just nothing, it makes nothing happen. You can't stop screwing yourself up, can't give yourself a break. Can't finish school or just stay around for me."

He reached up and touched her hand, but she shook her head and turned away. She let herself drop down facing the water again.

He said, "It's not a waste." He picked up a short length of stick and touched her back, trying to tickle her neck.

"Oh, please."

"No, you have to think of it that you're the only one who keeps me going at all. The only one who has anything good for me. I know I screw up, but without you it's just worse. You're the only one who cares whether I live or die."

"That's some fun for me."

"You say you don't matter, I'm telling you you're the only one who does."

"I can't do that alone, Ray. That's too much for me to take on by myself."

"Who else is there?" He sounded lost, and she turned and looked at him and her eyes were red.

"There's you, Ray. You have to care about yourself. I mean at least a little. Enough to stay out of prison and not, I don't know. Not mess with other people all the time. There has to be some small part of you that I could count on to keep on track."

They sat for a while, listening to the almost imperceptible sound of the water's edge, tiny breaking waves slapping at the rocks. Across the water a family poured out of vans and SUVs and set up a picnic in one of the pavilions. The low sounds of adult chatter and the high voices of children carried across the lake. One of the smaller kids made a beeline for the water, and a man who was maybe his father grabbed him at the water's edge and scooped him up into a giant whirling arc, the boy screaming. It took Ray a minute to hear that there was excitement in the whoop from the boy, not fear, and he heard the word "again" from the boy so that the man was forced to swing him out over the water again and again while the boy shrieked in mock terror and clutched at him. Ray looked down at his clenched hands.

After a minute he got up and walked the few yards to where Marletta sat and dropped down beside her, his arm brushing hers. She dug under her gown, brought a tissue out of the pocket of her jeans, and blew her nose.

"I love you, Marletta."

"I know you do."

Dennis Tafoya

"I'm sorry."

"You are. About the sorriest boy I ever knew." She shook her head at him.

"I knew I could make you smile."

"You always could, from the first time I ever saw you." She leaned over slowly and let her head settle on his shoulder. "Ray."

"I like to hear you say my name. You're the only one I want to hear say it." He kissed her, and she leaned into him and put her arms tight around him and breathed into his mouth; peppermint and strawberry lip balm. After a minute he said, "You're going to ruin that gown."

"You can always steal me a new one." She fitted herself against him, and he grew hard and pushed his face into her neck, opening his mouth and tasting the salt on her skin. She put her hand on his face and he closed his eyes.

"Take me somewhere, Ray."

"No one's home at Theresa's."

"Good. Take me there." He got a flash of her then in his darkened room the month before he got sent up, naked in his bed, her small, dark body next to his long pale one, her brown nipples hardening under his hand. Her lips parted as he moved with her, her fingers on his arm, grasping.

"Where does your dad think you are?" His voice husky, his breath ragged.

"At Carole's. There's a party there later." Her fingers brushed lightly over the hardness in his jeans.

"I don't know if I can wait till I get you home."

She put her mouth against his ear, her cheek grazing his. "All good things," she said.

CHAPTER TWELVE

"THERE HE IS. You awake, hon?" A nurse, big shoulders in green scrubs, a mask but kind-looking eyes under blue eye shadow. She turned to the door. "He's awake."

"Ray, how you doing?" Another nurse, this one small with blond hair framing the mask.

"I don't know." His eyes were leaking water. Fat tears that made him ashamed.

"You're in the hospital. Do you remember?"

"I don't."

"That's okay. We need to pull this tube out."

He blinked and tried to raise his arm. It was tethered to the bed with a soft strap. "I can't get my arm."

"Sorry about that, hon, you were pulling at the IV." The big nurse unwrapped his hand and it lifted, stiff and weightless as if reduced to denuded bone, and he brought it up to touch his face and felt stubble, then wiped at the gum in the corners of his eyes.

He wanted a drink, and they gave him ice chips. He felt like he was wrapped in someone else's flesh, a great swollen mass obscuring him, and he felt a distance between himself and his own wounded body. His arms were wrapped in gauze, and tubes ran under his blankets. He could smell himself, a rank smell of sweat and blood. In his leg he felt a sharp and constant stabbing as if there were still a knife blade in his thigh.

"I really hurt."

The nurse patted his hand and told him they had orders for him to get pain meds.

"I, uh, I have to go."

"You've got a colostomy, Ray. Do you know what I mean?"

"Christ."

"It's only for a while."

A third nurse, this one with red hair, came in, flicking a needle.

"No. I don't want that."

"It's okay, Ray. It's for the pain."

"No, it's okay."

"Is he, are you confused about what's going on?"

"No. It's okay, really."

"Well, if you don't feel you need it."

He turned his head to look at nothing. "I'm, uh. I have a problem with medication."

"Oh."

He heard them stop, all three, and felt them looking at him and each other.

"I can't. I shouldn't have anything like that." He could feel something, a wall going up. Something hardening in the air between them.

"Okay, Ray."

"Can you make a note or something? I just don't want them to ask me."

"I understand."

"'Cause I'll say yes. Right now I can say no, so please don't let them ask me again."

"We'll get someone in to talk to you about it."

HE FELL ASLEEP again and awoke, this time the pain sharp and clear and insistent, fingers poking his ribs, his belly, his arms and his leg clamped in a vise. He woke breathing hard, his head full of webs and haze. Bart and Theresa were there, sitting on two chairs pulled close together. Theresa was looking through her purse, and his father was dozing, his breath a raspy whisper. Ray watched them and tried to control his breathing. He held on to the bed rails with a shaking hand.

Theresa looked up, jumping from her chair when she caught his eyes. "Ray."

His father started awake and stood up, rubbing his face. They looked down at him, and he stared back, shaking and wracked.

"So," he said, his lips cracking, "who's watching the dog?"

Theresa put a hand to her eyes and choked, and Bart put his hand on her shoulder and patted her, the gesture clumsy and stiff.

"Look at you. Your heart stopped."

She couldn't say any more, and Bart helped her into her seat. He came back to look down at Ray, and they stared at each other a long time. Ray put his shuddering, dry hand on his father's arm. Bart looked down at his son's hand and then raised his head, and Ray saw him smile. It had been so long since he had seen his father smile it was almost disconcerting, as if he had become someone else for a moment, but in another moment Ray was smiling, too. He shook his head and he raised his eyebrows at his old man, at what they knew about each other. Ray grabbed the skinny rope of muscle over Bart's forearm, touching him where a heart was etched that had once been bright red but was slowly going green and black. It said CAROLINE.

His father shook his head and said, "So that's done, then?"

Ray nodded.

"You're kicking now?"

"I figure they got me strapped down anyway."

Bart nodded back, and his mouth opened and closed a few times like he wanted to say something else, but he just patted Ray's hand.

"I know," said Ray.

Bart held a hand out and took it back, then reached out again and touched Ray's head, patting him with a big hand of rough skin and loose bones. "We'll come back, and I'll keep her from cooking for you for a couple days."

"Yeah, that's good."

Theresa blew her nose, a long honk that echoed off the hard walls. "What's wrong with my cooking?"

"Nothing, girl," said Bart. "It's just the boy can't eat for a while."

"I'm not an idiot, Bart. I know that."

The shaking got worse, and Ray stuck his hands back under the sheet, sweat standing out on his forehead. Theresa stood up and held his cheek, and then they went out, Bart stooped and round-shouldered. Ray lay back and stared at the ceiling and bit his lips to keep from yelling out. After a few minutes of breathing through his mouth a nurse came in.

"How's it going?"

He just looked at her, his eyes wild, and she nodded and lifted his gown to check his dressing. For the first time he saw the criss-crossed lines of sutures and dark blood that reminded him of barbed wire, as if an army had fought a battle ranging across the white expanse of his abdomen and left fortifications abandoned in the field. There was a red tube that he realized was blood draining from one of the wounds and a flaccid plastic bag taped over a hole in his gut.

The nurse went to the sink and wet a washcloth and put it across his forehead. He nodded thanks at her, not trusting himself to say anything. He put his hand in his mouth and bit the fleshy part and growled, praying to pass out. The nurse told him things looked good. She said there was still a risk of infection but everything really did look good. He nodded without speaking, and she shook her head and left. It was more than he could stand, and he wanted to scream.

HE WOKE UP again and it was night. He had a sense of days going by, but nothing changed except the light, so he wasn't sure. He sat in the dark for a while getting used to himself, listening to the murmur of voices from the nurses' station, and then a dark shape filled the doorway and Manny came in and stood over him.

"Hey, man."

"Hey."

"How you making it?"

"Not good. Not good."

"Yeah, they giving you anything?"

"They wanted to. I told them no."

Manny shook his head violently. "What the fuck, Ray? You're missing your big chance here, man."

"I'm trying to kick."

"You're what? Are you kidding?"

"No, I figure I can get straightened out."

"Ah, bullshit." Manny stepped close, his voice a tense whisper.

"What? I've been high for two weeks. I want to get clean."

"You're not an addict, Ray."

"The fuck."

Manny got closer, pulled a chair up, and folded himself into it, his shoulders hunched. In the dark Ray could see pinpoints of light in the lenses of his sunglasses. "I'm an addict. I been in and out of rehab like six times. I'm a fucking dope addict. My mom was a dope addict. You . . ." He looked over his shoulder at the bright hallway and figures going by. "You're just, I don't know. Fucking with yourself."

Ray let out a long sigh and let his eyes close.

"You think you need to pay for something. Man, you paid. You went to jail for nothing, and your whole life was fucked."

"A lot of people are dead."

"Yeah, that's fucked up." He leaned in close, his voice dropping. "But you didn't kill anyone wasn't trying to kill you."

"My head is full of it. All this shit I done. I can't close my eyes."

Manny watched him and then turned his head to look out into the bright hallway for a while. "Listen to me." He turned back to look at Ray. "Listen to me. You ain't like me. Or Harlan. Or Cyrus or any of 'em. You can get clear of this and get a life. That guy you killed—"

Ray shook his head no, but Manny kept going.

"That guy you killed, he cut an old woman's throat and did worse for Danny. That doesn't mean you give up being a human being. Shit, if a cop had been there he'd have done the same."

"I threw it away."

"No, see, the fact you even think this way? That means something. Man, I never had two minutes worrying about any of the things I did. I say fuck 'em all and I mean it. You got all messed up with your dad going up and then the accident and that girl dying and then you came out of jail all fucked up. This money we got? I'm just gonna burn through it. In a couple of months it'll just be gone and I'll be broke again with nothing to show for it."

"What about Sherry?"

"I love Sherry, but she's as fucked as I am. She talks about kicking, having a kid, about buying a house, but at the end of the day she'd rather get high and watch TV and eat takeout food. We don't need that money. It's just going to kill us faster."

"What do I do?"

"Take the fucking money and go somewhere and do something. What do you do I have no fucking idea. I never been nothing but a convict or a thief. Whatever you coulda been you better start being it now. Fuck, man, your heart stopped. Twice, Theresa said. And here you are, breathing and talking and shit. That means something."

Ray shook his head. "It can't be that simple."

"It don't have to be complicated. You're thinking of the debt you owe? Then, I don't know, own it. Do something good for somebody. That money had blood on it long before we walked into that house. You want to help somebody, that's not wrong, but you got to help yourself. You got to want to. I remember enough of that crap from rehab to know you got to at least think you got a right to be alive, to get through the day. You did things wrong, do what you can to make things right."

Ray sat and listened, his head cocked. It was the most Manny had said in years that wasn't about wanting dope or girls or money, or getting dope or girls or money.

Manny grabbed Ray's upper arm and squeezed it tight. "Somebody's got to make it. We can't all die off. Somebody's got to get their shit together and get right." He let go of Ray's arm and grabbed his hand. "I got to go, I'm turning back into a pumpkin." He squeezed Ray's hand and got up, looming in the dark.

"Wait," Ray whispered. "What happened to our friend? From up north?"

Manny looked over his shoulder to check for anyone nearby in the hall, then turned back showing his teeth. "Bart finished the barbecue."

Ray flashed on the hole in the backyard, the pile of crumbling bricks.

"That thing's got the deepest foundation of any barbecue in the county. He's motivated, your old man works fast."

MORNING, AND A feeling of being hollowed out, a husk around air and bones. There were two men in the room, behind the nurses as they worked checking the IVs and drains and patting his hand. Ray watched the men, one tall, long limbs folded into a chair, black hair and a knowing smile like an assistant principal who figures you were the one who took a dump in the faculty lounge and he's just angling to prove it. He had a thick sheaf of papers and files in his lap.

The other one was short, gray-haired, moving around the back of the room with a dark energy, touching the pitiful bouquet from downstairs that Theresa had left, a card left thumbtacked to a board for somebody's grandma who had been in the room before Ray. The nurses left, and he sat and looked at them.

The younger one spoke. "Raymond!"

Cops.

"How are you, buddy? We thought we lost you there."

"Ah, you know. Making it, Officer."

"I'm Detective Nelson. This is Burt Grace, special investigator from the district attorney's office."

Ray nodded, and the gray-haired older man just looked at him.

"You know we're police officers."

Ray shrugged. Cheap sport coats and fraying collars, did anyone else dress like that?

"We wanted to talk to you about what happened."

"I don't really remember."

The older one shook his head, snorted. "Right."

"Well," said Nelson, acting the reasonable public servant. "What do you remember?"

"I was coming back to my apartment in Willow Grove, this guy jumped out of the bushes and stabbed me."

"You were home?"

"I guess. It's all pretty hazy."

"Did you know the man with the knife?"

"No, I didn't really see him."

"Lemme guess." The older cop again, Burt Grace. "It was a big black guy you never saw before."

"I didn't say that."

Grace turned to Nelson. "This is a waste of time." He pointed at Ray without looking at him. "This piece of shit is in the dope business, and he got stuck by some other piece of shit in the dope business."

Ray breathed through his nose, his body starting to hum with pain. "So is there something we have to talk about, or is this something you do for everybody gets stabbed in the county?"

Nelson leafed through the papers in front of him. "You've had quite a time, Raymond."

"You got my life story there, do you?"

"Three juvenile arrests, sent to Lima. Two arrests as an adult, both involving stolen cars. Sent up twice." He flipped pages. "You got a lot of interesting friends, Raymond. Emanuel Marchetti . . ."

Grace made a noise with his lips. "Manny Marchetti? That

Dennis Tafoya

scumbag? Isn't he the one his mother was a junkie retard got cut up in Bristol?"

Ray cocked his head. "Yeah, and you all did shit about that. It's been ten years. Any leads on that, Kojak?"

"Shut your mouth."

"Burt?" Nelson held up his hands.

"What?" Grace made a gesture of throwing something away. But he went to stand by the window.

"He's got anger management problems?"

"Detective Grace is a good cop."

"I never heard a cop say another cop was anything else."

Nelson was still paging through the files. "Harlan Maximuck. Jesus. Is he still alive?"

"Last I heard."

"Is that story they tell true? About the guy's head in his trunk?"

"I sure wasn't going to ask."

"Vietnamese organized crime figures. You get around."

He went in the folder, held something up to his eyes. A picture. Turned it to face Ray and there she was. Marletta Hicks, in her cap and gown. He wasn't prepared and turned his head.

"Pretty girl."

"Why are you here?" His eyes down, boring holes in the floor.

"Stole a car, smashed it up with the daughter of a state trooper in the passenger seat. Man, here's another one." He held up a picture of Ray, much younger with his eyes blackened, his arms in casts. "Off to adult prison that time, the first time. With your arms broken from the accident. That must have been fun. Of course, worse for the Hicks family."

Grace walked over and stood closer to Ray, and he thought the old man was going to take a swing at him. "You piece of shit. I knew I knew that name. You're the one killed Stan Hicks's kid. Jesus."

"That's what it says."

Nelson lifted his head. "You say different."

"Why would I?"

Grace said, "Oh, what the fuck. If this asshole is going to start lying again I'm going downstairs." He looked at Ray. "They should have punched your ticket ten years ago, shitbird." His footsteps moving away were like gunshots in the hall.

Nelson had a smile fixed on his face, waving pages from the file as if inviting him to continue. "You got something to say about all—this—I'm all ears. I never knew a convict who didn't like to spin a yarn."

"Okay, just be on your way." Ray's stomach cramped, and he gritted his teeth.

Nelson nodded and got up, pulling his card from his pocket. When he laid it on the bed table, Ray looked up, out of breath. "You got the file?"

Nelson held up the pile of papers. "Pretty much everything."

"Okay." Ray looked off, then back, breathing like he'd run a mile, spikes driven into him everywhere. "Okay, then." He grimaced and sucked in air. "You know it all."

"You got something to say about that?"

"Why would I?"

"Now's your chance." The cramp eased and Ray panted, open mouthed.

"No, my chance passed a long time ago. Just ask Stanard Hicks."

"Marletta's father? I know Stan Hicks."

"Yeah?"

"Why would I care about any of this?"

Ray shrugged. "No reason. I mean, you got the file, so you got the story."

"Raymond, you are a piece of work. Look at you." He went into the file, came out with the picture again, and laid it on the table. Marletta smiling in her cap and gown, her brown skin glowing. "Whatever else is true, Raymond, you're alive, still. You know, in my religion, they tell me everything happens with some kind of purpose. You're alive, and this beautiful girl is dead. I don't know, Ray. I can't see the purpose in that." He turned, but Ray grabbed his arm, hard.

Nelson looked at the white hand on his arm and then into Ray's eyes. "What do you want from me?"

"Not that. Forget all that."

"What?"

"There's a kid, down in Falls Township." Nelson nodded, got out a pen.

ALONE AGAIN, PAIN threading through his limbs and abdomen like hot wires, Ray just stared off into space and drifted. He was back in a car on a hot day in June when he was a kid with his arm around a girl in a bathing suit, he was lying in a black road starred like the night sky with broken glass, he was in prison with his back against a green tile wall and his broken arms held out like clubs, he was in the front yard of his father's house, watching the moon stab through the clouds and waiting to sleep.

THEY REPAIRED HIS gut, closed the hole from the colostomy, and discharged him quick, Theresa shouting after the clerk who came to tell him about his limited options. With no insurance, no job, no place to go, he found himself at the curb with a metal cane across the arms of his wheelchair, noticing trees across the parking lot starting to show bits of red. Theresa pulled up, and Bart waved from the passenger seat. They got out, and the orderly who had wheeled him to curb helped him into the backseat, where he sighed and fell in on himself like a derelict house. Bart pulled the seat belt across him, and he nodded thanks and let his head loll back. Bart stood back and pursed his lips, looked about to say something, but just nodded his head and closed the door gently.

At home Ray limped to the couch, still not comfortable on the cane, and Bart helped him down. The dog came and sat by his feet and watched him, and he leaned awkwardly down to pat the ancient head. His boots felt huge and stiff on his feet, and he swam in his clothes, gathering the empty expanse of his shirt in his hands. He watched Theresa empty his kit bag out, lining up his pill bottles on the TV while Bart got a pillow from the bedroom and brought it out and put it behind him.

"How's that, old man?"

"Good." Ray forced a smile, wished he was alone. "Thanks."

Dennis Tafoya

Couldn't bring himself to call his father by any name and didn't
know where to put his hands.

He wished for a book, a cigarette, a drink. Theresa put on the
TV and brought him the remote, a scepter for the new king of the
living room. He was afraid they'd sit down, but their work done,
they drifted to the kitchen while Ray flipped through the channels
with the volume off. He heard the rattle of pans and smelled coffee and something sweet baking. Warm and yeasty smells after
the antiseptic tang of the hospital.

He clicked through shows about decorating houses and planning weddings, watched men stumble around pitched decks in a
storm, cops standing over a humped sheet, one naked hand open
in the street. A broad red plain under a yellow sun, and jackals
tearing at a carcass, the dead thing jerking with a simulation of
life.

Thirty years and a month. It sounded like a sentence, something he'd been handed by a tough judge in a bad court. Well,
he'd served it and what? Was he out and free? Was he marking
time and dreaming of tunnels under the wall? He became aware
of Theresa standing in the kitchen doorway, watching him. She
was smiling.

"What do I do now, Ma?"

She stood and looked ahead, out the picture window at the
lawn and the street and the trees and two jets from the base moving together through the darkening sky, a kind of arcing steel
pantomime of love. Her eyes were lined and she looked tired, and
he felt a pang of guilt. Theresa had buried a husband when she
was young, been a knockaround girl who met Bart when she was

a dancer and he was stealing heavy equipment and stood by him through arrest and years of jail and tried to raise Ray, an angry kid who became a thief and hadn't told the plain truth to anyone about anything since he was eighteen.

She said, "How about some coffee?"

He laughed but said, "Sure, Ma."

She stopped at the doorway to the kitchen. "I know you're feeling bad, hon. I know. But it's good to have you home with us."

"Is it?"

"Yes, Ray."

CHAPTER THIRTEEN

LOST WEEKS OF watching television. Sometimes with Bart, sometimes with Theresa. Nature shows. Muscular cats stalking in a rage through long grass. Travel shows, small, neat women walking along brick streets in walled cities in Tuscany, taking dainty bites of mushroom and boar sausage under trees that looked like gauzy green spearheads. Ray got into a rhythm; reading the paper every day, eating little, his stomach cramping and sometimes blood in his shorts at the end of the day.

He woke up in the middle of the night tangled in his sheets and trying to explain himself to someone in uniform. Hot cramps knifed his thigh, and he threw the covers off and stood up, massaging his leg and leaning heavily on the night table. He walked stiff-legged into the bathroom and snapped on the light, taking stock in the mirror. His beard was streaked with white now, and his long face had the angular, distracted features he had seen in photographs of Civil War veterans staring into the middle distance of daguerreotypes, one pinned sleeve empty.

Anyway, he thought, they came home and went to work. Plowed fields and raised families and counted themselves lucky, no doubt, though they walked nightly over the dead bodies of friends and enemies and felt somehow apart from everyone who hadn't been where they'd been and done what they'd done. Still they got on with it.

He sat down in the living room in his underwear, clicked on the TV, and turned down the volume. He was watching the news without seeing it when he saw a familiar face and turned up the volume. It was an older woman, mousy brown hair. It took him a minute to remember. The house in Fairless Hills. The woman was in handcuffs. There were shots of evidence tape, a policewoman holding a blanket-wrapped bundle. Pictures of the yardbird Heston that looked like old arrest photos, shots of the police knee deep in fresh holes in the yard. Digging something up.

RAY WENT OUT the front door and blinked, leaning heavily on the cane. The street was empty; the sun was high and hot. Ray stretched and tried to enjoy moving more than the few steps from the bedroom to the kitchen to the living room. He tried to find a rhythm with the cane, popping the bottom out and then leaning into it, but he broke out in a sweat before he reached the sidewalk. September was winding down and it still felt like August. He made his way around to the car and opened the door, burning his hands on the hot metal of the door of Theresa's beat-up old Dodge. When he dropped into the seat he was panting like a dog and bathed in sweat.

He drove up 611, not knowing where to go. He passed school buses and saw one tree with leaves the red of clotted blood in a stand of oaks and maples on Street Road. The air conditioner gave a sigh and stopped with an exhalation of white mist, so Ray cranked the window down and breathed in the smell of road dust and exhaust and fried food from the Wendy's at 363. He was halfway to Doylestown before he realized that was where he was heading.

At Main and Court he turned right and made a slow loop on side streets, passing the courthouse, brick row homes converted to law offices, Victorian houses set back from the street. There were people out—men in business suits on cell phones, kids on cell phones, harried-looking moms pushing strollers and talking on cell phones. He realized he was looking more at the young mothers than at the girls preening in front of the Gap and thought of it as a sign of maturity. The street he was on ended, and he turned right and then left and wound up at the end of Pine Street. There the remains of the old county prison had been turned into an art center overlooking the local library. He parked and then tapped his way to the library door, his leg on fire.

Inside was a cool, quiet space filled with light, and the sweat dried on his arms as he moved slowly from shelf to shelf, canting his head and looking at titles. He worked his way through the westerns, finding a collection of Elmore Leonard novels he'd been wanting to read, working on the mechanics of carrying the books he was collecting while still using the cane at least some of the time.

He sat at a table with a stack of newspapers and made his way through them, starting with the day he and Manny went to the farm. There were pictures of fire engines and yellow evidence tape strung from trees, articles about biker clubs like the Pagans and the Angels and the dope business. He found more articles about the shooting and fire out in Kulpsville, and finally he sat and read about the man with white hair who had been shot by the men trying to take him on the street in Doylestown. The town hadn't seen violence like that in decades, and the story played over days on the front page. When he thought it had run its course, the articles getting thinner and the police having less to report due to the random nature of the act, there was a different kind of story about the man who had died.

His name had been Edward Gray, and he'd been a lawyer. In the days after he died, articles began to run about money missing from accounts and clients who had beefed to the local bar. There were increasingly confused quotes from his daughter, apparently his only surviving family; a spiky indignation in the early days smearing into anger and obvious shame. There was a picture that caught her getting out of a car and looking exhausted and empty, dark lines under her eyes.

He read other things, too. Announcements of weddings and obituaries, a kid getting a scholarship for football. He had a sense of life going by, a stream running while he sat on the bank and watched. He read the classifieds, then closed the paper and went back to the car and drove downtown.

There was a bookstore on State Street, half of a Victorian, and he sat in the car at the curb and looked at the window at a sign: FOR SALE.

The next day he went for the first time to the storage place in Willow Grove and angled the car in front of the door and picked through the keys on his ring, feeling the heat against his back. He found the key to the lock and snapped it open with a metallic ping and clumsily dropped to a knee to pry the door up. He had to put his back into the effort, his legs shaking and blood pulsing at his temples. The door groaned and lifted, and he lowered himself on a cracking knee to look inside.

Empty.

Or not quite. On the floor a pen or something, beyond the hard boundary of sunlight reaching under the open door. He bent closer, reached for it. A needle.

Manny.

RAY DROVE UP Street Road, letting the car take him, not sure what to think or feel. He crossed 263 and almost sideswiped a van that cut him off making a left into the diner, so he pulled into the parking lot of the bowling alley and went inside to think, figuring it was one place he wouldn't know anybody.

Inside it was bright and loud. He went into the small bar and sat at a chipped Formica table and let a Miller Lite go flat while he watched some kids clustered in one of the lanes. Two boys stood close to each other, knuckle-punching each other's arms and grimacing while a girl with braces shook her head and called them retards.

He knew he should feel angry, cheated, but that wasn't in him now. He'd wanted not the money but the freedom it might bring, but he knew in losing it he'd been relieved of a burden, and he'd never have been able to spend it on himself anyway. Part of him wanted to take it off Manny, not to keep it, but to keep Manny from killing himself with it. Yet he knew he wouldn't do that, either.

Whatever Ray was doing, wherever he'd end up, he knew Manny wouldn't be there, that he was as gone as the money, as whatever he'd been feeling when he racked the slide on his Colt and kicked in the door of the dope house in Ottsville. What they were to each other had a shape bordered by dope and guns, being desperate and hopeless and going down swinging, and none of that was in Ray anymore.

He imagined calling his friend, telling him something that might matter, but couldn't think what it would be. *Don't fuck up,* or *think about this,* or something, but they weren't things they could say to each other. The only way to get the money back would be to point a gun, and he wouldn't do that, either. In the end, he sat in the bar and watched the two boys through the smoked glass. One tripped the other, who dropped his ball with a detonating crack that made the girl with braces scream, and the boys laughed and gave each other hard high fives like they'd won a prize.

After that he would go and sit on the street and look at the bookstore and wait for the FOR SALE sign to disappear. Twice he went in, walked the stacks, bought a handful of paperbacks, and couldn't work up the nerve to ask the woman behind the counter about selling the store. One night during a commercial he said something to Theresa, who smacked her hands together and said, "Finally." She snapped off the TV and went back into her room. The Sanctuary. Off-limits to teenage boys and their dopehead friends. He couldn't remember the last time he was in there.

She came out with a bankbook and pressed it into his hand. He lifted it toward her, unopened.

"I don't want this."

"Open it."

"No."

"Is everyone in this family a hardhead every minute of every hour? Honest to Christ."

"Theresa."

"What?"

"Use it for yourself. Take a trip. Go on that Niagara Falls trip the Shrine is doing."

"Oh, that bunch of old ladies? I'd cut my throat." She took the book back but opened it in front of his eyes.

"Jesus, Theresa."

"That's my grandchildren money."

"So why spend it on this?"

"I'll tell you why. Because how the hell do I get grandchildren by you sitting on your ass watching *Jeopardy*?"

IT TOOK LESS time than he thought, and by the middle of November he was standing in the shop, jingling the keys to the front door and looking through the front window at people walking the street, now in jackets, and leaves blowing along the curbs.

Bart and Theresa stood in the little space near the cash register. Theresa was beaming and Bart looking shriveled in a sport coat two sizes too large, his hands in his pockets. Theresa's name was on the paper for the store, and she'd work the register. Ray walked down the aisles, already stocked with books the last owner had picked out and displayed. He was thinking about paint and some simple carpentry. The shelves were actually a mismatched bunch of secondhand bookcases and unpainted planks roughly nailed into the naked walls, sagging in their middles. There were small windows that looked into an alley and bluish fluorescent lights that gave off a low buzz.

On a whim, he went to the door and flipped the sign over, Theresa clapping and miming delight and Bart clumsily snapping a picture with the little digital camera she'd gotten for the occasion. Ray raised his eyebrows and shrugged, no idea what to do next except get to work. He looked at the street again. Clouds moved and their blue shadows pushed along the street, dividing the world into dark and light.

He was in the storeroom in the back sorting through unlabeled boxes of books when the little bell over the door rang and Theresa called to him, an edge of panic in her voice, to come out. He stood up, his bones cracking, and pulled himself out to the front where he had left his cane and found Theresa eyeing an even smaller, older woman with a baseball cap crusted with glass beads and a cast on one arm. Their first customer. The woman raised her eyebrows, looking from panicked Theresa to Ray with sweat standing out on his forehead and dust striping his work shirt to Bart, his lips pursed like he was expecting her to grab something and run.

The moment passed, and Theresa finally shook her head as if waking up and asked if they could help her.

Janet Evanovich, the woman said, and Ray waved her back to the mysteries, where she began to paw through the stock. She prattled on about her niece who had recommended the books and said she had one of them and wanted the next one and wasn't it great they took place in Trenton?

When she came to the register, Bart stepped behind the counter and opened a paper bag. Theresa opened the register, which was empty, and then the three of them patted their pockets until Theresa went into her purse and counted out the change. Bart took the woman's ten and stuck it in a small frame and balanced it on the windowsill, and Theresa took a picture. The woman with the cap got into the spirit of the thing and waved the book at them from the door.

The woman left, and the three of them stood in the silence afterward and shrugged at each other. How hard could it be? The bell over the door clanged again, but it was the woman, scowling. She held up the book.

"I read this one."

Ray shook his head. Theresa opened her hands helplessly. Bart grabbed the frame from the sill and smacked it open on the counter with a chime of thin glass breaking, then handed the woman back her ten.

WEEKS WENT BY and the days were dark and cold. Ray worked alone in the empty store, ripped the shelving out and replaced it in pieces, creating painted built-in shelves with finished edges and molding and painted a creamy white. He spent hours looking at track lighting at the Home Depot and finally settled on small, blue-shaded spots that he tied to a bank of dimmers near the register. He got up early each morning, made lists of tasks for himself on the backs of envelopes, and started noticing how the stores he visited were laid out and the merchandise displayed.

Bart got sicker, and Theresa stayed away more and more to

stay with him. Ray would open later and close earlier. He sat for hours in the back of the shop and heard people come by the front doors, sometimes rattling the handle. He took the books off the shelves and then restacked them, lining them up with soldierly precision and making lists of his stock. The woman who had sold him the store, a long, bent woman with a lesbian vibe named Elizabeth, had given him pages with long lists of contacts for book resellers who bought up stock from closing stores and libraries, a constant reminder that there was nothing guaranteed in what he had begun. With the shop closed he spent hours calling people, looking for more of the westerns and crime novels he loved, and every day brought cardboard boxes from Scottsdale or Presque Isle or Waukegan that smelled of ink and old paper and mold. But the store was open less and less.

In January Bart stopped getting out of bed, and Ray put a small sign in the window, HELP WANTED. Theresa had talked with him about a decent wage, and he added a few bucks to it in his head and the next Monday he sat in the store and tapped his cane against his boot and read *Hombre* for the ninth time, looking up occasionally to watch people moving down streets lashed by rain, their heads tucked into their chests.

He had just nodded off when the bell rang and he jerked upright and Michelle came in, shaking the rain off of a plastic kerchief and smiling at him as if this were the date they'd set up months before. He stood slowly, putting weight on his hands until he could get steady on the cane, and took one long step out from behind the counter.

She looked around and nodded her head. "Wow. It looks great."

"Oh," he said and raised one hand dismissively, "a little carpentry, new rugs."

"No, it looks wonderful. Liz would never spend any money on the place."

"You know her?"

"Oh, yeah. I worked here. Before the other place."

"So you know the operation."

"Sure. Well, the way Liz did things, anyway."

He nodded his head, keeping his hands down to resist the impulse to reach out and touch her.

She pointed to the sign in the window. "You need help?"

He let his smile get away from him, the muscles in his face stretching in unfamiliar ways until he brought a hand up and massaged his cheek. He did move, then. Leaned into the cane and reached past her and took down the sign. Waved it and threw it behind the counter.

He closed early that night, anxious for the time to pass and for Michelle to start. Couldn't bring himself to stop hoping, playing out different ways it could go. In the moment he'd stood on the sagging wooden porch watching her go up the street, head tucked against the rain, he let himself know he'd taken Theresa's money, bought the store, put up the sign, all of it hoping she'd walk in off the street. Let himself run a hundred changes in his mind, let himself feel stupid and impatient and something else that might be happiness at just breathing.

He stood on the street, looked back up at the store one last time to make sure the lights were off, and was nearly knocked off his unsteady feet by Edward Gray's daughter coming down the sidewalk, listing to one side and paddling at the air with one stiff arm. He searched his mind for her name. She held up her hands and spoke with deliberation.

"I'm so sorry." Adrienne, that was her name. She smelled like sour fruit and was underdressed for the weather in a sweater and scuffed jeans. She said, "A little dark out here tonight," and smiled. Drunk, he realized. Her eyes were shadowed pits in her head.

"My fault," he said and meant it. "Standing around in the middle of the sidewalk, blocking traffic."

She patted hair the color of foam on a lifeless pond. "Not at all. Not at all."

She kept moving along the street, downhill to wherever she lived, he hoped. He watched her go.

HE HAD AN open house in February and invited Manny, who didn't come, and Ho and Tina, who did. Theresa was there, and Bart, skin the color of mustard and sitting in a wheelchair, though he smiled and held a glass of white wine and snapped pictures with Theresa's little digital camera. Ray showed Ho the Web site Michelle had put together for the store and her brochures for the children's parties she wanted to host, letting the kids make books of their own. Ho looked from the computer to Ray and then at Michelle where she sat on the floor, her ankles tucked under her as she guided Ho's five-year-old, Ly, through an Alexandra Day book where a black dog danced with a smiling infant. Ho shook his head and smiled, and Ray opened his hands.

"What?"

"Nothing, nothing at all."

"Oh, you know? Don't start."

"Did I say a word?"

"I get this enough from Theresa." He inclined his head and dropped his voice, a hand held out as if to signal stop. "She doesn't know. Anything."

"So?"

"So I don't want to go down that road."

"Don't lie."

"I don't want to lie. I don't want to get into anything."

"You think what, she's here for six bucks an hour?"

"Fourteen. I can't dump my life on some kid from Ohio who works in a bookstore. That life? Where I've been and what I've done?"

"Then don't." Ho poured more wine into his glass, waved at his daughters. "But you got this far, man. You going to spend the next fifty years dating massage parlor girls?"

Ray dropped onto the sill of the window behind the counter, massaging his thigh and grimacing, and Ho stood with his back to the room.

"I'm just saying think about what you're going to say. You don't have to sign a full confession to tell someone you've been in trouble and aren't anymore. If you think you got to say anything except you own a bookstore in Doylestown."

Ray looked across at her, and she turned her head and smiled and then looked down, and he felt the floor dropping away and a thudding in his head.

Ho motioned him out to the porch and looked up and down the street, then told him Cyrus was dead.

"The guys from New England?"

"No. That's over."

"Over?"

"That guy, Scott? He was making this move on his own, took some of the guys from the Outlaws and came down here on his own. With his end of an armed robbery at an Indian casino. That's what the cash was."

"How do you know this?"

"A friend showed me some transcripts."

"Transcripts?"

Ho looked around again and lowered his head. "Federal wiretaps."

"Jesus."

"It was everything he had, his own money."

Ray nodded. It explained the way things played out. He shook his head. "How did it show up on wiretaps?"

"The FBI was on him up there. They scooped up everybody on the New Hampshire end of it."

"Then who got Cyrus?"

"That wasn't business." Ho smiled. "He was screwing around and his old lady caught him." Ray saw the woman at the abandoned house. Tattoos of the sun and moon on her hands and ice-blue eyes.

Ho turned to go back inside, shivering and pulling in his shoulders.

"Does this mean it's over?"

Ho shrugged but smiled. "There's no one left."

"How do we know?"

Ho looked at him. "The only people you got to worry about chasing you are all up here." He reached out and tapped Ray's forehead.

LATER HE WAS alone with Michelle, and he moved along the table they had set out, throwing empty plastic wineglasses into a plastic bag. Michelle fiddled at the CD player she had set up, and the gentle electronic music she liked started up. Quiet voices and lush sounds that were like being wrapped in something soft. It wasn't what he would have chosen, but he was getting used to it, starting even to depend on it. Like her sweet perfume and the quotes she put up on the board near the door every day. Admonitions to be brave and alive. Rilke and Emerson and Rumi. That made him secretly siphon off books and try to parse out the meaning of the poems she loved.

He became aware of her behind him and stopped. He turned and she took the plastic bag from his hand and dropped it on the floor and moved into his arms and they were dancing. He was stiff and moved slightly to the beat, and she rested her head on his shoulder, and after a minute he lost the sense of the music and just swayed with her. He tried out different things in his head. Telling her where he had been and what he had done. Wondering what she needed to know to know him.

She finally said, "What happened?"

"What?"

"In August?" She kept her head tucked against him, her breath warm on his chest. "Was it the accident?"

He had been waiting for this question since they day she had come in about the job but still wasn't ready for it. "Yes. No." He shook his head. "I was in trouble."

"What kind of trouble?" She picked her head up, and suddenly it was much more difficult and there was something guarded in her eyes.

His eyes flicked over her face and he looked down again. "I've made some mistakes in my life."

She stopped moving, and then he did, a beat too late.

"Tell me." But her face was different, harder, and it was an interrogation and his mind was blank.

The door chimed and they both looked up, Michelle pulling away and moving to the stacks, collecting paper plates left by Ho's kids. He looked after her, his hands still in the air, then turned to the door to see two kids, thirteen or fourteen or fifteen. One short and blond, the other long, with black hair hanging lank over his eyes. They moved to the counter and dropped a pillowcase on it, spilling hardback books, and Ray pawed through them while the short kid fidgeted and the tall kid stared hard at him. The tall one wore a thin black jacket with duct tape on the elbow, and Ray remembered he'd seen them before, by the side of the road in Warrington. The tall kid had a runny nose, and they both had red cheeks from the cold. The short one was just getting fuzz on his chin and had spots of something purple and sticky-looking on his army coat.

There were some old books that looked like they were worth something. Jack London, *The Iron Heel* and *Call of the Wild*. Fitzgerald's *Tender Is the Night*. Some others he didn't recognize. Some of them in plastic covers. First editions or something. He took more out of the pillowcase and found two candlesticks and a bell that looked to be real silver.

The short kid flicked the bell with his finger, miming pleasure at the bright sound. "Gimme a hundred bucks. And you can keep all that shit."

Ray looked them up and down and smiled.

"Yeah? That ain't much for all this swag."

"No, it's like a deal."

Ray put sunglasses on the tall kid in his head and laughed. Manny and Ray, a month out of Lima, scoring from empty houses near the Willow Grove mall and trying to dump the stuff in the pawnshops along 611.

The blond kid snapped his fingers under Ray's nose and pointed. "Fitzgerald, you know him?" He looked into the corner of the room as if something were painted there. " 'All good writing is swimming underwater and holding your breath.' " He pantomimed laughing, like a dog panting, and looked over his shoulder at his friend, who smiled and nodded as if the blond kid had done a card trick he'd seen before.

The tall one looked at Michelle, who had stopped what she was doing and stood listening. His face changed and he looked hard at

Ray. "Don't fuck with us, man. Just pay us or let us be on our way."

Ray nodded slowly. "Where did you get this stuff?"

The blond kid snorted, but the tall one reached over and started snapping the books back into the case. "We're out of here, Lynch."

Ray held up a hand. "Wait a minute, okay?"

The tall kid moved toward the door, wiping at his nose with his free hand, and Ray snapped the register open and he stopped. The shorter kid stood up and angled his head to see. Ray came out with two twenties and held them out to the kids. Michelle sighed and disappeared into the back of the store. The blond kid, Lynch, pointed at his friend and the pillowcase. For the first time, Ray noticed a bruise on the tall kid's face, the shape of a hand etched in faint and fading blue.

The blond kid said, "What? This shit is worth like ten times that."

"I don't want it."

"Then what?"

"Take the money."

The kids looked at each other, then reached for the money. Ray held out another two twenties, but when the kids reached for them, he jerked the bills back and held them high.

"This is to buy books with."

The kids looked at each other again, the blond one, Lynch, shrugging.

"Buy," Ray said again. He picked up the day's paper and dropped it where they could see he had circled half a dozen ads in red. "These are garage sales. Go by these places and buy whatever books you find. Don't pay more than a buck a book, and don't bring me CDs or DVDs or games or any other shit. Just books."

The tall kid shrugged and wiped at his nose with the back of his hand.

Ray said, "Get receipts."

He let the blond one take the money and watched it disappear into his coat and handed the tall one the newspaper. "Take that shit back where you found it and go buy me some books. Every book you bring me I'll pay you another buck. So drive hard bargains."

Ray watched them walk to the dark street through the front windows, heads together, talking and laughing. He saw a young blond girl come out from behind a column on the porch as if she'd been hiding there. She fell in beside the boys, and Lynch took her arm. When she turned one last time to look at the store, he saw a ring of livid purple around her right eye.

He turned to see Michelle in her coat. Her head was down.

"Okay, see you," she said.

"Wait."

"What?"

She looked at him and then away, and he had that feeling again of recognition he had had before on the street in August.

"What's wrong?"

"Nothing."

"Are you, you know. Coming back?"

"Why is Theresa's name on the store?"

"I told you I was . . . in trouble."

"Are you in trouble now?"

"No. I don't think so."

"Why do you pay me under the table?"

"What's going on? Isn't that better for you?" He looked around as if there were someone else he could bring into the conversation.

"Is it? Those kids stole that stuff."

"Yeah, but—"

"You thought it was funny or cute or something."

He smiled, saw at once that was the wrong thing. "They're kids, Michelle."

"Kids like you?"

"Once, yeah."

She was shaking her head and moving to the door. "So you're what? The cool guy who buys stolen stuff and maybe sells you some weed?"

"Where is this coming from?"

"I see you when there are policemen on the street."

"You see me?" He wanted to say, *I see you, too*, but wasn't sure what it was he saw.

"You get this look. And you move away from the window. One time that cop went next door and you hid in the stockroom."

"I didn't hide. I had shit to do." But he didn't believe himself, either. He was getting angry, felt something twisting out of his hands, the desire to restrain it somehow propelling it away.

"Yeah, okay. I'll see you, Ray."

He grabbed his cane and started after her, but she was through the door and down the street faster than he could cross the room. He stumped out to the top of the stairs, the cold gripping at him. Watched her moving under the lights away up the street toward Main. It began to snow, white flakes sticking to his hair and his shirt like nature trying to erase him from the scene.

CHAPTER FOURTEEN

SHE DIDN'T COME back the next day, or the next. He called her over the next three days, stammering vague messages to her voice mail and hanging up. He sat in the store and stared, reading the last quote she had put up over and over. "I hold this to be the highest task for a bond between two people: that each protects the solitude of the other." Rilke, one of her favorites. He got out *Letters to a Young Poet* when he was alone in the store and scoured it for traces of her, all the time willing himself to be smarter and more patient. When the store closed he sat in the light from the street and touched the pages and held it up to his face, hoping her scent would have lingered on the book.

STRANGE WEATHER MOVED in. Hot, damp days in which the sun furiously melted the last of the snow and kids built slick gray snowmen in their shirtsleeves. Bart moved into the hospital, and Ray would go there at the end the day, so Theresa could take a break. He'd bring his father crime novels. Elmore Leonard and Donald E. Westlake and John D. MacDonald. Bart loved anything with guys fighting over a briefcase full of money. Faithless women and smoking pistols. At first Ray would drop them on the nightstand and take the old ones, but after a week he noticed they were untouched and started reading them aloud. Bart would close his eyes and fall asleep, and Ray would stick a tongue depressor in the book and leave it on the nightstand.

One night, in the middle of *The Hunted,* during a long chase across the Negev, Bart put his hand on Ray's arm and held it there. Ray closed the book and waited, feeling the papery skin and the rocklike bones beneath.

"I always wanted to see the desert." Bart's voice was like something rimed with salt, gritty and brittle.

"Me, too."

"You should go."

"Maybe."

"Nah, just go. Take that girl from the store."

Ray thought about that, and about what to say. "That would be good."

"I never did nothing in my whole life."

Ray looked at him, but Bart was dry-eyed, just staring as if struck by the wonder of it.

"Nothing that was worth a damn to another living soul." Bart patted Ray's hand. "I can't tell you what to do. I ain't got that right anymore." Then his father smiled, that alien arrangement of muscles that made him unrecognizable. "But, maybe, take a lesson."

THE NEXT SATURDAY the kids came back, Lynch and the tall kid, who Ray found out was named Stevie. They were excited, dumping the books they'd found out on the counter, pushing them forward, Lynch talking about the ones he'd read, thumbing them open to show Ray passages he liked and that, eerily, he'd obviously memorized just by glancing at them. They shifted the books into piles, claiming finds and smacking the table and saying, pay me, bitch.

The blond girl, Andrea, came up and hovered at the door this time, and Lynch would look over at her as if he were making sure she was still there or checking to see if she was okay. She was tiny, lost in a parka that looked three sizes too large, her yellow hair seeping from under a hood and curling on her red cheeks. The bruise on her face had faded, but she was silent and looked off into the corners of the room, her hands in her pockets.

Ray caught her eye and, trying to look harmless, smiled and pointed back into the store. She dropped her head and moved down the aisles fast, as if she had been slapped.

Lynch watched her go, then called to her. "Hey, he's got some of those books, Andy."

Ray counted money out onto the counter. "What books?"

Stevie shook his head. He dropped his head and talked into his coat. "What a fucking loser."

"What books?"

Lynch smacked Stevie on the elbow. "Aw, man, you know. About babies and being pregnant and that shit."

Ray lost count. "Dude, what?"

"She's knocked up."

Ray picked up the small pile of money, feeling ridiculous. He had been thinking about two kids getting a couple of bucks for junk food and movies. "Jesus, man. Is she . . ." He shook his head. "I mean, where is she living? Do her parents know? I mean, where the fuck do you two live, anyway?"

Smiling, Stevie snatched the money from Ray. "We're covered, man." Lynch went into the back and came back with Andrea, who Ray could see now was pregnant, her small belly pressing against the inside of the parka. She had two books, *What to Expect When You're Expecting* and something called *Ten Little Fingers* with a cartoon of a baby with arms outstretched and an outsized, egglike head that made Ray wince with its fragility.

He gave them the books, gave them more money, couldn't stop himself from shaking his head every couple of seconds. He finally made them promise to take Andy to Lilly's, the sandwich shop around the corner, to get her something healthy to eat. On the porch Lynch turned and gave an apologetic shrug while Stevie fanned the air with dollar bills.

THE NEXT SUNDAY morning Ray couldn't bring himself to drive up and open the store, and instead he put a sport coat on and went to the low brick meetinghouse on Oakland Avenue. It was still hot, the street steaming and the lawns looking like wilted salad revealed by the melting snow.

He got there late, let himself in as quietly as he could, and sat near the door on an ancient, scarred bench half-covered with pamphlets about Darfur, capital punishment, and something called Peace Camp. It was quiet; the only sounds were passing traffic and the occasional sigh or sneeze. The room itself was plain, painted a sleep-inducing cream color and smelling faintly of wet ash, as if a fire had been put out just before he arrived. There was a mix of ages in the room, but Ray thought everyone had something indefinable in common. Expressed in uncombed hair and wrinkled clothes, maybe. Natural fibers and, he was guessing, nontoxic dyes.

In front of him two black-haired kids fidgeted next to their mother, who wore jeans and a peasant blouse. Ray realized he wore the only jacket in the room. He scanned faces but couldn't find Michelle in the crowd at first. Finally he spotted her between a large woman in a dress that looked like it was made from pink bedsheets and a small man with a bald head who kept clicking his dentures in his sleep. Michelle's eyes were closed.

He kept waiting for the service to begin, but it never seemed to. There would be a rustle of movement or an exhalation that he expected to signal the start of a prayer or a song, but it resolved itself into some small readjustment in the humid room. A tiny fan at the window blew a lank, tepid breeze past his face without cooling the air. A woman stood up, two rows away from him. She had short gray hair and a thickset body, and beside her sat Liz, who had sold Theresa the store and whom he hadn't seen since the closing. The woman who stood said she had sat on her porch and watched a spider build a web, working diligently and skillfully to make this delicately beautiful thing that would last only the day and then have to be rebuilt, and that there was some kind of message in that and she was trying to be open to it. She said her friend had given up something vitally important to her that she had worked a long time to get and very hard to keep, and wasn't there value in making something intricate and lovely, even if you knew it wasn't going to last? That there would only be more work at the end of it?

After her question, she just shrugged and sat down. Liz, whom Ray had never seen smile, beamed and squeezed the woman's hand, her eyes wet. Ray thought for a minute someone in authority would get up and answer her question, but there was just more silence leavened only by shifting and Quakers pinching at their damp clothes.

After another few minutes, he saw a tall gray-haired man turn and shake the hand of the person next to him, and then there was a sort of collective exhalation and everyone in the room turned and shook the hands of the people around them. The woman with the fidgety kids turned around to face him and offered him a damp red hand, and he smiled shyly and shook her fingers and nodded his head, wondering if there was some password he should know to say.

The man who had shaken the first hand stood and went to a table in the gap in the center of the room. He read some announcements. Someone named Betsy in the hospital who could use a visit, bulletins from various committees about an upcoming peace fair, a walk to protest the war, buses to a rally for Tibet.

The crowd drifted slowly toward the door. More handshaking, hugging. People catching up and remarking on the strange weather, stopping to eat gingersnaps and sip from tiny cups of cider from a table by the door. Michelle sat, not moving, her head down, though people touched her shoulder and whispered to her. Ray forced himself up and across the room and finally sat on the same bench at what he hoped was a respectful distance. When he was settled in she lifted her head but turned to watch people knotted at the door. She gave a shy wave to an older woman with a broad smile who might have been Filipino.

"Hello, Ray."

She didn't look at him. Her voice was low, and he moved closer and she didn't shift away. He looked down at her knees, conscious of his own quickened pulse. She had on a long skirt and the brown sweater he had seen her in when they met. They let a minute go by as the room emptied.

She said, "I worked in a lawyer's office in Massillon. You know where that is?" She kept her eyes on the door. "No. Anyway." The last people drifted out the door and they were alone.

"I fell in love with one of the associates. I was twenty-two." Empty, the room echoed with her voice. She lifted her hands and looked at them. Maybe seeing something that told her how long ago twenty-two was. "He was overwhelming. Smart, so smart. Funny and fun to be around. He took me places." Now her eyes went down. "We did a lot of coke. At first it was just fun, made us sharper and funnier and I thought more passionate. What it looked like at the time."

Ray was conscious of holding himself still, regulating his breathing. He waited, and she pulled her sweater around her.

"Then it became about the coke. Somehow. Everything turned on our getting high. We needed it to be together. He began to neglect everything else. Court dates, meetings. They were going to fire him." She shook her head, smiling at the wonder of it. "Me, too.

My mom got sick. Cancer. It didn't even register. Everything sort of shrank to this point." She made an open circle with her hands, closed it.

"We were full of this self-righteous anger, you know, just pumped up by the blow. How could they treat him this way, and how stupid and slow they all were. Life was so unfair. So when he told me about these accounts, and how he knew how to get access to them . . . Anyway, I stole sixty-eight thousand dollars." The smile again, a joke at her own expense. "And it was gone in, like, moments. It seems like so much money when you think of it in a pile. What you could do with it. In Massillon? But it came and went. Most of it. And it took them about a month to figure out what happened." Her voice got flatter now. Someone else's story. Ray took off the coat and threw it across the seat behind him, sweat in a line down his back.

"So, I'm twenty-two and stupid and he's thirty-five and a lawyer. So . . ." Now she finally turned to Ray. "Sixteen months at Trumbull Correctional Camp. My mom died while I was in there." Her voice broke, the sound catching somewhere in her chest. She cleared her throat, pushed up her sleeve, and showed him a tattoo, a cherry with a stem, crudely drawn and going blue now with age. "That was Cherry, a girl at the camp. I can't . . . I can't even describe that relationship now. She kept me from getting hurt. Hurting myself." Her eyes flicked to his. "But you don't need my prison stories, do you, Ray?"

"No."

" 'Cause you have your own."

"Yes." He tried to keep her eyes with him, but she turned her head. He kept going. "And not just prison. Juvie before that. Stupid things, stealing cars. Before it got more serious." He sat back, and she kept her hands flat in her lap, sitting straight upright as if waiting to be called to another room. "I wanted money, I can't even tell you why. It just sat there. My partner stole most of it, and I have to tell you I was . . ." He searched for the word. "Relieved. Like I was free of something. I wish to God I'd never seen it. Never wanted it."

They sat for a minute, and she looked into a far corner of the room.

"So," she finally said. "Are you another story that ends with 'she should have known better'? Or are you the one who sees me and knows who I am? Where I've been and what it means?"

He wondered where the girl he met in the street had gone, the bright-smiling girl who had looked him in the eye, and it cut him inside to think he was the reason she sat slumped next to him, her eyes empty and her head full of the banging echoes of cell doors and the thousand daily humiliations of being locked up.

He thought for a while, listened to cars moving in the street and the sounds of kids somewhere. "I know some things. Not a lot, maybe not enough."

"Tell me."

"I know I don't want any of it anymore. I know I want to sleep without the nightmares. Really rest, you know?"

She began to lean forward, her head lowering slowly. She put her hands on her face. He wanted to touch her but kept his hands in his lap though they twitched like wires. He kept going. "I wake up exhausted somehow. Like I never slept."

She looked down but nodded and shut her eyes tight, listening.

"I have these nightmares," he said. "Terrible things I can't control, people in trouble I can't help. And the terrible things are something I caused. Something I brought."

Michelle put her hand over her eyes.

"I know that you're ashamed. All the time."

She turned her head away and began to sob, a terrible strangled noise, her shoulders heaving.

"I know it because I am, too."

His eyes were dry, and he put his arms on her back and lowered his head to her hair. She gave a moan of pain that was dreadful to hear, a low, animal sound of loss, but clutched at his hand.

"You tell yourself all this . . . shit. Wrong place, wrong time. Not your fault. You were beat, or lied to, or hurt. But you know it doesn't matter and the things you did that were wrong were in you to do. Part of you. And you let them out and they destroyed every fucking thing you might have been. Wanted to be. Everyone who cared about you. Like you set this fire to burn down your own life."

She sat up and wrapped her arms around him, and he kissed her cheek and felt her tears soak into his shirt.

"I want to say it's going to be okay, but that's one of the things I don't know." Her breathing began to slow, to ease, and he kissed her cheek again, and she turned to him and covered his mouth with her own. Then they were quiet for a while.

They went back to her apartment, actually one big room over a garage. The first time he'd seen it. Candles and a warm vanilla smell of baking from the house next door. A miniature kitchen, a bank of small windows letting in the light and air. A photograph, torn from a magazine, of rolling green hills and a red stone house that made him think of Italy. More quotes from Rilke in her handwriting. Fat loops and swirls, like the way she moved her hands when she spoke and was animated.

They kissed in the doorway, their mouths open, and pulled at each other's clothing. She stood back and shucked off her sweater and then undid the buttons on his shirt as they moved to the bed. He put his hand on hers and stopped her from opening his shirt but hiked her skirt and pushed his hand inside the waistband of her pants. She moved under him, opening, and when he entered her, her eyes were still wet from crying. His breath hitched in his chest and she made a low noise in her throat and feeling the length of the space inside her for the first time he came, his teeth bared and her hands gripping his shoulders. He settled into her, breaking into pieces like a ship coming to rest in the sand at the bottom of the sea.

Later she opened his shirt. He stared at the ceiling when she put her cool fingers in the furrows left by the knife. He began to tell her, then. Everything that had happened, from when his mother left and Bart had gotten locked up. He told her about Marletta and the accident and how he couldn't get it all back. Bits and pieces would come to him but he couldn't hold it all his head at once. He told her how angry and stupid he'd been coming out of prison. About Harlan and Manny and Ho. About how it was all burned out or carved out by the things that had happened in August. Edward Gray dying, and the fire at the barn. He talked until it was dark and he was hoarse and his eyes burned, as if he'd been screaming instead of whispering.

When he woke in the night, his eyes wild, she was there with him and touched his head, and he fell asleep again, folded against her and smelling the warm bread scent of her skin and saying her name.

IT GOT COLDER again, and rainy. Wind tunneled down State Street in front of the store and kept the foot traffic lower than they would have liked. Michelle brought people in with kids' parties, and open mike night for bad poetry and white wine. A kid from the neighborhood noodling on a guitar while his black-haired girlfriend watched adoringly. People started to recognize them on the street. Ray began to stay most nights with Michelle in her room on Mary Street.

Bart died in April, and they buried him in a plot in Whitemarsh on a cool day when the shadows of clouds moving were sharp on the ground. They sat on folding chairs that sank into the spongy turf, and Michelle put her hand in his lap while he tried to fit everything that his father had been into his head. When the priest finished his generic prayers, Ray looked up and saw Manny, wearing his wraparound shades and a black jacket over jeans and standing back near his car. His face was whiter than Ray remembered. Something, a tremor, maybe, shifted his thin shoulders. Ray lifted his hand, and Manny nodded and turned away. When Ray held Theresa's arm to steady her on the marshy ground, he felt how thin and brittle she had become. He hadn't noticed against Bart's rapid dwindling, but soon she would be gone, too.

Dennis Tafoya

When he got to the store the next day the kids were there. Lynch and Stevie and Andy. Michelle called the boys Burke and Hare and teased them, and Stevie had begun to fall in love with her. Ray let them in, and they brought shopping bags in full of paperbacks and dropped their satisfying weight onto the floor by the register. Michelle took Andy into the storeroom to make coffee and ask her about the baby and came back with Entenmanns's cookies and a couple of paper plates. The boys were fighting over the last one, Stevie hanging back with feinted jabs and Lynch giving him dead eyes and saying, 'Don't even bother, dipshit,' when Ray's cell rang and it was Theresa.

"Someone's been here."

HE KNELT IN the entryway and could smell the bag. Cigarette smoke and hash oil and dog piss and air freshener and Lysol fighting, almost enough to make him gag. He picked it up and took it back to the bedroom while Theresa made coffee. When he was alone he unzipped it and dumped it out. Bundles of bills in rubber bands. He did a quick count and a lot of it was gone. There was about eighty thousand left.

He took money out, enough to cover what Theresa had spent on the store and then some, and tucked it into his pants. He closed the bag and took it to the front door and dropped it and went into Theresa's room and stuck the money from his pants in her top drawer. He saw the money now as a problem to be solved, but his life was getting crowded with people who needed help, and he'd think of some way to get rid of the rest of it.

Then he sat and had coffee and listened to Theresa talk about her latest trip to AC and her friend Evelyn who won six hundred dollars on a Wheel of Fortune machine. He made his eyes go wide. A lot of money.

CHAPTER
FIFTEEN

RAY AND MICHELLE drove up Holicong Road while he tried to get his bearings against the low hump of Buckingham Mountain starting to go green again. There were a few crocuses showing livid purple in the lawns they passed. The clouds moved fast in a wind that Ray could feel pulling at the car. The sky would show, blue-white between the clouds, then disappear again. He made two more turns, glancing down at a piece of paper Michelle had printed out for him.

She had been tense, watching the sheets print out, her shoulders drawn in, her eyes flicking over his. She shook her head. "If I said I didn't want you to do this, would it matter?"

"Nothing will happen." He smiled at her, or tried to, showed his teeth, but thought, how do I know that? "Anyway," he said. "Anyway, I have to go."

"Okay." She looked down. "Okay, but I'm driving you."

"No, it's okay."

"Fuck that. You're pretending you're handling shit. I get that. But I'm not sitting here and you go off and I never see you again."

He saw she was close to crying and thought about it for a minute and finally nodded. "Sure. Nothing is going to happen, but it's cool you come with me." He kissed the top of her head, and she held his arms.

NOW THEY WENT slowly by neat houses, looking at numbers painted on mailboxes. They came to a brick house with a lot of windows, nicer than he thought it would be, the lawn trimmed. Flower beds, hard rectangles of turned soil expecting something that was coming.

He didn't know exactly what he had expected. Dust and cracked windows, he guessed. Things rusting on a lawn. While they sat at the curb, the garage door lifted and there he was. Moving purposefully out across the driveway with a rake. Attacking a small pile of winter-dead leaves and pushing it into a black plastic bag.

He was still erect, and he matched the squared-away house. His hair was white etched with a few solid black lines, and his shoulders were broad. He looked like what he was, a state trooper. A cop. Retired, older, but still a cop.

Michelle opened her mouth, but Ray opened the door and pushed himself out, straightening slowly and then reaching back for the cane. She watched his face, showed him the cell phone. He winked.

He covered most of the distance to where Stan Hicks stood over the shrinking pile of leaves before the older man turned and faced him holding the rake loosely at his side. The eyes were pale gray and clear, focused. Ray wondered how old he was, comparing him mentally to the shriveled old man his father had been when they had finally let him out.

"I wondered if you'd ever come here."

Ray nodded, thought about putting his hand out. He felt Stan Hicks look him over, taking in the cane, the thin frame. When Hicks looked back at the car, Ray followed his eyes to see Michelle sitting in the open door, watching tensely, working the cell phone in her hands like a rosary.

"That's a pretty girl."

"Yessir."

"She looks a little like my girl."

Ray nodded; there was no denying it. Ray allowed himself to see it, and he did have to look at Michelle again. He smiled at her.

"Why did you come here, son?"

"I don't know."

"You bring a gun? Going to make me pay for something?" He didn't seem particularly worried about that possibility, and of the two of them seemed more able to defend himself.

"No, I thought maybe you already paid whatever you had to pay for."

"And what would that be?" He looked Ray in the eye. "You think I ruined your life?"

"No."

"You did that on your own."

"No, my life wasn't ruined." Ray stuck his hands in his pockets. "Took me a long time to see that. I'd have said it was, you asked me not long ago. But it wasn't." They both looked down at the wet pile of jagged leaf fragments at their feet.

"Why didn't you say what I did to you?"

"I wanted the same thing you wanted."

"I kept expecting they'd come. I was ready for it. When you told somebody what I did." He held the rake in his hands as if he were going to snap it. The way he'd snapped Ray's arms.

Ray could almost feel it again. Stan Hicks pushing him down on the cold asphalt, the rage spilling out of the older man in a torrent of screamed curses and spit. The metal bar falling once, twice on each arm.

Ray cocked his head. "What was that? That bar you used on me?"

"The tire iron from my patrol car. I was ready to account for it. I think I wanted to. I broke your arms. I lied, I made that dope addict Perry March say you stole his car. I was ready to tell it. I was proud of what I did. But no one ever came."

"No."

"You killed my girl."

"I loved her. A drunk driver killed her."

"You don't say that." His eyes were full of tears and his mouth worked. "You don't get to say that."

"No, Stan. I think that's why I went to prison. So I could say it. I think that's why I let everything come. The beating and the lies you told."

Stan Hicks sat on the ground and put his head in his hands. Ray got down slowly on one knee, the cold water from the grass soaking through his pants. He turned, to see Michelle standing now, watching intently, her eyes wet.

Stan Hicks spoke, his eyes hidden. "She'd have hated it. What I did."

"Yes. But she'd have wanted me to help you."

"I don't deserve it."

"No." Ray reached over and put his hand on the older man's arm. "That's why I had to do it. Come here and say it was okay. That it worked out okay. It's the same thing she did for me. Loved me. Wanted good things for me that I didn't deserve. She would have hated what you did. But she would have kept on loving you."

Ray got awkwardly to his feet, Michelle running across the lawn to help him. Together they helped Stan Hicks get up, and they went with him inside. The house was bright and empty, and there were pictures of Marletta and her mother. Michelle stood in the entryway and looked at them, and then at Stan Hicks and Ray standing in the kitchen. Ray got a glass from a cabinet and ran the water, filled it, and handed it to the older man.

Ray leaned back against the counter. "My mother always did that."

"Mine, too." Stan Hicks wiped at his eyes with his sleeve.

"It always helped."

They both looked at Michelle. For the first time, the older man smiled. "Just like my girl."

HE WAS IN the store late on a Wednesday night, unpacking boxes and thinking about locking the door, when one of the detectives from the hospital came in. The tall one, good cop, the one named Nelson. The detective looked around and rocked on his heels.

Ray waved from where he was kneeling in the space between the register and a display table, motioning him further in.

"Nice place, Raymond."

"Ray. Everyone calls me Ray, Detective." He stuck out his hand.

"Right. Ray."

Ray pointed down the stacks. "Take a look around. Help yourself to anything catches your eye."

Nelson scratched his ear, smiled.

Ray said, "If that's not a problem. Graft or something."

Nelson pulled out his notepad and gestured at a table and two chairs up against the far wall. "You got a second?"

Ray hesitated half a beat, then pointed to the chair nearest the door. "Sure. You want some coffee?"

Nelson said yes, and Ray went back to the storeroom, returning with two cups. Nelson had wedged his tall frame into the seat, and his notebook was open on the table. But Ray's eye was drawn by the paper-wrapped bottle that sat next to it. Green glass and a red cap that Nelson unscrewed. He poured a small dollop of the brown liquid into his coffee and held it out to Ray, who wagged his head for a second indecisively before saying sure, what the hell. Nelson sipped at his coffee, and they sat for a minute.

"You're seeing someone."

"You been keeping tabs."

Nelson laughed, holding up his hands to make peace. "No, really. Just saw you in the coffee shop with a woman."

"Michelle. She's usually here, but she's taking a writing class at Bucks."

Nelson nodded. "Nice. She seems like a nice lady, Ray." He looked sheepish. "Not doing so hot in that area myself."

Ray sipped at the coffee, made a face. "Forgot how bitter it is."

"Only at first." They sat in silence, Nelson tapping his pen on his cup.

"I gotta ask."

"Why am I here?"

"Well, yeah. Is it about the kid in the house in Falls Township?"

Nelson shook his head. "No, but thanks for that. They got the kid out."

"Good. I saw the news."

"They took two bodies out of the yard. Young girls who disappeared. At least we can tell the families something."

"That's good, I guess. And you got the kid out?"

"Yeah, into family services. I didn't think you'd want your name in it."

"No."

"But that's not why I came."

Ray raised his eyebrows. "Okay."

"I've been asking around. About what happened the year you went upstate." Ray stopped smiling, and waited. "I talked to Perry March's mother."

"His mother?"

"He's dead." Ray shook his head. Nelson tapped the notebook. "Overdose, two years ago. She told me some interesting things."

"Yeah?"

"She said Perry would get high and talk about Stan Hicks and you and the car. She said her son was afraid of Stan and that Perry told her he lied about you taking the car because he was jammed up on a possession thing." Ray put his coffee cup down and looked at his hands. "I looked at the records from the accident. And I looked at the medical records from the County Youth Authority the night you got your arms broken."

Ray rubbed his arms then, an old reflex. Feeling the thickened bones that ached when it was cold.

Nelson said, "I talked to Stan Hicks."

Ray looked up now. "How did that go?"

"He told me you'd been there. He told me everything."

"I guess he's ready to tell it."

"He laid it all out. How he pressured Perry March with the possession beef and got him to say you stole his car. The guy who hit you and Marletta? The guy who was killed? He was a drunk. Blood alcohol well over the line. Your blood screen was clean. Stan pressured the DA, made her life hell until she made you a priority. Then he took you out of County in the middle of the night and broke your arms with something, I can't figure out what. You went to prison with busted arms at seventeen. Stayed for two years for something you didn't do."

Ray was quiet. "The jack from his car. He said. It was dark. He told the Youth Authority I ran away from him in the dark and fell off a loading dock. I said, sure, whatever. I didn't care."

"So, what do you want to do?"

"Do?"

"About Stan Hicks. What do you want to do?"

Ray shook his head, surprised. "Nothing." He picked up the coffee again. "I really forgot. It does kind of grow on you."

"You might be able to press charges, I don't know. Maybe sue, collect some money."

"No, I'm not doing that." Ray looked into the cup.

Nelson looked at him and rocked a little in his chair. "Okay, so . . ."

"You never knew her?"

"Marletta? No."

Ray looked at his pale hand. "She was, I don't know the words. There was a light inside her. Ever know anyone like that? She glowed." He smiled and closed his eyes. "She was one of those people. You just liked her. And she was the only one who cared about me."

"You feel guilty?"

"I was driving. I can't remember now, but I know what I was like then. Looking at her and not the road? I can't remember, and I don't want to anymore. Anyway, I can imagine what it was like for him. If she was my family? And then to lose her like that? I was Stan Hicks I would have done the same." His eyes clouded over. "Worse."

"You got hit by a drunk driver, Ray. You can't think she'd have wanted you to go to jail."

"No, she'd have hated that."

"How did you make it? With broken arms?"

"Harlan Maximuck." Nelson shook his head, not getting it. Ray said, "Harlan had a younger brother died in prison in Maine."

He conjured Harlan then, tall and lopsided, walking with a hitched step, a staccato lope from where a statie had tagged him with shotgun pellets in the thighs when he and an even crazier friend had robbed a pawnshop and killed two people. Broad across the chest and wild brown hair that he'd stab at with oddly delicate hands, trying to keep it out of his eyes.

"So he, what? Adopted you?"

Ray pursed his lips. "Guys like you? Like anyone I guess hasn't been sent up. You see Harlan as a scumbag. As, I don't know. Evil, I guess."

"And you think, what? He was misunderstood?"

"No. No." Ray looked at the books on the shelves and tried to stretch for the words. "He kept me alive. He didn't have to. He didn't take anything off me. Except what he took off everybody." Ray smiled at a memory. "He'd be talking to you and, like, going through your pockets. Looking for cigarettes, whatever. I even saw him start to do it to a CO once." Nelson picked up the bottle again and offered it to Ray, who waved him off. "But he was crazy. I mean he was *crazy*. I saw him, well . . . One time this guy flicked cigarette ash in his oatmeal? Harlan shanked him with a fucking pork chop bone."

"Jesus."

"Yeah. So it's not like I don't know who he is. Would he rat me out if that was in his best interest? Yes. Would he fuck me over in a deal? Yes, if by some tragic fucking wheel of fortune miscalculation he ever gets out again." Ray leaned in. "But he *also* did this. He's also this." Made a circle in the air to include himself, the body saved. "Guys like Harlan? And Manny? Me, too? We're more and we're less than you think. Worse and better. And the thing is, all you people are, too."

"So what does a cop do about that?"

Ray smiled wide. "Lock us up. What the hell else can you do? But maybe know, too. You lock up the good and the bad and sometimes both in the same person."

Nelson squinted, not entirely convinced. "Maybe."

"You think a person is defined by the worst thing he ever did? The most desperate, the most terrible day in his life?" He got a glimpse of himself in the farmhouse in Ottsville, the smoke hanging in the air, the milk and blood pooled on the floor and his head on fire.

"That's how the law sees it."

"What about Stan Hicks? He probably locked up a lot of guys who broke the law, bad guys who hurt people. You're willing to send him away, too?"

"It's the law, Ray. Without the law, what do we have?"

Ray lifted his shoulders. "I don't know. Just a lot of fucked-up people trying to get through a day."

ADRIENNE GRAY STAGGERED home at two o'clock on a Saturday morning, and Ray was sitting on her steps in a bright cone of light. She started when she saw him and stepped back, holding her keys out. Her eyes were wide but red and bleary.

"Adrienne."

"Is that you, Ray?"

"Yes, it's me." She put a hand on her heart.

"Jesus Christ. You scared the crap out of me."

"Sorry." He thumped the cold stair next to him. "Come sit and talk to me."

She lifted her shoulders, patted her arms. "It's cold out, hon. Can't we talk tomorrow? I'll come by the store."

"No. Come here." She made a gesture of giving up with her spread arms and slowly navigated the step and parked herself on the step below him, holding her arms in her thin coat. Ray took off his parka and put it over her shoulders, and she smiled at him and pulled the sleeves together.

They had started talking, Ray finding her coming out of Kelly's or Chambers and walking her home. Trying to pull her into the store instead of letting her go back up the hill to the bars. Bringing her books she didn't read.

"Adrienne."

"What can I do for you, hon? You lonely?"

"No. Adrienne, you need help."

She stood up slowly and turned to look down at him. "And you're going to help me?"

"I'll do what I can." He lifted a shoulder, not sure how this should go.

In the cold light he saw her face close up, a subtle shift in her muscles, the way a closed hand becomes a fist. "Who the fuck are you?"

"Nobody. But you need a friend."

"I got all the fucking friends I need. The bars are full of them." She shucked the coat and threw it down at his feet.

"I don't think those are your friends, Adrienne."

"What the hell do you know about it? What the hell do you want from me anyway?"

He jammed up, not ready for her to be so amped up, ready to fight. "Don't you want to get right? Get clean?"

"So I can be what, like you? Your life's a picnic and I'm invited?"

"No, man. I don't know."

"You don't know is right." She stalked up the steps, her small, hard shins banging his bad leg. "You don't know what the hell you're talking about. You don't know me."

"Adrienne."

She took a couple of steps back down toward him, and he retreated, almost losing the rail.

"I lost my father. One day he's a lawyer and he's got money and respect and he takes care of me and the next day he's dead, and his name gets dragged through the mud, and now he's a shitbag who stole money, and how do I even know what's true? Everyone knows but me. Everyone knows he's a shitbag. And me? I'm the shitbag's daughter. You going to make that go away? Are you?"

"No."

"And how do you even know my name? Where did you come from?"

"I'm nobody. I just thought . . ."

"Yeah, you just thought."

"I'm sorry."

"Go home, Ray."

"Adrienne. Goddammit."

"Go home."

TWO O'CLOCK IN the morning and Ray's cell rang at the apartment on Mary Street. He looked at the number and didn't recognize it.

He whispered, "Hello?" Michelle sat up, widening her eyes to clear the sleep, her hair rucked to one side from sleeping on it. He kissed her and winked while he listened. Then his face changed and he started nodding.

HE HADN'T BEEN inside Manny's in almost a year. It was a narrow apartment fronting 611, quiet now at three in the morning. He looked right and left moving through the dark parking lot, the careful habits of his old life slow to desert him.

Sherry met him at the door, small and pale under unwashed black hair, speed-rapping about how she couldn't get him up and he was just so lazy and she thought about an ambulance but who was paying for that? He put her in a chair in front of the television, noticing the scattered potato chip wrappers, the empty beer cans on the table, the smell. The same smell he'd got off the bag Manny'd left at Theresa's. Sherry chewed her nail and watched an infomercial with couples in Hawaii wearing flower print shirts and looking painted into the scenery, tapped her feet on the table, blinking.

He made his way back to the bedroom where Manny was stretched out, blue and still. The orange sodium lamps on the street half lit the room, a salvage diver's light illuminating a tiny wedge of a wreck in black water. He was facing up, naked to the waist, and Ray sat down next to him and touched an arm like cold putty. He got out his cell, called an ambulance, and waited. Heard Sherry muttering to herself about getting a dog, about money she was owed by her sister in Kutztown.

Manny's mom had died when they were in Juvie. Abducted from some bar in Bristol, left in plastic bags by the side of the road. When he heard the CO say it, Manny slugged him in the face and ran for the fence. Three guards brought him down, got him in a choke hold and threw him into Isolation, and Ray went that night, one of the female guards taking him back to the door to try to calm Manny down. Ray banged on the door, called out, and looked through the tiny, smudged window, seeing nothing. Finally he slid open the chute and stuck his arm through and grabbed Manny around his skinny bicep and just held on, feeling the muscle vibrate and hearing his friend's ragged breath.

On the nightstand he found Manny's sunglasses and put them over his eyes, smoothed the hair away from his face. Fit his hand around Manny's bicep and squeezed.

HE STAYED UP all night, first emptying dope and guns out of the apartment and Manny's car before the cops came through, then finding Sherry's sister and getting her to come down to pick her up at the hospital where they took Manny. When he left Abington Memorial it was nearly dawn, so he drove up to the Eagle and got a cup of coffee and some toast. When he paid, he went outside and the sky was just starting to go blue at the edges.

He'd have to get Sherry into rehab, have to watch her and take care of her, and it would probably all be for nothing, but that's how it would go and there wasn't anything to be done about it. He was starting to see an outline of the life in front of him. It was different than the one behind, harder to dope out, but he had to think it would be better. He had to believe in it, the way Theresa believed that prayers to St. Jude had brought him home safe from prison. Even if what he did never worked, if he was no good at it.

It would be where the money went, where his days got used up. Taking care of all the fucked-up people around him. Maybe because he'd been given this other chance he never earned. Because somebody loved him and he never understood why. Because the alternative was endless black night and dope dreams and there wasn't anything else he could do.

AT DAWN HE took a bag into the garage at Theresa's house. He went through Bart's scarred wood worktable, pulling tools out of the drawers and laying them quietly on the floor. A hammer, a punch gone black with age. A speckled boning knife, still carrying a faint, vinegary tang.

He dumped a dozen guns out on the floor, then knelt slowly, the cold from the cement grabbing at the bones in his knees. He looked at the guns a long time, picking up each one and putting it down. He held up the Colt, ejected the clip, worked the slide to spit a dull brass shell onto the floor. He worked methodically, removing the barrel, the slide. Working the firing pin out with the punch, his fingers feeling thick and slow in the weak blue light from the window.

He separated the parts into two piles, then centered each part in front of him in turn and covered it with a decaying terrycloth rag. He raised the hammer and smacked each piece a few times, denting the barrel, snapping the magazine spring with his fingers. He had to get up periodically and work his knees, flex at the hips to keep from getting locked up. As the sun came up he began to sweat, and his hands got slick and black with old gun oil and grit.

He finally walked into the house and went into Theresa's linen closet and got a bunch of pillowcases for his bed, moving quietly in the dark house.

She called from the kitchen. "What are you going to do with those guns?"

He jumped and banged the cane against the doorjamb. "Jesus Christ, don't you sleep?"

"Not anymore." She came to the hallway and handed him a mug of coffee.

He shook his head. "I'm getting rid of them. I smashed them up, so no one can find them and get hurt."

"Come in when you're done, sit down like a person and have some coffee." She reached into the closet, straightened the mess he'd made. "Sneaking around the house in the middle of the night. You're lucky *I* don't have a gun."

"Old habits." He smiled, and she rolled her eyes.

THREE WEEKS AFTER Manny's funeral, Ray stood at the store's counter, sorting through invoices. Michelle sat cross-legged on the floor in a storm of packing material and bright paper, her new laptop open. She had them selling books online. It more than doubled their income but meant shipping and tracking and dealing with people over the phone, which Ray left to her. He loved her openness to the new world but felt he couldn't be much help and just admired the work from a distance. He told her they had gotten far out of his commercial comfort zone, which was sticking a gun in someone's face and demanding money.

The shop was doing good, she said, and he trusted her to be right. He felt himself being drawn forward into life, and some days that was good and some days he'd pull back against it. He'd smell dope on Stevie and instead of giving him crap about it, he'd want to get high. Or a customer would get in his shit and he'd have to leave the store, drive around and listen to music and let the tide in his blood shift until he was drawn home again to find Michelle waiting for him, and when he tried to apologize or explain she'd shake her head and hold him and he'd believe in it again.

Theresa crouched in the back pawing the new romances before they went out onto the shelves, pulling each one to her face to squint at the covers, thumbing them open and mouthing a few words.

Michelle smiled. "Finding everything, Theresa?"

"I'm an old lady, hearts and flowers don't do it for me. I like the ones where they get laid."

Ray said, "We should get you some little stars to put on the ones where they get their cookies. We won't be able to keep them on the shelves. The little old ladies who come down from the shrine after mass'll clean us out." He looked outside, saw Andy launching herself up the stairs, one hand around her belly. She pushed through the door hard, the noise scaring Michelle, who ran to the front.

The girl was sobbing. "Has Lynch been here? Is he here?" Michelle put her arm around the girl, but she slid away to stand in the corner, her head swiveling. "Get him out here."

"He's not here, Andy." Ray held up his hands. "What's going on?" The girl was hugely pregnant now, her belly projecting over the small hand she kept on the waistband of the oversized jeans Michelle had helped her pick out. They had been trying to figure out her living situation, which seemed to be on- and off-again at home and occasionally in the basements of friends. They had even tried to get her into a cheap rental, but Lynch just waved them off and shrugged, and the girl volunteered nothing, though the bruises that occasionally appeared on her face made Michelle drop her eyes and shake her head.

They were standing there, Ray at the counter, Michelle hovering in the empty space between the door and the register, her arms outstretched as if Andy were a cat she was trying to coax off the windowsill, when Lynch ran up the street and into the store, Stevie a few steps behind him, the two of them out of breath.

The door banged on the wall, and Theresa got up and slapped the stack of books with an open hand. "Jesus Christ, can't anyone open and close a door?"

Stevie bent over, wheezing, and hit his knees with his fist. Lynch put his arms around Andy, his back to the room, and she stood still and white. Ray could see the boy's hands were shaking.

"What's going on?" Ray looked from one to the other. Michelle touched Stevie's arm and he jumped, his eyes moving wild in his head.

Theresa said, "Is it the baby? We need to call an ambulance?"

Stevie shook his head, pointed at his friend. "Man."

Lynch turned, and they saw he was crying and there was a fine spray of blood across his eyes. Michelle sucked in a breath and stood up straight. They were all still for a moment. There were muted traffic sounds and a distant siren, and Andy, quiet now, turned to look at the street.

Lynch made a motion with his upper body, flexing his arms as if the sleeves of his thin jacket were too small. He smeared at his face with his hand, looked into his palm, but the blood had dried to rust. "I told that fucker. I told him he fucked with Andy again . . ."

Stevie spoke to the floor. "You told him. But man, Lynch."

"No, I told him, he touched her again."

Michelle pulled her arms around her as if she were cold. "You have to tell us what happened. Andy, what happened?"

The young girl moved closer to the window, breathed on it. She traced something no one else could see onto the window in the fine mist from her breath, watched it evaporate. Ray thought it might have been a heart.

Stevie said, "Andy's old man was wailing on her again. He kicked her in the stomach."

"Jesus." Ray covered his face with his hands and spat out the words. "Jesus."

He heard a rustling, and when he opened his eyes Lynch had produced a pistol from his oversized thrift store parka. It was comically large, a long barrel like something from a western.

Michelle said, "Bradley." It was the boy's first name, and Ray had never heard her say it out loud before. Lynch turned to her and his eyes were dull. "Honey, put that away."

Ray came from around the counter. Theresa was standing, her hand over her mouth, her eyes wide. He moved deliberately, slowly, imagining each terrible way this could play out. He put himself in front of Michelle and backed up, moving her into the aisles and toward the rear of the store. Then he stepped forward, one arm extended.

Michelle's eyes filled with tears and she grabbed at a bookshelf, her knuckles showing up white against her dark skin. She said, "Andrea, honey, come stand by me," but her voice was strange, rounded and hoarse.

"Lynch, man, you are among friends." He turned to Michelle, who reached past him and grabbed Stevie by the sleeve and pulled him and Theresa toward the back door. "Think, kid, you don't want a gun around Andy or the baby."

Lynch turned and looked at Andy, who sighed as if she were bored by an argument she had heard before and stared out at the street.

She said, "Lynch, we have to go."

"We need money." He lifted the pistol and pointed it at Ray, who put up his hands. Behind him he heard Michelle stifle a scream, clapping her hand over her mouth. He turned and smiled at her, or thought he did, watching through the rear window at Theresa stumbling across the parking lot toward the borough hall and the sign that said POLICE.

"I know, man, you can have whatever you need, we just have

to talk about what's going to happen, and you need for Christ's sake to put away the gun."

The pistol went off then, always a different sound than Ray expected, not that resonant bang they dub into the movies but a concussive pop that slapped at his head and made his ears ring. The bullet cracked a display case behind him that showered glass onto the floor. Michelle jumped forward into the room, scuffling with Stevie, who was panting and trying to pull her back out to the parking lot.

Andy sighed again, and Lynch said, "I shot her old man. I told him and told him, but he was such a dumb-ass. You can't keep beating on people. You can't."

Ray dropped his head. "Lynch."

"Don't fuck with us. Just give us some money and we'll get out of here."

"You don't have to do this. Tell me what happened."

"I just fucking told you."

"No, I mean everything, everything, the whole story. He was hitting her, right?" Ray had only glimpses of their lives, Stevie and Lynch and Andrea. Drug abuse and alcoholism, suicide and abandonment and rage that chased the kids into the street to live in alleys and abandoned cars, camp in the woods, or cling to each other in wet sleeping bags in half-built houses and vanish into the forest like deer when the Mexican and Guatemalan construction crews came to work in the morning.

"I don't have time to tell you no story. Me and Andy are going to Idaho. We're going to do comics. Andy can draw. Man, she draws everything, and no one knows it but me."

Ray's head snapped up as Nelson appeared on the porch, and he turned behind him to see another cop, this one in a uniform, muscle past Michelle in the rear of the store and stand rigid. He saw Nelson, Glock in hand, take up a position just outside the front door. He heard the cop behind him draw his gun, the creak of the leather holster. Through the window he could see people on the street. A couple stopped in front of the building, pulling apart a soft pretzel from the place across the street, the man feeding the woman the soft white flesh with the tips of his fingers while she laughed.

"Lynch, man, listen to me."

"Drop your weapon, son." The cop in uniform edged forward, his arms locked, the pistol a few feet from Ray's head.

Ray circled, his arms wide. "Wait a minute, will you fucking please?" He watched the door swing slowly behind Lynch, Nelson holding his blocky automatic, his face transfixed, hard. Ray shook his head, held his hand out, palm up, at first the boy, then the cops each in turn.

"It's all okay, right? This is just okay, all right?" He swallowed, his brain firing and his sinuses full of a strange ozone smell as his heart hammered and sweat began to form in a line on his back. "There's a story here. You have to know the story. It's not, you know. This is not," he said, but Lynch raised the pistol and Michelle screamed and Ray didn't know what to do and he was launching himself at the boy, his arms wide, crossing the floor without being conscious of moving his legs as if he were pulled on a wire.

There were shots, *pop, pop, pop,* loud, and glass breaking, and later Ray could never be sure of the order of things as he gathered Bradley Lynch in his arms and they went over together, everything happening at once, blood pouring onto the floor, following the cracks in the hardwood, eddying in hollow scuff marks. Michelle screaming, and Stevie yelling his friend's name, and Andy giving one long banshee shriek that sounded like she had been saving it her whole life. Ray's cheek was against the floor, and he saw the blood as a dark tide that came to carry him away to drown. When he lifted his head, his face was dripping, and he looked down at Lynch, his coat open and his T-shirt wound around his thin chest, and saw the boy's white flank torn open, shattered like glass.

The room around him exploded into more screaming and shouted orders, and he saw movement and lights out of the corners of his eyes. He looked over at Andy. She was hunched in the corner, her mouth working soundlessly, her arms around her belly and her jeans stained with dark water and flecked with foam.

He put his hands over the wound in Lynch's side and pressed, put his blood-painted face inches from the boy's and tried to hold his gaze, and he was screaming something but he never knew what it was, holding the boy's eyes with his and willing him to stay in the room, stay connected, pushing hard on Lynch's frail chest, as if he could hold his life in by force, hold him together, keep him alive.

August

It was a long drive into the hills, out past Valley Forge and through quiet towns where no one stirred on the street, and when they finally got out of the van everyone stretched and squinted, pulling at themselves in the heat like athletes before a long run.

Dennis Tafoya

They started across a long stretch of grass, and small insects opened white wings and vaulted ahead of them.

It took a while to get them all in, Ray and Michelle taking turns holding the baby while Andy and Stevie signed the visitation forms and passing each other the mealy, lopsided bread that Andy had made herself the day before and an unwieldy bowl of peppery chicken salad. Theresa's offering, though she herself was down with a cold and propped up in bed with a stack of romances, some DVDs of a cop show she liked, and a carton of cigarettes, which she claimed were necessary to keep her throat clear.

They put everything out on a long table in the visiting room, shyly watching the other families. They were black and white and other colors and nationalities that Ray couldn't guess, clustered in knots, heads together, voices quiet except for the occasional murmuring cry from a baby or screech from two kids roughhousing in front of the vending machines.

Lynch was buzzed into the visiting room in his blue DOC jumpsuit, his arms out for his son, and they clustered around him and touched his shoulders, which were getting broad. Andy fingered his thin growth of beard while Lynch held his head up, his teeth showing and his bright eyes flicking back and forth between Andy and the baby, who observed everything with a wry and satisfied look. He reached for his father's bright lapel and worked it in the minute and impossible fingers Ray could never stop looking at.

Michelle, hovering, organized plates of food and went into the diaper bag for a bottle. Ray caught Stevie checking out her ass and gave him yard eyes that had mellowed sufficiently to make the boy lift one shoulder and smile. The room was hot and close with bodies, but through the long windows they could see bright grass divided by rolling coils of wire and beyond that the Pennsylvania hills. They sat to eat, Lynch holding the baby across his lap and watching his son work his mouth and blink his eyes.

Ray knelt near him and kept his voice low. "How you making it?"

Lynch never took his eyes off the baby but nodded. "I read a lot, write letters. Stay in my house, out of the shit on the tiers. It's okay."

"No, it's not, it's fucked every minute, but it's twenty-four months. Not even. We can do twenty-four months." He balled some of the loose material of the jumpsuit and put his lips inches from the boy's pale ear. "Listen to me. Never think any of this shit is okay. Never think it's what you got coming."

Lynch shrugged, and Ray put a hand on his arm. "No, man. Twenty-four months and out, no fucking around in here, no ganging up, none of that slopbucket meth. Seven hundred and thirty days and you're home with your boy and Andy and this is all behind you."

"Yeah, it's less time than middle school, huh?" Ray nodded, lifted one brown hand and touched Lynch at his temple, and was almost overcome. He cleared his throat and rubbed at his reddened eyes, trying to think of the light sentence as lucky for nearly killing Andy's father, who had lived through the bullet in his back but who would never leave a wheelchair.

WHILE STEVIE AND Lynch walked around the visiting room and talked about TV shows and movies, DVDs that Stevie was putting aside for his friend to watch when he was out, Michelle sat by Ray and massaged his tense shoulders, swiveling her head to watch for the guards.

She put her head down into the back of his neck and whispered into his hair. "Fuck, I hate this."

"You and me both." They watched Stevie lift his T-shirt, show Lynch a new tattoo: barbed wire encircling his arm. Lynch rolled his eyes and slapped his friend lightly on the forehead.

Michelle said, "I keep expecting a couple of guards to cut me out of the herd and take me back to my cell." She shivered, and Ray covered her hand with his and then lifted it to his lips. "How's he doing, Ray?"

"He'll be okay. If he was fucking up, we'd know it." He looked to the gate, saw the COs checking clipboards and counting heads. He watched through the smeared glass as the shadows of clouds moved over the low hills and the towers and gauzy rolls of wire, painting them with a dark wash like ink dissolved in water.

Michelle slid onto the bench beside him and pressed against his hip, and they watched Andy feed the baby, the mother making small sympathetic movements of her lips as she held the minute spoon to the boy's puckered mouth. While they watched, Michelle took Ray's hand and pressed it against her, low on her stomach inside her jeans, and he felt the heat in her belly and the palms of her hands.

She said, "Do you want that, Ray? Do you want that for us?"

"I don't know."

He watched a man in a blue jumpsuit serving tuna salad to his family from a foil pan, his brow thick with scar tissue. A heavy woman with blond hair like a suspended wave watched him, her eyes wary, and when the plastic spoon snapped in his hands she winced and grabbed involuntarily at the frail, pink-eyed girl in her lap.

Michelle waited, and he finally said, "I just don't." He made a movement with his free hand that took in the room. "Trust that things will be okay. That they'll be good."

"They won't, always." She smiled. Lifted one hand and touched the baby's white hair. "But we'll do the best we can, and we'll have a good life."

"Do I deserve that?"

She pressed against him, and Ray could feel pain in his arm from where he'd had his tattoo burned, the laser turning the heavy black letters into an oblique scar so that he'd shaken his head, laughed at himself for wasting the money. He'd marked himself; he'd always be marked.

He said, "Who am I now?" but there was a change in the room, a collective sighing and pauses in conversation, and it was time to go, and Michelle hadn't heard what he'd said.

They packed up, Andy clinging for a long moment to Lynch, their eyes closed, swaying in the heat as if at one of the high school dances they'd all missed, though it was Stevie who teared up and had to go stand in front of a vending machine and pretend to pick out orange soda, working quarters in his red fist.

Ray walked Lynch back to the door and handed him two cartons of cigarettes. Hugged him hard, feeling the knot of scar tissue at his side through the jumpsuit, then stood while the boy

288

went through the gate to stand patiently with his arms out to be wanded by a short woman with wide hips who laughed at something the boy said.

While Ray was watching, an older man came down the hall from the tiers in the brown jumpsuit of a lifer, his shoulders riding in a lopsided wave and one long hand pushing at a mass of graying hair. When the man got to Lynch the younger man turned, smiled, and said something lost to Ray behind the glass. He patted the older man's mountainous shoulder and pointed through at Ray, shaking his head, mouthed a word that might have been "bad-ass." When the door nearest him was buzzed open, Ray could hear the distant shouting and banging of the tiers.

Ray lifted a hand and waved at Harlan and Lynch as they turned to go back. Harlan went into Lynch's pockets while they walked, pulled a cigarette out, and stuck it behind his ear. He turned and nodded at Ray, made a scooting motion to send him on his way.

Ray knew he couldn't fix everything, couldn't stop every bad thing just by his love for Michelle or these broken kids. He'd failed with Adrienne Gray, and he'd let Manny slide away into the dark. The rest of the money had all gone to legal bills for Lynch and medical bills for Andy and rehab for Sherry, and he saw they'd always struggle to stay ahead. But there were good, clear days, too, and sometimes he came home tired and slept without dreams.

Ray knew Lynch would come out with tattoos and scars, but Michelle had said it would be a map only of where he had been, not where he was headed. Ray hoped it was true, though he sometimes saw her staring into the middle distance and knew she saw her mother's untended grave in the flat Ohio earth, a boy she had loved in high school walking down a tree-lined street with his children.

Ray turned to the rest of his pickup family, clutching bags and blankets as they clustered by the door, and looked out into the daylight with the hooded and set-upon eyes of refugees. In the parking lot he had to keep himself from running, and Michelle laced her fingers through his and kissed his cheek.

In Phoenixville they stopped at a Dairy Queen, and he bought sodas for the kids and soft serve for the baby. The clouds had piled up overhead into a hard ceiling threaded with black and softening the light to a muted blue. He stood at the eroded curb and watched them all, Stevie draped over the seats and flipping through the CDs, Andy furiously texting one of her girlfriends from work, Michelle cradling the baby and smiling at him with her crooked smile.

They looked okay, and he let himself believe they would be. They looked hungry and tired. They looked like any family by the side of the road, and he had the thought that if they locked him up again this would be the image he'd remember. At night on his bunk, when the lights would go out, this moment, these few quiet seconds, would be the thing he'd hold on to to keep himself sane.

There was a low, drumming rumble behind him, and he turned as a motorcycle appeared on the street and drifted to a stop at the light. The noise grew louder, bouncing and echoing off the buildings around him, and then there were a dozen more bikes strung out along the road. Ray stood silent, watching them come. Men in leather jackets, some wearing chromed helmets, most with nothing on their heads but bandannas or long hair in matted plaits.

At the back of the line, a young guy with black hair and a goatee turned and looked at Ray, his face shadowed and unreadable. Ray felt naked, exposed, blinking away the sweat from his eyes. His heart worked faster, but he stood up straight, put his chin out. Thought to himself, *take what comes*. The bike coasted; the man leaned forward, reached a hand behind him. Touched a small form there. A boy, pressed against his back, wearing goggles and an oversized helmet the blue of a robin's egg. White-blond hair framing a heart-shaped face. The boy held a hand up and gave Ray a quick, shy wave. Then the light changed, and they were gone.